AGAINST THE LEGIONS OF ROME!

"Here is a prince of Erin," said Bran. "Will you fight for the Westerner?"

"We fight under no Celt, West or East," growled the Viking, and a low rumble of approval rose from the onlookers. "It is enough to fight by their side."

The hot Gaelic blood rose in Cormac's brain and he pushed past Bran, his hand on his sword. "How mean you that, pirate?"

Before Wulfhere could reply Bran interposed: "Have done! Will you fools throw away the battle before it is fought, by your madness? What of your oath, Wulfhere?"

"We swore it under Rognar; when he died from a Roman arrow we were absolved of it. We will follow only a king – against the legions."

"But your comrades will follow you – against the heather people!" snapped Bran.

"Aye," the Northman's eyes met his brazenly. "Send us a king or we join the Romans tomorrow."

Bran snarled. In his rage he dominated the scene, dwarfing the huge men who towered over him.

"Traitors! Liars! I hold your lives in my hand! Aye, draw your swords if you will – Cormac, keep your blade in its sheath. These wolves will not bite a king! Wulfhere – I spared your lives when I could have taken them.You came to raid the countries of the South, sweeping down from the northern sea in your galleys. You ravaged the coasts and the smoke of burning villages hung like a cloud over the shores of Caledon. I trapped you all when you were pillaging and burning – with the blood of my people on your hands. I burned your long ships and ambushed you when you followed. With thrice your number of bowmen who burned for your lives hidden in the heathered hills about you, I spared you when we could have shot you down like trapped wolves. Because I spared you, you swore to come and fight for me."

"And shall we die because the Picts fight Rome?" rumbled a bearded raider.

"Your lives are forfeit to me; you came to ravage the South. I did not promise to send you all back to your homes in the North unharmed and loaded with loot. Your vow was to fight one battle against Rome under my standard. Then I will aid your survivors to build ships and you may go where you will, with a goodly share of the plunder we take from the legions . . ."

ALSO BY ROBERT E. HOWARD

The Complete Action Stories

Gates of Empire

Treasures of Tartary

Graveyard Rats and Others

Waterfront Fists and Others

THE WEIRD WORKS OF ROBERT E. HOWARD

Shadow Kingdoms

Moon of Skulls

People of the Dark

Wings in the Night

Valley of the Worm

PEOPLE OF THE DARK

ROBERT E. HOWARD

EDITED BY
PAUL HERMAN

INTRODUCTION BY
JOE R. LANSDALE

PEOPLE OF THE DARK

Published by:
Wildside Press
9710 Traville Gateway Dr.
Rockville, MD 20850
www.wildsidepress.com

Distributed by Diamond Book Distribusion.

Printed in Canada.

CONTENTS

HOWARD — THE TEXAS PHOENIX FLAMES IN DARKNESS

by Joe R. Lansdale

It's easy for me to relate to Robert E. Howard. At least in many ways. Because I too grew up in a small Texas town, East instead of West, and in that respect, less bleak, but still, a small town. A town populated by good, solid people, but a small corner of the earth cursed with a kind of raw wound of ignorance, a black hole void of the possibilities of a bigger universe.

In spite of all the bad things said about television, it must be said that it brought to the small back waters of civilization a broader view of the world and opinions and beliefs other than those held by the residents of those stagnant back waters.

But in Howard's time there was more darkness than light, and without interference, these wounds were left to fester in a cultural vacuum that must have sucked the very air out of Howard's lungs.

At least it felt that way if you were born with a creative fire in your belly, a razor-eye, a vision that looked not only at what it saw, but around corners, and saw backwards into the past and dressed it up in a manner that fit no past at all, except that which existed in the head, and was, as all spirited imagineers will tell you, far more real than any past that had been or any future that might be.

I suspect that this kind of thinking is not subject only to Texas, but to any area where culture is thought to be a ornament, or something sissy, and that in such places a fist fight is of more importance than a poem. But whatever the case, Howard's cross to bear, his hole in the world, was a bleak little spot of West Texas dirt that to this day is little more than a hole in the road with a Dairy Queen, a library, and finally, his home, now a museum dedicated to the imaginings of its most prominent and well known citizen, who during his life time was thought, at best, eccentric, and at the extreme, just plain old nuts.

I discovered Howard in 1970. It was my first marriage, and my first year of college. I was going to Tyler Junior College, wanting to write, wondering if it would ever happen, and not thinking my wife understood this at all.

Or maybe I understood her not at all.

But the point was this. I was feeling high and dry and lonely and bleak as Howard must have felt when he sat down to type many of his stories. And during the time this feeling was on me, hanging around my shoulders like some heavy poison-laced cloak, I found a paperback called *Wolfshead*. It was a collection of stories, and the first thing that struck me was the introduction (and if the introduction was, in fact, part of some other Howard book, don't tell me, let me have my lie of memory). In this introduction he talked about the fact that he had made his living from his wits, from work of his own choosing, and he didn't have some sonofabitch standing over him, telling him what to do.

As a young man who had worked every odd job imaginable so that I could go to college and not end up a permanent ditch digger, or aluminum chair factory worker, or field worker, or handyman who was not so handy, this struck a chord.

Deep down inside of me a string throbbed, and there was a kind of high note hit, and I felt a sudden kinship to this man. I knew of what he spoke.

Then there was the fiction. It was on fire, and full of sparks and smoke, lightning and thunder, primary colors cranked up bright.

I hadn't had this much pure fun as a reader since Edgar Rice Burroughs kicked my ass as a kid.

This man was pulpy and raw and powerful, and it was obvious that, like Burroughs, he believed in what he wrote. In the next couple of years, I discovered Conan, which I still believe to be his best work, and many other stories by Howard, but the thing that sticks with me, Conan aside, are the non-series stories. The ones that thrilled me and made my skin crawl, and yet somehow tied me to the Texas world I grew up in. Because no matter how wild the story, how bizarre the idea, or what location he claimed for it, I assure you, Howard was always writing about Texas and Texans.

These stories are full of Howard's piss and vinegar, Howard's heart and soul.

This collection contains many fine tales. One of my favorites is "The Horror from the Mound." I've read it many times, but when I first read "The Horror from the Mound," I was certain I had never read a horror story quite like it. It wasn't the usual tale of a monster and a hapless protagonist, but that of a Western hero confronted with a problem, and like all true Western heroes, he had to just go out and do what he had to do, which was face off with the thing and try to defeat it.

Self-reliance.

Courage.

Confidence.

These are all hallmarks of Howard's fiction, and of Texans, and they are its main appeal. It's especially powerful to readers below the age of twenty-five, because from adolescence to the mid-twenties, we may feign these feelings, but if we are truthful, it is hard for us to embrace them with the fullness we would like. Therefore, we experience them through others, or through the beautiful lies of fiction.

It's good to have heroes.

Or at least heroics. Howard's characters were not always heroes. Not in the classic sense. Conan was really quite a turd, if you think about it. But, somehow Howard was able to give him such a sheen of power and verisimilitude and energy that, on some level, we all wished to be him.

I know that his introduction, his words, eventually led me to drop out of college and write. Just go for it. Because, I too, like Howard, did not want to end up with some sonofabitch standing over me telling me what to do, and also like Howard, I wanted to make my own way by my wits, doing work of my choosing.

I thank his shade for that.

And readers should thank his shade for all the work that exists. Including the fine hot-pulp stories in this volume. And maybe, just maybe, we should be angry with that same shade for taking himself from us so soon. Killed not, in my view, by his inability to accept his mothers expected death, but, by a series of events.

The loss of a woman he really cared about, Novalyne Price, someone who was an intellectual stimulant, as well as possibly his one true love. Add to this, the soon to be loss of his mother, who never judged him and always encouraged him, and finally add in this certain knowledge: Now he would be sitting alone dangling his feet over the rim of a lonesome abyss.

If he had had the courage to stand up to that, how much more of his fiction would we have seen?

How much greater would his mind have developed, and how much greater would his writer skills have become in time?

As it were, trapped in a sort of permanent adolescence, fueled primarily by his own energies, intelligence, and creativity, he gave us much. And even now, long gone, the echo of his voice, and ultimately of the .38 he used to take his life, resound forever.

* * *

Read these stories and enjoy. Dip into the exciting horrors and adventures of Robert E. Howard.

Do not come to them with an academic mind.

Come to them with an eager heart. That way they will give you much. Because they know little of logic, and much of desire – and desire drives us.

Howard knew that. Let him share this knowledge with you.

And finally, if you're someone sitting in some bleak place with nothing but the hungry sounds of the inner gnawings of creative desire chewing at your head, here is something to feed the beast within until you too can rise up Phoenix-like and leave it all behind in your wing-flapping wake, minus the suicidal gun fire, of course.

KINGS OF THE NIGHT

Weird Tales, November 1930

The Caesar lolled on his ivory throne –
His iron legions came
To break a king in a land unknown,
And a race without a name.
– The Song of Bran

The dagger flashed downward. A sharp cry broke in a gasp. The form on the rough altar twitched convulsively and lay still. The jagged flint edge sawed at the crimsoned breast, and thin bony fingers, ghastly dyed, tore out the still-twitching heart. Under matted white brows, sharp eyes gleamed with a ferocious intensity.

Besides the slayer, four men stood about the crude pile of stones that formed the altar of the God of Shadows. One was of medium height, lithely built, scantily clad, whose black hair was confined by a narrow iron band in the center of which gleamed a single red jewel. Of the others, two were dark like the first. But where he was lithe, they were stocky and misshapen, with knotted limbs, and tangled hair falling over sloping brows. His face denoted intelligence and implacable will; theirs merely a beast-like ferocity. The fourth man had little in common with the rest. Nearly a head taller, though his hair was black as theirs, his skin was comparatively light and he was gray-eyed. He eyed the proceedings with little favor.

And, in truth, Cormac of Connacht was little at ease. The Druids of his own isle of Erin had strange dark rites of worship, but nothing like this. Dark trees shut in this grim scene, lit by a single torch. Through the branches moaned an eerie night-wind. Cormac was alone among men of a strange race and he had just seen the heart of a man ripped from his still pulsing body. Now the ancient priest, who looked scarcely human, was glaring at the throbbing thing. Cormac shuddered, glancing at him who wore the jewel. Did Bran Mak Morn, king of the Picts, believe that this white-bearded old butcher could foretell events by scanning a bleeding human heart? The dark eyes of the king were inscrutable.

There were strange depths to the man that Cormac could not fathom, nor any other man.

"The portents are good!" exclaimed the priest wildly, speaking more to the two chieftains than to Bran. "Here from the pulsing heart of a captive Roman I read – defeat for the arms of Rome! Triumph for the sons of the heather!"

The two savages murmured beneath their breath, their fierce eyes smoldering.

"Go and prepare your clans for battle," said the king, and they lumbered away with the ape-like gait assumed by such stunted giants. Paying no more heed to the priest who was examining the ghastly ruin on the altar, Bran beckoned to Cormac. The Gael followed him with alacrity. Once out of that grim grove, under the starlight, he breathed more freely. They stood on an eminence, looking out over long swelling undulations of gently waving heather. Near at hand a few fires twinkled, their fewness giving scant evidence of the hordes of tribesmen who lay close by. Beyond these were more fires and beyond these still more, which last marked the camp of Cormac's own men, hard-riding, hard-fighting Gaels, who were of that band which was just beginning to get a foothold on the western coast of Caledonia – the nucleus of what was later to become the kingdom of Dalriadia. To the left of these, other fires gleamed.

And far away to the south were more fires – mere pinpoints of light. But even at that distance the Pictish king and his Celtic ally could see that these fires were laid out in regular order.

"The fires of the legions," muttered Bran. "The fires that have lit a path around the world. The men who light those fires have trampled the races under their iron heels. And now – we of the heather have our backs at the wall. What will fall on the morrow?"

"Victory for us, says the priest," answered Cormac.

Bran made an impatient gesture. "Moonlight on the ocean. Wind in the fir tops. Do you think that I put faith in such mummery? Or that I enjoyed the butchery of a captive legionary? I must hearten my people; it was for Gron and Bocah that I let old Gonar read the portents. The warriors will fight better."

"And Gonar?"

Bran laughed. "Gonar is too old to believe – anything. He was high priest of the Shadows a score of years before I was born. He claims direct descent from that Gonar who was a wizard in the days of Brule the Spear-slayer who was the first of my line. No man knows how old he is – sometimes I think he is the original Gonar himself!"

"At least," said a mocking voice, and Cormac started as a dim shape appeared at his side, "at least I have learned that in order to keep the faith and trust of the people, a wise man must appear to be a fool. I know secrets that would blast even your brain, Bran, should I speak them. But in order that the people may believe in me, I must descend to such things as they think proper magic – and prance and yell and rattle snakeskins, and dabble about in human blood and chicken livers."

Cormac looked at the ancient with new interest. The semi-madness of his appearance had vanished. He was no longer the charlatan, the spell-mumbling shaman. The starlight lent him a dignity which seemed to increase his very height, so that he stood like a white-bearded patriarch.

"Bran, your doubt lies there." The lean arm pointed to the fourth ring of fires.

"Aye," the king nodded gloomily. "Cormac – you know as well as I. Tomorrow's battle hinges upon that circle of fires. With the chariots of the Britons and your own Western horsemen, our success would be certain, but – surely the devil himself is in the heart of every Northman! You know how I trapped that band – how they swore to fight for me against Rome! And now that their chief, Rognar, is dead, they swear that they will be led only by a king of their own race! Else they will break their vow and go over to the Romans. Without them we are doomed, for we can not change our former plan."

"Take heart, Bran," said Gonar. "Touch the jewel in your iron crown. Mayhap it will bring you aid."

Bran laughed bitterly. "Now you talk as the people think. I am no fool to twist with empty words. What of the gem? It is a strange one, truth, and has brought me luck ere now. But I need now no jewels, but the allegiance of three hundred fickle Northmen who are the only warriors among us who may stand the charge of the legions on foot."

"But the jewel, Bran, the jewel!" persisted Gonar.

"Well, the jewel!" cried Bran impatiently. "It is older than this world. It was old when Atlantis and Lemuria sank into the sea. It was given to Brule, the Spear-slayer, first of my line, by the Atlantean Kull, king of Valusia, in the days when the world was young. But shall that profit us now?"

"Who knows?" asked the wizard obliquely. "Time and space exist not. There was no past, and there shall be no future. *Now* is all. All things that ever were, are, or ever will be, transpire *now*. Man is forever at the center of what we call time and space. I have gone into yesterday and tomorrow and both were as real as today – which is like the dreams of ghosts! But let me sleep and talk with Gonar. Mayhap he shall aid us."

"What means he?" asked Cormac, with a slight twitching of his shoulders, as the priest strode away in the shadows.

"He has ever said that the first Gonar comes to him in his dreams and talks with him," answered Bran. "I have seen him perform deeds that seemed beyond human ken. I know not. I am but an unknown king with an iron crown, trying to lift a race of savages out of the slime into which they have sunk. Let us look to the camps."

As they walked Cormac wondered. By what strange freak of fate had such a man risen among this race of savages, survivors of a darker, grimmer age? Surely he was an atavism, an original type of the days when the Picts ruled all Europe, before their primitive empire fell before the bronze swords of the Gauls. Cormac knew how Bran, rising by his own efforts from the negligent position of the son of a Wolf clan chief, had to an extent united the tribes of the heather and now claimed kingship over all Caledon. But his rule was loose and much remained before the Pictish clans would forget their feuds and present a solid front to foreign foes. On the battle of the morrow, the first pitched battle between the Picts under their king and the Romans, hinged the future of the rising Pictish kingdom.

Bran and his ally walked through the Pictish camp where the swart warriors lay sprawled about their small fires, sleeping or gnawing half-cooked food. Cormac was impressed by their silence. A thousand men camped here, yet the only sounds were occasional low guttural intonations. The silence of the Stone Age rested in the souls of these men.

They were all short – most of them crooked of limb. Giant dwarfs; Bran Mak Morn was a tall man among them. Only the older men were bearded and they scantily, but their black hair fell about their eyes so that they peered fiercely from under the tangle. They were barefoot and clad scantily in wolfskins. Their arms consisted in short barbed swords of iron, heavy black bows, arrows tipped with flint, iron and copper, and stone-headed mallets.

Defensive armor they had none, save for a crude shield of hide-covered wood; many had worked bits of metal into their tangled manes as a slight protection against sword-cuts. Some few, sons of long lines of chiefs, were smooth-limbed and lithe like Bran, but in the eyes of all gleamed the unquenchable savagery of the primeval.

These men are fully savages, thought Cormac, worse than the Gauls, Britons and Germans. Can the old legends be true – that they reigned in a day when strange cities rose where now the sea rolls? And that they survived the flood that washed those gleaming empires under, sinking again into that savagery from which they once had risen?

Close to the encampment of the tribesmen were the fires of a group of Britons – members of fierce tribes who lived south of the Roman Wall but who dwelt in the hills and forests to the west and defied the power of Rome. Powerfully built men they were, with blazing blue eyes and shocks of tousled yellow hair, such men as had thronged the Ceanntish beaches when Caesar brought the Eagles into the Isles. These men, like the Picts, wore no armor, and were clad scantily in coarse-worked cloth and deerskin sandals. They bore small round bucklers of hard wood, braced with bronze, to be worn on the left arm, and long heavy bronze swords with blunt points. Some had bows, though the Britons were indifferent archers. Their bows were shorter than the Picts' and effective only at close range. But ranged close by their fires were the weapons that had made the name Briton a word of terror to Pict, Roman and Norse raider alike. Within the circle of firelight stood fifty bronze chariots with long cruel blades curving out from the sides. One of these blades could dismember half a dozen men at once. Tethered close by under the vigilant eyes of their guards grazed the chariot horses – big, rangy steeds, swift and powerful.

"Would that we had more of them!" mused Bran. "With a thousand chariots and my bowmen I could drive the legions into the sea."

"The free British tribes must eventually fall before Rome," said Cormac. "It would seem they would rush to join you in your war."

Bran made a helpless gesture. "The fickleness of the Celt. They can not forget old feuds. Our ancient men have told us how they would not even unite against Caesar when the Romans first came. They will not make head against a common foe together. These men came to me because of some dispute with their chief, but I can not depend on them when they are not actually fighting."

Cormac nodded. "I know; Caesar conquered Gaul by playing one tribe against another. My own people shift and change with the waxing and waning of the tides. But of all Celts, the Cymry are the most changeable, the least stable. Not many centuries ago my own Gaelic ancestors wrested Erin from the Cymric Danaans, because though they outnumbered us, they opposed us as separate tribes, rather than as a nation."

"And so these Cymric Britons face Rome," said Bran. "These will aid us on the morrow. Further I can not say. But how shall I expect loyalty from alien tribes, who am not sure of my own people? Thousands lurk in the hills, holding aloof. I am king in name only. Let me win tomorrow and they will flock to my standard; if I lose, they will scatter like birds before a cold wind."

A chorus of rough welcome greeted the two leaders as they entered the camp of Cormac's Gaels. Five hundred in number they were, tall rangy men, black-haired and gray-eyed mainly, with the bearing of men who lived by war alone. While there was nothing like close discipline among them, there was an air of more system and practical order than existed in the lines of the Picts and Britons. These men were of the last Celtic race to invade the Isles and their barbaric civilization was of much higher order than that of their Cymric kin. The ancestors of the Gaels had learned the arts of war on the vast plains of Scythia and at the courts of the Pharaohs where they had fought as mercenaries of Egypt, and much of what they learned they brought into Ireland with them. Excelling in metal work, they were armed, not with clumsy bronze swords, but with high-grade weapons of iron.

They were clad in well-woven kilts and leathern sandals. Each wore a light shirt of chain mail and a vizorless helmet, but this was all of their defensive armor. Celts, Gaelic or Brythonic, were prone to judge a man's valor by the amount of armor he wore. The Britons who faced Caesar deemed the Romans cowards because they cased themselves in metal, and many centuries later the Irish clans thought the same of the mail-clad Norman knights of Strongbow.

Cormac's warriors were horsemen. They neither knew nor esteemed the use of the bow. They bore the inevitable round, metal-braced buckler, dirks, long straight swords and light single-handed axes. Their tethered horses grazed not far away – big-boned animals, not so ponderous as those raised by the Britons, but swifter.

Bran's eyes lighted as the two strode through the camp. "These men are keen-beaked birds of war! See how they whet their axes and jest of the morrow! Would that the raiders in yon camp were as staunch as your men, Cormac! Then would I greet the legions with a laugh when they come up from the south tomorrow."

They were entering the circle of the Northmen fires. Three hundred men sat about gambling, whetting their weapons and drinking deep of the heather ale furnished them by their Pictish allies. These gazed upon Bran and Cormac with no great friendliness. It was striking to note the difference between them and the Picts and Celts – the difference in their cold eyes, their strong moody faces, their very bearing. Here was ferocity, and savagery, but not of the wild, upbursting fury of the Celt. Here was fierceness backed by grim determination and stolid stubbornness. The charge of the British clans was terrible, overwhelming. But they had no patience; let them be balked of immediate victory and they were likely to lose heart and scatter or fall to bickering among themselves. There was the patience of the cold blue North in these seafarers – a lasting determination that would keep them steadfast to the bitter end, once their face was set toward a definite goal.

As to personal stature, they were giants; massive yet rangy. That they did not share the ideas of the Celts regarding armor was shown by the fact that they were clad in heavy scale mail shirts that reached below mid-thigh, heavy horned helmets and hardened hide leggings, reinforced, as were their shoes, with plates of iron. Their shields were huge oval affairs of hard wood, hide and brass. As to weapons, they had long iron-headed spears, heavy iron axes, and daggers. Some had long wide-bladed swords.

Cormac scarcely felt at ease with the cold magnetic eyes of these flaxen-haired men fixed upon him. He and they were hereditary foes, even though they did chance to be fighting on the same side at present – but were they?

A man came forward, a tall gaunt warrior on whose scarred, wolfish face the flickering firelight reflected deep shadows. With his wolfskin mantle flung carelessly about his wide shoulders, and the great horns on his helmet adding to his height, he stood there in the swaying shadows, like some half-human thing, a brooding shape of the dark barbarism that was soon to engulf the world.

"Well, Wulfhere," said the Pictish king, "you have drunk the mead of council and have spoken about the fires – what is your decision?"

The Northman's eyes flashed in the gloom. "Give us a king of our own race to follow if you wish us to fight for you."

Bran flung out his hands. "Ask me to drag down the stars to gem your helmets! Will not your comrades follow you?"

"Not against the legions," answered Wulfhere sullenly. "A king led us on the Viking path – a king must lead us against the Romans. And Rognar is dead."

"I am a king," said Bran. "Will you fight for me if I stand at the tip of your fight wedge?"

"A king of our own race," said Wulfhere doggedly. "We are all picked men of the North. We fight for none but a king, and a king must lead us – against the legions."

Cormac sensed a subtle threat in this repeated phrase.

"Here is a prince of Erin," said Bran. "Will you fight for the Westerner?"

"We fight under no Celt, West or East," growled the Viking, and a low rumble of approval rose from the onlookers. "It is enough to fight by their side."

The hot Gaelic blood rose in Cormac's brain and he pushed past Bran, his hand on his sword. "How mean you that, pirate?"

Before Wulfhere could reply Bran interposed: "Have done! Will you fools throw away the battle before it is fought, by your madness? What of your oath, Wulfhere?"

"We swore it under Rognar; when he died from a Roman arrow we were absolved of it. We will follow only a king – against the legions."

"But your comrades will follow you – against the heather people!" snapped Bran.

"Aye," the Northman's eyes met his brazenly. "Send us a king or we join the Romans tomorrow."

Bran snarled. In his rage he dominated the scene, dwarfing the huge men who towered over him.

"Traitors! Liars! I hold your lives in my hand! Aye, draw your swords if you will – Cormac, keep your blade in its sheath. These wolves will not bite a king! Wulfhere – I spared your lives when I could have taken them.

"You came to raid the countries of the South, sweeping down from the northern sea in your galleys. You ravaged the coasts and the smoke of burning villages hung like a cloud over the shores of Caledon. I trapped you all when you were pillaging and burning – with the blood of my people on your hands. I burned your long ships and ambushed you when you followed. With thrice your number of bowmen who burned for your lives hidden in the heathered hills about you, I spared you when we could have shot you down like trapped wolves. Because I spared you, you swore to come and fight for me."

"And shall we die because the Picts fight Rome?" rumbled a bearded raider.

"Your lives are forfeit to me; you came to ravage the South. I did not promise to send you all back to your homes in the North unharmed and loaded with loot. Your vow was to fight one battle against Rome under my standard. Then I will aid your survivors to build ships and you may go where you will, with a goodly share of the plunder we take from the legions. Rognar had kept his oath. But Rognar died in a skirmish with Roman scouts and now you, Wulfhere the Dissension-breeder, you stir up your comrades to dishonor themselves by that which a Northman hates – the breaking of the sworn word."

"We break no oath," snarled the Viking, and the king sensed the basic Germanic stubbornness, far harder to combat than the fickleness of the fiery Celts. "Give us a king, neither Pict, Gael nor Briton, and we will die for you. If not – then we will fight tomorrow for the greatest of all kings – the emperor of Rome!"

For a moment Cormac thought that the Pictish king, in his black rage, would draw and strike the Northman dead. The concentrated fury that blazed in Bran's dark eyes caused Wulfhere to recoil and drop a hand to his belt.

"Fool!" said Mak Morn in a low voice that vibrated with passion. "I could sweep you from the earth before the Romans are near enough to hear your death howls. Choose – fight for me on the morrow – or die tonight under a black cloud of arrows, a red storm of swords, a dark wave of chariots!"

At the mention of the chariots, the only arm of war that had ever broken the Norse shield-wall, Wulfhere changed expression, but he held his ground.

"War be it," he said doggedly. "Or a king to lead us!"

The Northmen responded with a short deep roar and a clash of swords on shields. Bran, eyes blazing, was about to speak again when a white shape glided silently into the ring of firelight.

"Soft words, soft words," said old Gonar tranquilly. "King, say no more. Wulfhere, you and your fellows will fight for us if you have a king to lead you?"

"We have sworn."

"Then be at ease," quoth the wizard; "for ere battle joins on the morrow I will send you such a king as no man on earth has followed for a hundred thousand years! A king neither Pict, Gael nor Briton, but one to whom the emperor of Rome is as but a village headman!"

While they stood undecided, Gonar took the arms of Cormac and Bran. "Come. And you, Northmen, remember your vow, and my promise which I have never broken. Sleep now, nor think to steal away in the darkness to the Roman camp, for if you escaped our shafts you would not escape either my curse or the suspicions of the legionaries."

So the three walked away and Cormac, looking back, saw Wulfhere standing by the fire, fingering his golden beard, with a look of puzzled anger on his lean evil face.

The three walked silently through the waving heather under the faraway stars while the weird night wind whispered ghostly secrets about them.

"Ages ago," said the wizard suddenly, "in the days when the world was young, great lands rose where now the ocean roars. On these lands thronged mighty nations and kingdoms. Greatest of all these was Valusia – Land of Enchantment. Rome is as a village compared to the splendor of the cities of Valusia. And the greatest king was Kull, who came from the land of Atlantis to wrest the crown of Valusia from a degenerate dynasty. The Picts who dwelt in the isles which now form the mountain peaks of a strange land upon the Western Ocean, were allies of Valusia, and the greatest of all the Pictish war-chiefs was Brule the Spear-slayer, first of the line men call Mak Morn.

"Kull gave to Brule the jewel which you now wear in your iron crown, oh king, after a strange battle in a dim land, and down the long ages it has come to us, ever a sign of the Mak Morn, a symbol of former greatness. When at last the sea rose and swallowed Valusia, Atlantis and Lemuria, only the Picts survived and they were scattered and few. Yet they began again the slow climb upward, and though many of the arts of civilization were lost in the great flood, yet they progressed. The art of metalworking was lost, so they excelled in the working of flint. And they ruled all the new lands flung up by the sea and now called Europe, until down from the north came younger tribes who had scarce risen from the ape when Valusia reigned in her glory, and who, dwelling in the icy lands about the Pole, knew naught of the lost splendor of the Seven Empires and little of the flood that had swept away half a world.

"And still they have come – Aryans, Celts, Germans, swarming down from the great cradle of their race which lies near the Pole. So again was the growth of the Pictish nation checked and the race hurled into savagery. Erased from the earth, on the fringe of the world with our backs to the wall we fight. Here in Caledon is the last stand of a once mighty race. And we change. Our people have mixed with the savages of an elder age which we drove into the North when we came into the Isles, and now, save for their chieftains, such as thou, Bran, a Pict is strange and abhorrent to look upon."

"True, true," said the king impatiently, "but what has that to do –"

"Kull, king of Valusia," said the wizard imperturbably, "was a barbarian in his age as thou art in thine, though he ruled a mighty empire by the weight of his sword. Gonar, friend of Brule, your first ancestor, has been dead a hundred thousand years as we reckon time. Yet I talked with him a scant hour agone."

"You talked with his ghost –"

"Or he with mine? Did I go back a hundred thousand years, or did he come forward? If he came to me out of the past, it is not I who talked with a dead man, but he who talked with a man unborn. Past, present and future are one to a wise man. I talked to Gonar while he was alive; likewise was I alive. In a timeless, spaceless land we met and he told me many things."

The land was growing light with the birth of dawn. The heather waved and bent in long rows before the dawn wind as bowing in worship of the rising sun.

"The jewel in your crown is a magnet that draws down the eons," said Gonar. "The sun is rising – and who comes out of the sunrise?"

Cormac and the king started. The sun was just lifting a red orb above the eastern hills. And full in the glow, etched boldly against the golden rim, a man suddenly appeared. They had not seen him come. Against the golden birth of day he loomed colossal; a gigantic god from the dawn of creation. Now as he strode toward them the waking hosts saw him and sent up a sudden shout of wonder.

"Who – or what is it?" exclaimed Bran.

"Let us go to meet him, Bran," answered the wizard. "He is the king Gonar has sent to save the people of Brule."

2

"I have reached these lands but newly
From an ultimate dim Thule;
From a wild weird clime that lieth sublime
Out of Space – out of Time."
– Poe.

The army fell silent as Bran, Cormac and Gonar went toward the stranger who approached in long swinging strides. As they neared him the illusion of monstrous size vanished, but they saw he was a man of great stature. At first Cormac thought him to be a Northman but a second glance told him that nowhere before had he seen such a man. He was built much like the Vikings, at once massive and lithe – tigerish. But his features were not as theirs, and his square-cut, lion-like mane of hair was as black as Bran's own. Under heavy brows glittered eyes gray as steel and cold as ice. His bronzed face, strong and inscrutable, was clean-shaven, and the broad forehead betokened a high intelligence, just as the firm jaw and thin lips showed willpower and courage. But more than all, the bearing of him, the unconscious lion-like stateliness, marked him as a natural king, a ruler of men.

Sandals of curious make were on his feet and he wore a pliant coat of strangely meshed mail which came almost to his knees. A broad belt with a great golden buckle encircled his waist, supporting a long straight sword in a heavy leather scabbard. His hair was confined by a wide, heavy golden band about his head.

Such was the man who paused before the silent group. He seemed slightly puzzled, slightly amused. Recognition flickered in his eyes. He spoke in a strange archaic Pictish which Cormac scarcely understood. His voice was deep and resonant.

"Ha, Brule, Gonar did not tell me I would dream of you!"

For the first time in his life Cormac saw the Pictish king completely thrown off his balance. He gaped, speechless. The stranger continued:

"And wearing the gem I gave you, in a circlet on your head! Last night you wore it in a ring on your finger."

"Last night?" gasped Bran.

"Last night or a hundred thousand years ago – all one!" murmured Gonar in evident enjoyment of the situation.

"I am not Brule," said Bran. "Are you mad to thus speak of a man dead a hundred thousand years? He was first of my line."

The stranger laughed unexpectedly. "Well, now I know I am dreaming! This will be a tale to tell Brule when I waken on the morrow! That I went into the future and saw men claiming descent from the Spear-slayer who is, as yet, not even married. No, you are not Brule, I see now, though you have his eyes and his bearing. But he is taller and broader in the shoulders. Yet you have his jewel – oh, well – anything can happen in a dream, so I will not quarrel with you. For a time I thought I had been transported to some other land in my sleep, and was in reality awake in a strange country, for this is the clearest dream I ever dreamed. Who are you?"

"I am Bran Mak Morn, king of the Caledonian Picts. And this ancient is Gonar, a wizard, of the line of Gonar. And this warrior is Cormac na Connacht, a prince of the isle of Erin."

The stranger slowly shook his lion-like head. "These words sound strangely to me, save Gonar – and that one is not Gonar, though he too is old. What land is this?"

"Caledon, or Alba, as the Gaels call it."

"And who are those squat ape-like warriors who watch us yonder, all agape?"

"They are the Picts who own my rule."

"How strangely distorted folk are in dreams!" muttered the stranger. "And who are those shock-headed men about the chariots?"

"They are Britons – Cymry from south of the Wall."

"What Wall?"

"The Wall built by Rome to keep the people of the heather out of Britain."

"Britain?" the tone was curious. "I never heard of that land – and what is Rome?"

"What!" cried Bran. "You never heard of Rome, the empire that rules the world?"

"No empire rules the world," answered the other haughtily. "The mightiest kingdom on Earth is that wherein I reign."

"And who are you?"

"Kull of Atlantis, king of Valusia!"

Cormac felt a coldness trickle down his spine. The cold gray eyes were unswerving – but this was incredible – monstrous – unnatural.

"Valusia!" cried Bran. "Why, man, the sea waves have rolled above the spires of Valusia for untold centuries!"

Kull laughed outright. "What a mad nightmare this is! When Gonar put on me the spell of deep sleep last night – or this night! – in the secret room of the inner palace, he told me I would dream strange things, but this is more fantastic than I reckoned. And the strangest thing is, I know I am dreaming!"

Gonar interposed as Bran would have spoken. "Question not the acts of the gods," muttered the wizard. "You are king because in the past you have seen and seized opportunities. The gods or the first Gonar have sent you this man. Let me deal with him."

Bran nodded, and while the silent army gaped in speechless wonder, just within earshot, Gonar spoke: "Oh great king, you dream, but is not all life a dream? How reckon you but that your former life is but a dream from which you have just awakened? Now we dream-folk have our wars and our peace, and just now a great host comes up from the south to destroy the people of Brule. Will you aid us?"

Kull grinned with pure zest. "Aye! I have fought battles in dreams ere now, have slain and been slain and was amazed when I woke from my visions. And at times, as now, dreaming I have known I dreamed. See, I pinch myself and feel it, but I know I dream for I have felt the pain of fierce wounds, in dreams. Yes, people of my dream, I will fight for you against the other dream-folk. Where are they?"

"And that you enjoy the dream more," said the wizard subtly, "forget that it is a dream and pretend that by the magic of the first Gonar, and the quality of the jewel you gave Brule, that now gleams on the crown of the Morni, you have in truth been transported forward into another, wilder age where the people of Brule fight for their life against a stronger foe."

For a moment the man who called himself king of Valusia seemed startled; a strange look of doubt, almost of fear, clouded his eyes. Then he laughed.

"Good! Lead on, wizard."

But now Bran took charge. He had recovered himself and was at ease. Whether he thought, like Cormac, that this was all a gigantic hoax arranged by Gonar, he showed no sign.

"King Kull, see you those men yonder who lean on their long-shafted axes as they gaze upon you?"

"The tall men with the golden hair and beards?"

"Aye – our success in the coming battle hinges on them. They swear to go over to the enemy if we give them not a king to lead them – their own having been slain. Will you lead them to battle?"

Kull's eyes glowed with appreciation. "They are men such as my own Red Slayers, my picked regiment. I will lead them."

"Come then."

The small group made their way down the slope, through throngs of warriors who pushed forward eagerly to get a better view of the stranger, then pressed back as he approached. An undercurrent of tense whispering ran through the horde.

The Northmen stood apart in a compact group. Their cold eyes took in Kull and he gave back their stares, taking in every detail of their appearance.

"Wulfhere," said Bran, "we have brought you a king. I hold you to your oath."

"Let him speak to us," said the Viking harshly.

"He can not speak your tongue," answered Bran, knowing that the Northmen knew nothing of the legends of his race. "He is a great king of the South –"

"He comes out of the past," broke in the wizard calmly. "He was the greatest of all kings, long ago."

"A dead man!" The Vikings moved uneasily and the rest of the horde pressed forward, drinking in every word. But Wulfhere scowled: "Shall a ghost lead living men? You bring us a man you say is dead. We will not follow a corpse."

"Wulfhere," said Bran in still passion, "you are a liar and a traitor. You set us this task, thinking it impossible. You yearn to fight under the Eagles of Rome. We have brought you a king neither Pict, Gael nor Briton and you deny your vow!"

"Let him fight me, then!" howled Wulfhere in uncontrollable wrath, swinging his ax about his head in a glittering arc. "If your dead man overcomes me – then my people will follow you. If I overcome him, you shall let us depart in peace to the camp of the legions!"

"Good!" said the wizard. "Do you agree, wolves of the North?"

A fierce yell and a brandishing of swords was the answer. Bran turned to Kull, who had stood silent, understanding nothing of what was said. But the Atlantean's eyes gleamed. Cormac felt that those cold eyes had looked on too many such scenes not to understand something of what had passed.

"This warrior says you must fight him for the leadership," said Bran, and Kull, eyes glittering with growing battle-joy, nodded: "I guessed as much. Give us space."

"A shield and a helmet!" shouted Bran, but Kull shook his head.

"I need none," he growled. "Back and give us room to swing our steel!"

Men pressed back on each side, forming a solid ring about the two men, who now approached each other warily. Kull had drawn his sword and the great blade shimmered like a live thing in his hand. Wulfhere, scarred by a hundred savage fights, flung aside his wolfskin mantle and came in cautiously, fierce eyes peering over the top of his out-thrust shield, ax half-lifted in his right hand.

Suddenly when the warriors were still many feet apart Kull sprang. His attack brought a gasp from men used to deeds of prowess; for like a leaping tiger he shot through the air and his sword crashed on the quickly lifted shield. Sparks flew and Wulfhere's ax hacked in, but Kull was under its sweep and as it swished viciously above his head he thrust upward and sprang out again, cat-like. His motions had been too quick for the eye to follow. The upper edge of Wulfhere's shield showed a deep cut, and there was a long rent in his mail shirt where Kull's sword had barely missed the flesh beneath.

Cormac, trembling with the terrible thrill of the fight, wondered at this sword that could thus slice through scale-mail. And the blow that gashed the shield should have shattered the blade. Yet not a notch showed in the Valusian steel! Surely this blade was forged by another people in another age!

Now the two giants leaped again to the attack and like double strokes of lightning their weapons crashed. Wulfhere's shield fell from his arm in two pieces as the Atlantean's sword sheared clear through it, and Kull staggered as the Northman's ax, driven with all the force of his great body, descended on the golden circlet about his head. That blow should have sheared through the gold like butter to split the skull beneath, but the ax rebounded, showing a great notch in the edge. The next instant the Northman was overwhelmed by a whirlwind of steel – a storm of strokes delivered with such swiftness and power that he was borne back as on the crest of a wave, unable to launch an attack of his own. With all his tried skill he sought to parry the singing steel with his ax. But he could only avert his doom for a few seconds; could only for an instant turn the whistling blade that hewed off bits of his mail, so close fell the blows. One of the horns flew from his helmet; then the ax-head itself fell away, and the same blow that severed the handle, bit through the Viking's helmet into the scalp beneath. Wulfhere was dashed to his knees, a trickle of blood starting down his face.

Kull checked his second stroke, and tossing his sword to Cormac, faced the dazed Northman weaponless. The Atlantean's eyes were blazing with ferocious joy and he roared something in a strange tongue. Wulfhere gathered his legs under him and bounded up, snarling like a wolf, a dagger flashing into his hand. The watching horde gave tongue in a yell that ripped the skies as the two bodies clashed. Kull's clutching hand missed the Northman's wrist but the desperately lunging dagger snapped on the Atlantean's mail, and dropping the useless hilt, Wulfhere locked his arms about his foe in a bear-like grip that would have crushed the ribs of a lesser man. Kull grinned tigerishly and returned the grapple, and for a moment the two swayed on their feet. Slowly the black-haired warrior bent his foe backward until it seemed his spine would snap. With a howl that had nothing of the human in it, Wulfhere clawed frantically at Kull's face, trying to tear out his eyes, then turned his head and snapped his fang-like teeth into the Atlantean's arm. A yell went up as a trickle of blood started: "He bleeds! He bleeds! He is no ghost, after all, but a mortal man!"

Angered, Kull shifted his grip, shoving the frothing Wulfhere away from him, and smote him terrifically under the ear with his right hand. The Viking landed on his back a dozen feet away. Then, howling like a wild man, he leaped up with a stone in his hand and flung it. Only Kull's incredible quickness saved his face; as it was, the rough edge of the missile tore his cheek and inflamed him to madness. With a lion-like roar he bounded upon his foe, enveloped him in an irresistible blast of sheer fury, whirled him high above his head as if he were a child and cast him a dozen feet away. Wulfhere pitched on his head and lay still – broken and dead.

Dazed silence reigned for an instant; then from the Gaels went up a thundering roar, and the Britons and Picts took it up, howling like wolves, until the echoes of the shouts and the clangor of sword on shield reached the ears of the marching legionaries, miles to the south.

"Men of the gray North," shouted Bran, "will you hold by your oath *now*?"

The fierce souls of the Northmen were in their eyes as their spokesman answered. Primitive, superstitious, steeped in tribal lore of fighting gods and mythical heroes, they did not doubt that the black-haired fighting man was some supernatural being sent by the fierce gods of battle.

"Aye! Such a man as this we have never seen! Dead man, ghost or devil, we will follow him, whether the trail lead to Rome or Valhalla!"

Kull understood the meaning, if not the words. Taking his sword from Cormac with a word of thanks, he turned to the waiting Northmen and silently held the blade toward them high above his head, in both hands, before he returned it to its scabbard. Without understanding, they appreciated the action. Bloodstained and disheveled, he was an impressive picture of stately, magnificent barbarism.

"Come," said Bran, touching the Atlantean's arm; "a host is marching on us and we have much to do. There is scant time to arrange our forces before they will be upon us. Come to the top of yonder slope."

There the Pict pointed. They were looking down into a valley which ran north and south, widening from a narrow gorge in the north until it debouched upon a plain to the south. The whole valley was less than a mile in length.

"Up this valley will our foes come," said the Pict, "because they have wagons loaded with supplies and on all sides of this vale the ground is too rough for such travel. Here we plan an ambush."

"I would have thought you would have had your men lying in wait long before now," said Kull. "What of the scouts the enemy is sure to send out?"

"The savages I lead would never have waited in ambush so long," said Bran with a touch of bitterness. "I could not post them until I was sure of the Northmen. Even so I had not dared to post them ere now – even yet they may take panic from the drifting of a cloud or the blowing of a leaf, and scatter like birds before a cold wind. King Kull – the fate of the Pictish nation is at stake. I am called king of the Picts, but my rule as yet is but a hollow mockery. The hills are full of wild clans who refuse to fight for me. Of the thousand bowmen now at my command, more than half are of my own clan.

"Some eighteen hundred Romans are marching against us. It is not a real invasion, but much hinges upon it. It is the beginning of an attempt to extend their boundaries. They plan to build a fortress a day's march to the north of this valley. If they do, they will build other forts, drawing bands of steel about the heart of the free people. If I win this battle and wipe out this army, I will win a double victory. Then the tribes will flock to me and the next invasion will meet a solid wall of resistance. If I lose, the clans will scatter, fleeing into the north until they can no longer flee, fighting as separate clans rather than as one strong nation.

"I have a thousand archers, five hundred horsemen, fifty chariots with their drivers and swordsmen – one hundred fifty men in all – and, thanks to you, three hundred heavily armed Northern pirates. How would you arrange your battle lines?"

"Well," said Kull, "I would have barricaded the north end of the valley – no! That would suggest a trap. But I would block it with a band of desperate men, like those you have given me to lead. Three hundred could hold the gorge for a time against any number. Then, when the enemy was engaged with these men to the narrow part of the valley, I would have my archers shoot down into them until their ranks are broken, from both sides of the vale. Then, having my horsemen concealed behind one ridge and my chariots behind the other, I would charge with both simultaneously and sweep the foe into a red ruin."

Bran's eyes glowed. "Exactly, king of Valusia. Such was my exact plan –"

"But what of the scouts?"

"My warriors are like panthers; they hide under the noses of the Romans. Those who ride into the valley will see only what we wish them to see. Those who ride over the ridge will not come back to report. An arrow is swift and silent.

"You see that the pivot of the whole thing depends on the men that hold the gorge. They must be men who can fight on foot and resist the charges of the heavy legionaries long enough for the trap to close. Outside these Northmen I had no such force of men. My naked warriors with their short swords could never stand such a charge for an instant. Nor is the armor of the Celts made for such work; moreover, they are not foot-fighters, and I need them elsewhere.

"So you see why I had such desperate need of the Northmen. Now will you stand in the gorge with them and hold back the Romans until I can spring the trap? Remember, most of you will die."

Kull smiled. "I have taken chances all my life, though Tu, chief councilor, would say my life belongs to Valusia and I have no right to so risk it –" His voice trailed off and a strange look flitted across his face. "By Valka," said he, laughing uncertainly, "sometimes I forget this is a dream! All seems so real. But it is – of course it is! Well, then, if I die I will but awaken as I have done in times past. Lead on, king of Caledon!"

Cormac, going to his warriors, wondered. Surely it was all a hoax; yet – he heard the arguments of the warriors all about him as they armed themselves and prepared to take their posts. The black-haired king was Neid himself, the Celtic war-god; he was an antediluvian king brought out of the past by Gonar; he was a mythical fighting man out of Valhalla. He was no man at all but a ghost! No, he was mortal, for he had bled. But the gods themselves bled, though they did not die. So the controversies raged. At least, thought Cormac, if it was all a hoax to inspire the warriors with the feeling of supernatural aid, it had succeeded. The belief that Kull was more than a mortal man had fired Celt, Pict and Viking alike into a sort of inspired madness. And Cormac asked himself – what did he himself believe? This man was surely one from some far land – yet in his every look and action there was a vague hint of a greater difference than mere distance of space – a hint of alien Time, of misty abysses and gigantic gulfs of eons lying between the black-haired stranger and the men with whom he walked and talked. Clouds of bewilderment mazed Cormac's brain and he laughed in whimsical self-mockery.

3

"And the two wild peoples of the north
Stood fronting in the gloam,
And heard and knew each in his mind
A third great sound upon the wind,
The living walls that hedge mankind,
The walking walls of Rome."
– Chesterton.

The sun slanted westward. Silence lay like an invisible mist over the valley. Cormac gathered the reins in his hand and glanced up at the ridges on both sides. The waving heather which grew rank on those steep slopes gave no evidence of the hundreds of savage warriors who lurked there. Here in the narrow gorge which widened gradually southward was the only sign of life. Between the steep walls three hundred Northmen were massed solidly in their wedge-shaped shield-wall, blocking the pass. At the tip, like the point of a spear, stood the man who called himself Kull, king of Valusia. He wore no helmet, only the great, strangely worked head-band of hard gold, but he bore on his left arm the great shield borne by the dead Rognar; and in his right hand he held the heavy iron mace wielded by the sea-king. The Vikings eyed him in wonder and savage admiration. They could not understand his language, or he theirs. But no further orders were necessary. At Bran's directions they had bunched themselves in the gorge, and their only order was – hold the pass!

Bran Mak Morn stood just in front of Kull. So they faced each other, he whose kingdom was yet unborn, and he whose kingdom had been lost in the mists of Time for unguessed ages. Kings of darkness, thought Cormac, nameless kings of the night, whose realms are gulfs and shadows.

The hand of the Pictish king went out. "King Kull, you are more than king – you are a man. Both of us may fall within the next hour – but if we both live, ask what you will of me."

Kull smiled, returning the firm grip. "You too are a man after my own heart, king of the shadows. Surely you are more than a figment of my sleeping imagination. Mayhap we will meet in waking life some day."

Bran shook his head in puzzlement, swung into the saddle and rode away, climbing the eastern slope and vanishing over the ridge.

Cormac hesitated: "Strange man, are you in truth of flesh and blood, or are you a ghost?"

"When we dream, we are all flesh and blood – so long as we are dreaming," Kull answered. "This is the strangest nightmare I have ever known – but you, who will soon fade into sheer nothingness as I awaken, seem as real to me *now,* as Brule, or Kananu, or Tu, or Kelkor."

Cormac shook his head as Bran had done, and with a last salute, which Kull returned with barbaric stateliness, he turned and trotted away. At the top of the western ridge he paused. Away to the south a light cloud of dust rose and the head of the marching column was in sight. Already he believed he could feel the earth vibrate slightly to the measured tread of a thousand mailed feet beating in perfect unison. He dismounted, and one of his chieftains, Domnail, took his steed and led it down the slope away from the valley, where trees grew thickly. Only an occasional vague movement among them gave evidence of the five hundred men who stood there, each at his horse's head with a ready hand to check a chance nicker.

Oh, thought Cormac, *the gods themselves made this valley for Bran's ambush!* The floor of the valley was treeless and the inner slopes were bare save for the waist-high heather. But at the foot of each ridge on the side facing away from the vale, where the soil long washed from the rocky slopes had accumulated, there grew enough trees to hide five hundred horsemen or fifty chariots.

At the northern end of the valley stood Kull and his three hundred Vikings, in open view, flanked on each side by fifty Pictish bowmen. Hidden on the western side of the western ridge were the Gaels. Along the top of the slopes, concealed in the tall heather, lay a hundred Picts with their shafts on string. The rest of the Picts were hidden on the eastern slopes beyond which lay the Britons with their chariots in full readiness. Neither they nor the Gaels to the west could see what went on in the vale, but signals had been arranged.

Now the long column was entering the wide mouth of the valley and their scouts, light-armed men on swift horses, were spreading out between the slopes. They galloped almost within bowshot of the silent host that blocked the pass, then halted. Some whirled and raced back to the main force, while the others deployed and cantered up the slopes, seeking to see what lay beyond. This was the crucial moment. If they got any hint of the ambush, all was lost.

Cormac, shrinking down into the heather, marveled at the ability of the Picts to efface themselves from view so completely. He saw a horseman pass within three feet of where he knew a bowman lay, yet the Roman saw nothing.

The scouts topped the ridges, gazed about; then most of them turned and trotted back down the slopes. Cormac wondered at their desultory manner of scouting. He had never fought Romans before, knew nothing of their arrogant self-confidence, of their incredible shrewdness in some ways, their incredible stupidity in others. These men were overconfident; a feeling radiating from their officers. It had been years since a force of Caledonians had stood before the legions. And most of these men were but newly come to Britain; part of a legion which had been quartered in Egypt. They despised their foes and suspected nothing.

But stay – three riders on the opposite ridge had turned and vanished on the other side. And now one, sitting his steed at the crest of the western ridge, not a hundred yards from where Cormac lay, looked long and narrowly down into the mass of trees at the foot of the slope. Cormac saw suspicion grow on his brown, hawk-like face. He half turned as though to call to his comrades, then instead reined his steed down the slope, leaning forward in his saddle. Cormac's heart pounded. Each moment he expected to see the man wheel and gallop back to raise the alarm. He resisted a mad impulse to leap up and charge the Roman on foot. Surely the man could feel the tenseness in the air – the hundreds of fierce eyes upon him. Now he was halfway down the slope, out of sight of the men in the valley. And now the twang of an unseen bow broke the painful stillness. With a strangled gasp the Roman flung his hands high, and as the steed reared, he pitched headlong, transfixed by a long black arrow that had flashed from the heather. A stocky dwarf sprang out of nowhere, seemingly, and seized the bridle, quieting the snorting horse, and leading it down the slope. At the fall of the Roman, short crooked men rose like a sudden flight of birds from the grass and Cormac saw the flash of a knife. Then with unreal suddenness all had subsided. Slayers and slain were unseen and only the still-waving heather marked the grim deed.

The Gael looked back into the valley. The three who had ridden over the eastern ridge had not come back and Cormac knew they never would. Evidently the other scouts had borne word that only a small band of warriors was ready to dispute the passage of the legionaries. Now the head of the column was almost below him and he thrilled at the sight of these men who were doomed, swinging along with their superb arrogance. And the sight of their splendid armor, their hawk-like faces and perfect discipline awed him as much as it is possible for a Gael to be awed.

Twelve hundred men in heavy armor who marched as one so that the ground shook to their tread! Most of them were of middle height, with powerful chests and shoulders and bronzed faces – hard-bitten veterans of a hundred campaigns. Cormac noted their javelins, short keen swords and heavy shields; their gleaming armor and crested helmets, the eagles on the standards. These were the men beneath whose tread the world had shaken and empires crumbled! Not all were Latins; there were Romanized Britons among them and one century or hundred was composed of huge yellow-haired men – Gauls and Germans, who fought for Rome as fiercely as did the native-born, and hated their wilder kinsmen more savagely.

On each side was a swarm of cavalry, outriders, and the column was flanked by archers and slingers. A number of lumbering wagons carried the supplies of the army. Cormac saw the commander riding in his place – a tall man with a lean, imperious face, evident even at that distance. Marcus Sulius – the Gael knew him by repute.

A deep-throated roar rose from the legionaries as they approached their foes. Evidently they intended to slice their way through and continue without a pause, for the column moved implacably on. Whom the gods destroy they first make mad – Cormac had never heard the phrase but it came to him that the great Sulius was a fool. Roman arrogance! Marcus was used to lashing the cringing peoples of a decadent East; little he guessed of the iron in these western races.

A group of cavalry detached itself and raced into the mouth of the gorge, but it was only a gesture. With loud jeering shouts they wheeled three spears length away and cast their javelins, which rattled harmlessly on the overlapping shields of the silent Northmen. But their leader dared too much; swinging in, he leaned from his saddle and thrust at Kull's face. The great shield turned the lance and Kull struck back as a snake strikes; the ponderous mace crushed helmet and head like an eggshell, and the very steed went to its knees from the shock of that terrible blow. From the Northmen went up a short fierce roar, and the Picts beside them howled exultantly and loosed their arrows among the retreating horsemen.

First blood for the people of the heather! The oncoming Romans shouted vengefully and quickened their pace as the frightened horse raced by, a ghastly travesty of a man, foot caught in the stirrup, trailing beneath the pounding hoofs.

Now the first line of the legionaries, compressed because of the narrowness of the gorge, crashed against the solid wall of shields – crashed and recoiled upon itself. The shield-wall had not shaken an inch. This was the first time the Roman legions had met with that unbreakable formation – that oldest of all Aryan battle-lines – the ancestor of the Spartan regiment – the Theban phalanx – the Macedonian formation – the English square.

Shield crashed on shield and the short Roman sword sought for an opening in that iron wall. Viking spears bristling in solid ranks above, thrust and reddened; heavy axes chopped down, shearing through iron, flesh and bone. Cormac saw Kull, looming above the stocky Romans in the forefront of the fray, dealing blows like thunderbolts. A burly centurion rushed in, shield held high, stabbing upward. The iron mace crashed terribly, shivering the sword, rending the shield apart, shattering the helmet, crushing the skull down between the shoulders – in a single blow.

The front line of the Romans bent like a steel bar about the wedge, as the legionaries sought to struggle through the gorge on each side and surround their opposers. But the pass was too narrow; crouching close against the steep walls the Picts drove their black arrows in a hail of death. At this range the heavy shafts tore through shield and corselet, transfixing the armored men. The front line of battle rolled back, red and broken, and the Northmen trod their few dead underfoot to close the gaps their fall had made. Stretched the full width of their front lay a thin line of shattered forms – the red spray of the tide which had broken upon them in vain.

Cormac had leaped to his feet, waving his arms. Domnail and his men broke cover at the signal and came galloping up the slope, lining the ridge. Cormac mounted the horse brought him and glanced impatiently across the narrow vale. No sign of life appeared on the eastern ridge. Where was Bran – and the Britons?

Down in the valley, the legions, angered at the unexpected opposition of the paltry force in front of them, but not suspicious, were forming in more compact body. The wagons which had halted were lumbering on again and the whole column was once more in motion as if it intended to crash through by sheer weight. With the Gaulish century in the forefront, the legionaries were advancing again in the attack. This time, with the full force of twelve hundred men behind, the charge would batter down the resistance of Kull's warriors like a heavy ram; would stamp them down, sweep over their red ruins. Cormac's men trembled in impatience. Suddenly Marcus Sulius turned and gazed westward, where the line of horsemen was etched against the sky. Even at that distance Cormac saw his face pale. The Roman at last realized the metal of the men he faced, and that he had walked into a trap. Surely in that moment there flashed a chaotic picture through his brain – defeat – disgrace – red ruin!

It was too late to retreat – too late to form into a defensive square with the wagons for barricade. There was but one possible way out, and Marcus, crafty general in spite of his recent blunder, took it. Cormac heard his voice cut like a clarion through the din, and though he did not understand the words, he knew that the Roman was shouting for his men to smite that knot of Northmen like a blast – to hack their way through and out of the trap before it could close!

Now the legionaries, aware of their desperate plight, flung themselves headlong and terribly on their foes. The shield-wall rocked, but it gave not an inch. The wild faces of the Gauls and the hard brown Italian faces glared over locked shields into the blazing eyes of the North. Shields touching, they smote and slew and died in a red storm of slaughter, where crimsoned axes rose and fell and dripping spears broke on notched swords.

Where in God's name was Bran with his chariots? A few minutes more would spell the doom of every man who held that pass. Already they were falling fast, though they locked their ranks closer and held like iron. Those wild men of the North were dying in their tracks; and looming among their golden heads the black lion-mane of Kull shone like a symbol of slaughter, and his reddened mace showered a ghastly rain as it splashed brains and blood like water.

Something snapped in Cormac's brain.

"These men will die while we wait for Bran's signal!" he shouted. "On! Follow me into Hell, sons of Gael!"

A wild roar answered him, and loosing rein he shot down the slope with five hundred yelling riders plunging headlong after him. And even at that moment a storm of arrows swept the valley from either side like a dark cloud and the terrible clamor of the Picts split the skies. And over the eastern ridge, like a sudden burst of rolling thunder on Judgment Day, rushed the war-chariots. Headlong down the slope they roared, foam flying from the horses' distended nostrils, frantic feet scarcely seeming to touch the ground, making naught of the tall heather. In the foremost chariot, with his dark eyes blazing, crouched Bran Mak Morn, and in all of them the naked Britons were screaming and lashing as if possessed by demons. Behind the flying chariots came the Picts, howling like wolves and loosing their arrows as they ran. The heather belched them forth from all sides in a dark wave.

So much Cormac saw in chaotic glimpses during that wild ride down the slopes. A wave of cavalry swept between him and the main line of the column. Three long leaps ahead of his men, the Gaelic prince met the spears of the Roman riders. The first lance turned on his buckler, and rising in his stirrups he smote downward, cleaving his man from shoulder to breastbone. The next Roman flung a javelin that killed Domnail, but at that instant Cormac's steed crashed into his, breast to breast, and the lighter horse rolled headlong under the shock, flinging his rider beneath the pounding hoofs.

Then the whole blast of the Gaelic charge smote the Roman cavalry, shattering it, crashing and rolling it down and under. Over its red ruins Cormac's yelling demons struck the heavy Roman infantry, and the whole line reeled at the shock. Swords and axes flashed up and down and the force of their rush carried them deep into the massed ranks. Here, checked, they swayed and strove. Javelins thrust, swords flashed upward, bringing down horse and rider, and greatly outnumbered, leaguered on every side, the Gaels had perished among their foes, but at that instant, from the other side the crashing chariots smote the Roman ranks. In one long line they struck almost simultaneously, and at the moment of impact the charioteers wheeled their horses side-long and raced parallel down the ranks, shearing men down like the mowing of wheat. Hundreds died on those curving blades in that moment, and leaping from the chariots, screaming like blood-mad wildcats, the British swordsmen flung themselves upon the spears of the legionaries, hacking madly with their two-handed swords. Crouching, the Picts drove their arrows point-blank and then sprang in to slash and thrust. Maddened with the sight of victory, these wild peoples were like wounded tigers, feeling no wounds, and dying on their feet with their last gasp a snarl of fury.

But the battle was not over yet. Dazed, shattered, their formation broken and nearly half their number down already, the Romans fought back with desperate fury. Hemmed in on all sides they slashed and smote singly, or in small clumps, fought back to back, archers, slingers, horsemen and heavy legionaries mingled into a chaotic mass. The confusion was complete, but not the victory. Those bottled in the gorge still hurled themselves upon the red axes that barred their way, while the massed and serried battle thundered behind them. From one side Cormac's Gaels raged and slashed; from the other chariots swept back and forth, retiring and returning like iron whirlwinds. There was no retreat, for the Picts had flung a cordon across the way they had come, and having cut the throats of the camp followers and possessed themselves of the wagons, they sent their shafts in a storm of death into the rear of the shattered column. Those long black arrows pierced armor and bone, nailing men together. Yet the slaughter was not all on one side. Picts died beneath the lightning thrust of javelin and shortsword, Gaels pinned beneath their falling horses were hewed to pieces, and chariots, cut loose from their horses, were deluged with the blood of the charioteers.

And at the narrow head of the valley still the battle surged and eddied. Great gods – thought Cormac, glancing between lightning-like blows – do these men still hold the gorge? Aye! They held it! A tenth of their original number, dying on their feet, they still held back the frantic charges of the dwindling legionaries.

Over all the field went up the roar and the clash of arms, and birds of prey, swift-flying out of the sunset, circled above. Cormac, striving to reach Marcus Sulius through the press, saw the Roman's horse sink under him, and the rider rise alone in a waste of foes. He saw the Roman sword flash thrice, dealing a death at each blow; then from the thickest of the fray bounded a terrible figure. It was Bran Mak Morn, stained from head to foot. He cast away his broken sword as he ran, drawing a dirk. The Roman struck, but the Pictish king was under the thrust, and gripping the sword-wrist, he drove the dirk again and again through the gleaming armor.

A mighty roar went up as Marcus died, and Cormac, with a shout, rallied the remnants of his force about him and, striking in the spurs, burst through the shattered lines and rode full speed for the other end of the valley.

But as he approached he saw that he was too late. As they had lived, so had they died, those fierce sea-wolves, with their faces to the foe and their broken weapons red in their hands. In a grim and silent band they lay, even in death preserving some of the shield-wall formation. Among them, in front of them and all about them lay high-heaped the bodies of those who had sought to break them, in vain. *They had not given back a foot!* To the last man, they had died in their tracks. Nor were there any left to stride over their torn shapes; those Romans who had escaped the Viking axes had been struck down by the shafts of the Picts and swords of the Gaels from behind.

Yet this part of the battle was not over. High up on the steep western slope Cormac saw the ending of that drama. A group of Gauls in the armor of Rome pressed upon a single man – a black-haired giant on whose head gleamed a golden crown. There was iron in these men, as well as in the man who had held them to their fate. They were doomed – their comrades were being slaughtered behind them – but before their turn came they would at least have the life of the black-haired chief who had led the golden-haired men of the North.

Pressing upon him from three sides they had forced him slowly back up the steep gorge wall, and the crumpled bodies that stretched along his retreat showed how fiercely every foot of the way had been contested. Here on this steep it was task enough to keep one's footing alone; yet these men at once climbed and fought. Kull's shield and the huge mace were gone, and the great sword in his right hand was dyed crimson. His mail, wrought with a forgotten art, now hung in shreds, and blood streamed from a hundred wounds on limbs, head and body. But his eyes still blazed with the battle-joy and his wearied arm still drove the mighty blade in strokes of death.

But Cormac saw that the end would come before they could reach him. Now at the very crest of the steep, a hedge of points menaced the strange king's life, and even his iron strength was ebbing. Now he split the skull of a huge warrior and the backstroke shore through the neck-cords of another; reeling under a very rain of swords he struck again and his victim dropped at his feet, cleft to the breastbone. Then, even as a dozen swords rose above the staggering Atlantean for the death stroke, a strange thing happened. The sun was sinking into the western sea; all the heather swam red like an ocean of blood. Etched in the dying sun, as he had first appeared, Kull stood, and then, like a mist lifting, a mighty vista opened behind the reeling king. Cormac's astounded eyes caught a fleeting gigantic glimpse of other climes and spheres – as if mirrored in summer clouds he saw, instead of the heather hills stretching away to the sea, a dim and mighty land of blue mountains and gleaming quiet lakes – the golden, purple and sapphirean spires and towering walls of a mighty city such as the earth has not known for many a drifting age.

Then like the fading of a mirage it was gone, but the Gauls on the high slope had dropped their weapons and stared like men dazed – *For the man called Kull had vanished and there was no trace of his going!*

As in a daze Cormac turned his steed and rode back across the trampled field. His horse's hoofs splashed in lakes of blood and clanged against the helmets of dead men. Across the valley the shout of victory was thundering. Yet all seemed shadowy and strange. A shape was striding across the torn corpses and Cormac was dully aware that it was Bran. The Gael swung from his horse and fronted the king. Bran was weaponless and gory; blood trickled from gashes on brow, breast and limb; what armor he had worn was clean hacked away and a cut had shorn halfway through his iron crown. But the red jewel still gleamed unblemished like a star of slaughter.

"It is in my mind to slay you," said the Gael heavily and like a man speaking in a daze, "for the blood of brave men is on your head. Had you given the signal to charge sooner, some would have lived."

Bran folded his arms; his eyes were haunted. "Strike if you will; I am sick of slaughter. It is a cold mead, this kinging it. A king must gamble with men's lives and naked swords. The lives of all my people were at stake; I sacrificed the Northmen – yes; and my heart is sore within me, for they were men! But had I given the order when you would have desired, all might have gone awry. The Romans were not yet massed in the narrow mouth of the gorge, and might have had time and space to form their ranks again and beat us off. I waited until the last moment – and the rovers died. A king belongs to his people, and can not let either his own feelings or the lives of men influence him. Now my people are saved; but my heart is cold in my breast."

Cormac wearily dropped his sword-point to the ground.

"You are a born king of men, Bran," said the Gaelic prince.

Bran's eyes roved the field. A mist of blood hovered over all, where the victorious barbarians were looting the dead, while those Romans who had escaped slaughter by throwing down their swords and now stood under guard, looked on with hot smoldering eyes.

"My kingdom – my people – are saved," said Bran wearily. "They will come from the heather by the thousands and when Rome moves against us again, she will meet a solid nation. But I am weary. What of Kull?"

"My eyes and brain were mazed with battle," answered Cormac. "I thought to see him vanish like a ghost into the sunset. I will seek his body."

"Seek not for him," said Bran. "Out of the sunrise he came – into the sunset he has gone. Out of the mists of the ages he came to us, and back into the mists of the eons has he returned – to his own kingdom."

Cormac turned away; night was gathering. Gonar stood like a white specter before him.

"To his own kingdom," echoed the wizard. "Time and Space are naught. Kull has returned to his own kingdom – his own crown – his own age."

"Then he was a ghost?"

"Did you not feel the grip of his solid hand? Did you not hear his voice – see him eat and drink, laugh and slay and bleed?"

Still Cormac stood like one in a trance.

"Then if it be possible for a man to pass from one age into one yet unborn, or come forth from a century dead and forgotten, whichever you will, with his flesh-and-blood body and his arms – then he is as mortal as he was in his own day. Is Kull dead, then?"

"He died a hundred thousand years ago, as men reckon time," answered the wizard, "but in his own age. He died not from the swords of the Gauls of this age. Have we not heard in legends how the king of Valusia traveled into a strange, timeless land of the misty future ages, and there fought in a great battle? Why, so he did! A hundred thousand years ago, or today!

"And a hundred thousand years ago – or a moment agone! – Kull, king of Valusia, roused himself on the silken couch in his secret chamber and laughing, spoke to the first Gonar, saying: 'Ha, wizard, I have in truth dreamed strangely, for I went into a far clime and a far time in my visions, and fought for the king of a strange shadow-people!' And the great sorcerer smiled and pointed silently at the red, notched sword, and the torn mail and the many wounds that the king carried. And Kull, fully woken from his 'vision' and feeling the sting and the weakness of these yet bleeding wounds, fell silent and mazed, and all life and time and space seemed like a dream of ghosts to him, and he wondered thereat all the rest of his life. For the wisdom of the Eternities is denied even unto princes and Kull could no more understand what Gonar told him than you can understand my words."

"And then Kull lived despite his many wounds," said Cormac, "and has returned to the mists of silence and the centuries. Well – he thought us a dream; we thought him a ghost. And sure, life is but a web spun of ghosts and dreams and illusion, and it is in my mind that the kingdom which has this day been born of swords and slaughter in this howling valley is a thing no more solid than the foam of the bright sea."

THE SONG OF THE MAD MINSTREL

Weird Tales, February-March 1931

I am the thorn in the foot, I am the blur in the sight;
I am the worm at the root, I am the thief in the night.
I am the rat in the wall, the leper that leers at the gate;
I am the ghost in the hall, herald of horror and hate.

I am the rust on the corn, I am the smut on the wheat,
Laughing man's labor to scorn, weaving a web for his feet.
I am canker and mildew and blight, danger and death and decay;
The rot of the rain by night, the blast of the sun by day.

I warp and wither with drought, I work in the swamp's foul yeast;
I bring the black plague from the south and the leprosy in from the east.
I rend from the hemlock boughs wine steeped in the petals of dooms;
Where the fat black serpents drowse I gather the Upas blooms.

I have plumbed the northern ice for a spell like frozen lead;
In lost gray fields of rice, I have learned from Mongol dead.
Where a bleak black mountain stands I have looted grisly caves;
I have digged in the desert sands to plunder terrible graves.

Never the sun goes forth, never the moon glows red,
But out of the south or the north, I come with the slavering dead.
I come with hideous spells, black chants and ghastly tunes;
I have looted the hidden hells and plundered the lost black moons.

There was never a king or priest to cheer me by word or look,
There was never a man or beast in the blood-black ways I took.
There were crimson gulfs unplumbed, there were black wings over a sea;
There were pits where mad things drummed, and foaming blasphemy.

There were vast ungodly tombs where slimy monsters dreamed;
There were clouds like blood-drenched plumes where unborn demons
screamed.
There were ages dead to Time, and lands lost out of Space;
There were adders in the slime, and a dim unholy Face.

Oh, the heart in my breast turned stone, and the brain froze in my skull –
But I won through, I alone, and poured my chalice full
Of horrors and dooms and spells, black buds and bitter roots –
From the hells beneath the hells, I bring you my deathly fruits.

THE CHILDREN OF THE NIGHT

Weird Tales, April-May 1931

There were, I remember, six of us in Conrad's bizarrely fashioned study, with its queer relics from all over the world and its long rows of books which ranged from the Mandrake Press edition of Boccaccio to a *Missale Romanum*, bound in clasped oak boards and printed in Venice, 1740. Clemants and Professor Kirowan had just engaged in a somewhat testy anthropological argument: Clemants upholding the theory of a separate, distinct Alpine race, while the professor maintained that this so-called race was merely a deviation from an original Aryan stock – possibly the result of an admixture between the southern or Mediterranean races and the Nordic people.

"And how," asked Clemants, "do you account for their brachycephalicism? The Mediterraneans were as long-headed as the Aryans: would admixture between these dolichocephalic peoples produce a broad-headed intermediate type?"

"Special conditions might bring about a change in an originally long-headed race," snapped Kirowan. "Boaz has demonstrated, for instance, that in the case of immigrants to America, skull formations often change in one generation. And Flinders Petrie has shown that the Lombards changed from a long-headed to a round-headed race in a few centuries."

"But what caused these changes?"

"Much is yet unknown to science," answered Kirowan, "and we need not be dogmatic. No one knows, as yet, why people of British and Irish ancestry tend to grow unusually tall in the Darling district of Australia – Cornstalks, as they are called – or why people of such descent generally have thinner jaw-structures after a few generations in New England. The universe is full of the unexplainable."

"And therefore the uninteresting, according to Machen," laughed Taverel.

Conrad shook his head. "I must disagree. To me, the unknowable is most tantalizingly fascinating."

"Which accounts, no doubt, for all the works on witchcraft and demonology I see on your shelves," said Ketrick, with a wave of his hand toward the rows of books.

And let me speak of Ketrick. Each of the six of us was of the same breed – that is to say, a Briton or an American of British descent. By British, I include all natural inhabitants of the British Isles. We represented various strains of English and Celtic blood, but basically, these strains are the same after all. But Ketrick: to me the man always seemed strangely alien. It was in his eyes that this difference showed externally. They were a sort of amber, almost yellow, and slightly oblique. At times, when one looked at his face from certain angles, they seemed to slant like a Chinaman's.

Others than I had noticed this feature, so unusual in a man of pure Anglo-Saxon descent. The usual myths ascribing his slanted eyes to some pre-natal influence had been mooted about, and I remember Professor Hendrik Brooler once remarked that Ketrick was undoubtedly an atavism, representing a reversion of type to some dim and distant ancestor of Mongolian blood – a sort of freak reversion, since none of his family showed such traces.

But Ketrick comes of the Welsh branch of the Cetrics of Sussex, and his lineage is set down in the *Book of Peers*. There you may read the line of his ancestry, which extends unbroken to the days of Canute. No slightest trace of Mongoloid intermixture appears in the genealogy, and how could there have been such intermixture in old Saxon England? For Ketrick is the modern form of Cedric, and though that branch fled into Wales before the invasion of the Danes, its male heirs consistently married with English families on the border marches, and it remains a pure line of the powerful Sussex Cedrics – almost pure Saxon. As for the man himself, this defect of his eyes, if it can be called a defect, is his only abnormality, except for a slight and occasional lisping of speech. He is highly intellectual and a good companion except for a slight aloofness and a rather callous indifference which may serve to mask an extremely sensitive nature.

Referring to his remark, I said with a laugh: "Conrad pursues the obscure and mystic as some men pursue romance; his shelves throng with delightful nightmares of every variety."

Our host nodded. "You'll find there a number of delectable dishes – Machen, Poe, Blackwood, Maturin – look, there's a rare feast – *Horrid Mysteries*, by the Marquis of Grosse – the real Eighteenth Century edition."

Taverel scanned the shelves. "Weird fiction seems to vie with works on witchcraft, voodoo and dark magic."

True; historians and chronicles are often dull; tale-weavers never – the masters, I mean. A voodoo sacrifice can be described in such a dull manner as to take all the real fantasy out of it, and leave it merely a sordid murder. I will admit that few writers of fiction touch the true heights of horror – most of their stuff is too concrete, given too much earthly shape and dimensions. But in such tales as Poe's *Fall of the House of Usher*, Machen's *Black Seal* and Lovecraft's *Call of Cthulhu* – the three master horror-tales, to my mind – the reader is borne into dark and *outer* realms of imagination.

"But look there," he continued, "there, sandwiched between that nightmare of Huysmans', and Walpole's *Castle of Otranto* – Von Junzt's *Nameless Cults*. There's a book to keep you awake at night!"

"I've read it," said Taverel, "and I'm convinced the man is mad. His work is like the conversation of a maniac – it runs with startling clarity for awhile, then suddenly merges into vagueness and disconnected ramblings."

Conrad shook his head. "Have you ever thought that perhaps it is his very sanity that causes him to write in that fashion? What if he dares not put on paper all he knows? What if his vague suppositions are dark and mysterious hints, keys to the puzzle, to those who know?"

"Bosh!" This from Kirowan. "Are you intimating that any of the nightmare cults referred to by Von Junzt survive to this day – if they ever existed save in the hag-ridden brain of a lunatic poet and philosopher?"

"Not he alone used hidden meanings," answered Conrad. "If you will scan various works of certain great poets you may find double meanings. Men have stumbled onto cosmic secrets in the past and given a hint of them to the world in cryptic words. Do you remember Von Junzt's hints of 'a city in the waste'? What do you think of Flecker's line:

"'Pass not beneath! Men say there blows in stony deserts still a rose

But with no scarlet to her leaf – and from whose heart no perfume flows.'

"Men may stumble upon secret things, but Von Junzt dipped deep into forbidden mysteries. He was one of the few men, for instance, who could read the *Necronomicon* in the original Greek translation."

Taverel shrugged his shoulders, and Professor Kirowan, though he snorted and puffed viciously at his pipe, made no direct reply; for he, as well as Conrad, had delved into the Latin version of the book, and had found there things not even a cold-blooded scientist could answer or refute.

"Well," he said presently, "suppose we admit the former existence of cults revolving about such nameless and ghastly gods and entities as Cthulhu, Yog Sothoth, Tsathoggua, Gol-goroth, and the like, I can not find it in my mind to believe that survivals of such cults lurk in the dark corners of the world today."

To our surprise Clemants answered. He was a tall, lean man, silent almost to the point of taciturnity, and his fierce struggles with poverty in his youth had lined his face beyond his years. Like many another artist, he lived a distinctly dual literary life, his swashbuckling novels furnishing him a generous income, and his editorial position on *The Cloven Hoof* affording him full artistic expression. *The Cloven Hoof* was a poetry magazine whose bizarre contents had often aroused the shocked interest of the conservative critics.

"You remember Von Junzt makes mention of a so-called Bran cult," said Clemants, stuffing his pipe-bowl with a peculiarly villainous brand of shag tobacco. "I think I heard you and Taverel discussing it once."

"As I gather from his hints," snapped Kirowan, "Von Junzt includes this particular cult among those still in existence. Absurd."

Again Clemants shook his head. "When I was a boy working my way through a certain university, I had for roommate a lad as poor and ambitious as I. If I told you his name, it would startle you. Though he came of an old Scotch line of Galloway, he was obviously of a non-Aryan type.

"This is in strictest confidence, you understand. But my roommate talked in his sleep. I began to listen and put his disjointed mumbling together. And in his mutterings I first heard of the ancient cult hinted at by Von Junzt; of the king who rules the Dark Empire, which was a revival of an older, darker empire dating back into the Stone Age; and of the great, nameless cavern where stands the Dark Man – the image of Bran Mak Morn, carved in his likeness by a master-hand while the great king yet lived, and to which each worshipper of Bran makes a pilgrimage once in his or her lifetime. Yes, that cult lives today in the descendants of Bran's people – a silent, unknown current it flows on in the great ocean of life, waiting for the stone image of the great Bran to breathe and move with sudden life, and come from the great cavern to rebuild their lost empire."

"And who were the people of that empire?" asked Ketrick.

"Picts," answered Taverel, "doubtless the people known later as the wild Picts of Galloway were predominantly Celtic – a mixture of Gaelic, Cymric, aboriginal and possibly Teutonic elements. Whether they took their name from the older race or lent their own name to that race, is a matter yet to be decided. But when Von Junzt speaks of Picts, he refers specifically to the small, dark, garlic-eating peoples of Mediterranean blood who brought the Neolithic culture into Britain. The first settlers of that country, in fact, who gave rise to the tales of earth spirits and goblins."

"I can not agree to that last statement," said Conrad. "These legends ascribe a deformity and inhumanness of appearances to the characters. There was nothing about the Picts to excite such horror and repulsion in the Aryan peoples. I believe that the Mediterraneans were preceded by a Mongoloid type, very low in the scale of development, whence these tales –"

"Quite true," broke in Kirowan, "but I hardly think they preceded the Picts, as you call them, into Britain. We find troll and dwarf legends all over the Continent, and I am inclined to think that both the Mediterranean and Aryan people brought these tales with them from the Continent. They must have been of extremely inhuman aspect, those early Mongoloids."

"At least," said Conrad, "here is a flint mallet a miner found in the Welsh hills and gave to me, which has never been fully explained. It is obviously of no ordinary Neolithic make. See how small it is, compared to most implements of that age; almost like a child's toy; yet it is surprisingly heavy and no doubt a deadly blow could be dealt with it. I fitted the handle to it, myself, and you would be surprized to know how difficult it was to carve it into a shape and balance corresponding with the head."

We looked at the thing. It was well made, polished somewhat like the other remnants of the Neolithic I had seen, yet as Conrad said, it was strangely different. Its small size was oddly disquieting, for it had no appearance of a toy, otherwise. It was as sinister in suggestion as an Aztec sacrificial dagger. Conrad had fashioned the oaken handle with rare skill, and in carving it to fit the head, had managed to give it the same unnatural appearance as the mallet itself had. He had even copied the workmanship of primal times, fixing the head into the cleft of the haft with rawhide.

"My word!" Taverel made a clumsy pass at an imaginary antagonist and nearly shattered a costly Shang vase. "The balance of the thing is all off-center; I'd have to readjust all my mechanics of poise and equilibrium to handle it."

"Let me see it," Ketrick took the thing and fumbled with it, trying to strike the secret of its proper handling. At length, somewhat irritated, he swung it up and struck a heavy blow at a shield which hung on the wall nearby. I was standing near it; I saw the hellish mallet twist in his hand like a live serpent, and his arm wrenched out of line; I heard a shout of alarmed warning – then darkness came with the impact of the mallet against my head.

Slowly I drifted back to consciousness. First there was dull sensation with blindness and total lack of knowledge as to where I was or what I was; then vague realization of life and being, and a hard something pressing into my ribs. Then the mists cleared and I came to myself completely.

I lay on my back half-beneath some underbrush and my head throbbed fiercely. Also my hair was caked and clotted with blood, for the scalp had been laid open. But my eyes traveled down my body and limbs, naked but for a deerskin loincloth and sandals of the same material, and found no other wound. That which pressed so uncomfortably into my ribs was my ax, on which I had fallen.

Now an abhorrent babble reached my ears and stung me into clear consciousness. The noise was faintly like language, but not such language as men are accustomed to. It sounded much like the repeated hissing of many great snakes.

I stared. I lay in a great, gloomy forest. The glade was overshadowed, so that even in the daytime it was very dark. Aye – that forest was dark, cold, silent, gigantic and utterly grisly. And I looked into the glade.

I saw a shambles. Five men lay there – at least, what had been five men. Now as I marked the abhorrent mutilations my soul sickened. And about clustered the – Things. Humans they were, of a sort, though I did not consider them so. They were short and stocky, with broad heads too large for their scrawny bodies. Their hair was snaky and stringy, their faces broad and square, with flat noses, hideously slanted eyes, a thin gash for a mouth, and pointed ears. They wore the skins of beasts, as did I, but these hides were but crudely dressed. They bore small bows and flint-tipped arrows, flint knives and cudgels. And they conversed in a speech as hideous as themselves, a hissing, reptilian speech that filled me with dread and loathing.

Oh, I hated them as I lay there; my brain flamed with white-hot fury. And now I remembered. We had hunted, we six youths of the Sword People, and wandered far into the grim forest which our people generally shunned. Weary of the chase, we had paused to rest; to me had been given the first watch, for in those days, no sleep was safe without a sentry. Now shame and revulsion shook my whole being. I had slept – I had betrayed my comrades. And now they lay gashed and mangled – butchered while they slept, by vermin who had never dared to stand before them on equal terms. I, Aryara, had betrayed my trust.

Aye – I remembered. I had slept and in the midst of a dream of the hunt, fire and sparks had exploded in my head and I had plunged into a deeper darkness where there were no dreams. And now the penalty. They who had stolen through the dense forest and smitten me senseless, had not paused to mutilate me. Thinking me dead they had hastened swiftly to their grisly work. Now perhaps they had forgotten me for a time. I had sat somewhat apart from the others, and when struck, had fallen half-under some bushes. But soon they would remember me. I would hunt no more, dance no more in the dances of hunt and love and war, see no more the wattle huts of the Sword People.

But I had no wish to escape back to my people. Should I slink back with my tale of infamy and disgrace? Should I hear the words of scorn my tribe would fling at me, see the girls point their contemptuous fingers at the youth who slept and betrayed his comrades to the knives of vermin?

Tears stung my eyes, and slow hate heaved up in my bosom, and my brain. I would never bear the sword that marked the warrior. I would never triumph over worthy foes and die gloriously beneath the arrows of the Picts or the axes of the Wolf People or the River People. I would go down to death beneath a nauseous rabble, whom the Picts had long ago driven into forest dens like rats.

And mad rage gripped me and dried my tears, giving in their stead a berserk blaze of wrath. If such reptiles were to bring about my downfall, I would make it a fall long remembered – if such beasts had memories.

Moving cautiously, I shifted until my hand was on the haft of my ax; then I called on Il-marinen and bounded up as a tiger springs. And as a tiger springs I was among my enemies and mashed a flat skull as a man crushes the head of a snake. A sudden wild clamor of fear broke from my victims and for an instant they closed round me, hacking and stabbing. A knife gashed my chest but I gave no heed. A red mist waved before my eyes, and my body and limbs moved in perfect accord with my fighting brain. Snarling, hacking and smiting, I was a tiger among reptiles. In an instant they gave way and fled, leaving me bestriding half a dozen stunted bodies. But I was not satiated.

I was close on the heels of the tallest one, whose head would perhaps come to my shoulder, and who seemed to be their chief. He fled down a sort of runway, squealing like a monstrous lizard, and when I was close at his shoulder, he dived, snake-like, into the bushes. But I was too swift for him, and I dragged him forth and butchered him in a most gory fashion.

And through the bushes I saw the trail he was striving to reach – a path winding in and out among the trees, almost too narrow to allow the traversing of it by a man of normal size. I hacked off my victim's hideous head, and carrying it in my left hand, went up the serpent-path, with my red ax in my right.

Now as I strode swiftly along the path and blood splashed beside my feet at every step from the severed jugular of my foe, I thought of those I hunted. Aye – we held them in so little esteem, we hunted by day in the forest they haunted. What they called themselves, we never knew; for none of our tribe ever learned the accursed hissing sibilances they used as speech; but we called them Children of the Night. And night-things they were indeed, for they slunk in the depths of the dark forests, and in subterraneous dwellings, venturing forth into the hills only when their conquerors slept. It was at night that they did their foul deeds – the quick flight of a flint-tipped arrow to slay cattle, or perhaps a loitering human, the snatching of a child that had wandered from the village.

But it was for more than this we gave them their name; they were, in truth, people of night and darkness and the ancient horror-ridden shadows of bygone ages. For these creatures were very old, and they represented an outworn age. They had once overrun and possessed this land, and they had been driven into hiding and obscurity by the dark, fierce little Picts with whom we contested now, and who hated and loathed them as savagely as did we.

The Picts were different from us in general appearance, being shorter of stature and dark of hair, eyes and skin, whereas we were tall and powerful, with yellow hair and light eyes. But they were cast in the same mold, for all of that. These Children of the Night seemed not human to us, with their deformed dwarfish bodies, yellow skin and hideous faces. Aye – they were reptiles – vermin.

And my brain was like to burst with fury when I thought that it was these vermin on whom I was to glut my ax and perish. Bah! There is no glory slaying snakes or dying from their bites. All this rage and fierce disappointment turned on the objects of my hatred, and with the old red mist waving in front of me I swore by all the gods I knew, to wreak such red havoc before I died as to leave a dread memory in the minds of the survivors.

My people would not honor me, in such contempt they held the Children. But those Children that I left alive would remember me and shudder. So I swore, gripping savagely my ax, which was of bronze, set in a cleft of the oaken haft and fastened securely with rawhide.

Now I heard ahead a sibilant, abhorrent murmur, and a vile stench filtered to me through the trees, human, yet less than human. A few moments more and I emerged from the deep shadows into a wide open space. I had never before seen a village of the Children. There was a cluster of earthen domes, with low doorways sunk into the ground; squalid dwelling-places, half-above and half-below the earth. And I knew from the talk of the old warriors that these dwelling-places were connected by underground corridors, so the whole village was like an ant-bed, or a system of snake holes. And I wondered if other tunnels did not run off under the ground and emerge long distances from the villages.

Before the domes clustered a vast group of the creatures, hissing and jabbering at a great rate.

I had quickened my pace, and now as I burst from cover, I was running with the fleetness of my race. A wild clamor went up from the rabble as they saw the avenger, tall, bloodstained and blazing-eyed leap from the forest, and I cried out fiercely, flung the dripping head among them and bounded like a wounded tiger into the thick of them.

Oh, there was no escape for them now! They might have taken to their tunnels but I would have followed, even to the guts of Hell. They knew they must slay me, and they closed around, a hundred strong, to do it.

There was no wild blaze of glory in my brain as there had been against worthy foes. But the old berserk madness of my race was in my blood and the smell of blood and destruction in my nostrils.

I know not how many I slew. I only know that they thronged about me in a writhing, slashing mass, like serpents about a wolf, and I smote until the ax-edge turned and bent and the ax became no more than a bludgeon; and I smashed skulls, split heads, splintered bones, scattered blood and brains in one red sacrifice to Il-marinen, god of the Sword People.

Bleeding from half a hundred wounds, blinded by a slash across the eyes, I felt a flint knife sink deep into my groin and at the same instant a cudgel laid my scalp open. I went to my knees but reeled up again, and saw in a thick red fog a ring of leering, slant-eyed faces. I lashed out as a dying tiger strikes, and the faces broke in red ruin.

And as I sagged, overbalanced by the fury of my stroke, a taloned hand clutched my throat and a flint blade was driven into my ribs and twisted venomously. Beneath a shower of blows I went down again, but the man with the knife was beneath me, and with my left hand I found him and broke his neck before he could writhe away.

Life was waning swiftly; through the hissing and howling of the Children I could hear the voice of Il-marinen. Yet once again I rose stubbornly, through a very whirlwind of cudgels and spears. I could no longer see my foes, even in a red mist. But I could feel their blows and knew they surged about me. I braced my feet, gripped my slippery ax-haft with both hands, and calling once more on Il-marinen I heaved up the ax and struck one last terrific blow. And I must have died on my feet, for there was no sensation of falling; even as I knew, with a last thrill of savagery, that slew, even as I felt the splintering of skulls beneath my ax, darkness came with oblivion.

I came suddenly to myself. I was half-reclining in a big armchair and Conrad was pouring water on me. My head ached and a trickle of blood had half-dried on my face. Kirowan, Taverel and Clemants were hovering about, anxiously, while Ketrick stood just in front of me, still holding the mallet, his face schooled to a polite perturbation which his eyes did not show. And at the sight of those cursed eyes a red madness surged up in me.

"There," Conrad was saying, "I told you he'd come out of it in a moment; just a light crack. He's taken harder than that. All right now, aren't you, O'Donnel?"

At that I swept them aside, and with a single low snarl of hatred launched myself at Ketrick. Taken utterly by surprize he had no opportunity to defend himself. My hands locked on his throat and we crashed together on the ruins of a divan. The others cried out in amazement and horror and sprang to separate us – or rather, to tear me from my victim, for already Ketrick's slant eyes were beginning to start from their sockets.

"For God's sake, O'Donnel," exclaimed Conrad, seeking to break my grip, "what's come over you? Ketrick didn't mean to hit you – let go, you idiot!"

A fierce wrath almost overcame me at these men who were my friends, men of my own tribe, and I swore at them and their blindness, as they finally managed to tear my strangling fingers from Ketrick's throat. He sat up and choked and explored the blue marks my fingers had left, while I raged and cursed, nearly defeating the combined efforts of the four to hold me.

"You fools!" I screamed. "Let me go! Let me do my duty as a tribesman! You blind fools! I care nothing for the paltry blow he dealt me – he and his dealt stronger blows than that against me, in bygone ages. You fools, he is marked with the brand of the beast – the reptile – the vermin we exterminated centuries ago! I must crush him, stamp him out, rid the clean earth of his accursed pollution!"

So I raved and struggled and Conrad gasped to Ketrick over his shoulder: "Get out, quick! He's out of his head! His mind is unhinged! Get away from him."

Now I look out over the ancient dreaming downs and the hills and deep forests beyond and I ponder. Somehow, that blow from that ancient accursed mallet knocked me back into another age and another life. While I was Aryara I had no cognizance of any other life. It was no dream; it was a stray bit of reality wherein I, John O'Donnel, once lived and died, and back into which I was snatched across the voids of time and space by a chance blow. Time and times are but cogwheels, unmatched, grinding on oblivious to one another. Occasionally – oh, very rarely! – the cogs fit; the pieces of the plot snap together momentarily and give men faint glimpses beyond the veil of this everyday blindness we call reality.

I am John O'Donnel and I was Aryara, who dreamed dreams of war-glory and hunt-glory and feast-glory and who died on a red heap of his victims in some lost age. But in what age and where?

The last I can answer for you. Mountains and rivers change their contours; the landscapes alter; but the downs least of all. I look out upon them now and I remember them, not only with John O'Donnel's eyes, but with the eyes of Aryara. They are but little changed. Only the great forest has shrunk and dwindled and in many, many places vanished utterly. But here on these very downs Aryara lived and fought and loved and in yonder forest he died. Kirowan was wrong. The little, fierce, dark Picts were not the first men in the Isles. There were beings before them – aye, the Children of the Night. Legends – why, the Children were not unknown to us when we came into what is now the isle of Britain. We had encountered them before, ages before. Already we had our myths of them. But we found them in Britain. Nor had the Picts totally exterminated them.

Nor had the Picts, as so many believe, preceded us by many centuries. We drove them before us as we came, in that long drift from the East. I, Aryara, knew old men who had marched on that century-long trek; who had been borne in the arms of yellow-haired women over countless miles of forest and plain, and who as youths had walked in the vanguard of the invaders.

As to the age – that I cannot say. But I, Aryara, was surely an Aryan and my people were Aryans – members of one of the thousand unknown and unrecorded drifts that scattered yellow-haired blue-eyed tribes all over the world. The Celts were not the first to come into western Europe. I, Aryara, was of the same blood and appearance as the men who sacked Rome, but mine was a much older strain. Of the language spoke, no echo remains in the waking mind of John O'Donnel, but I knew that Aryara's tongue was to ancient Celtic what ancient Celtic is to modern Gaelic.

Il-marinen! I remember the god I called upon, the ancient, ancient god who worked in metals – in bronze then. For Il-marinen was one of the base gods of the Aryans from whom many gods grew; and he was Wieland and Vulcan in the ages of iron. But to Aryara he was Il-marinen.

And Aryara – he was one of many tribes and many drifts. Not alone did the Sword People come or dwell in Britain. The River People were before us and the Wolf People came later. But they were Aryans like us, light-eyed and tall and blond. We fought them, for the reason that the various drifts of Aryans have always fought each other, just as the Achaeans fought the Dorians, just as the Celts and Germans cut each other's throats; aye, just as the Hellenes and the Persians, who were once one people and of the same drift, split in two different ways on the long trek and centuries later met and flooded Greece and Asia Minor with blood.

Now understand, all this I did not know as Aryara. I, Aryara, knew nothing of all these world-wide drifts of my race. I knew only that my people were conquerors, that a century ago my ancestors had dwelt in the great plains far to the east, plains populous with fierce, yellow-haired, light-eyed people like myself; that my ancestors had come westward in a great drift; and that in that drift, when my tribesmen met tribes of other races, they trampled and destroyed them, and when they met other yellow-haired, light-eyed people, of older or newer drifts, they fought savagely and mercilessly, according to the old, illogical custom of the Aryan people. This Aryara knew, and I, John O'Donnel, who know much more and much less than I, Aryara, knew, have combined the knowledge of these separate selves and have come to conclusions that would startle many noted scientists and historians.

Yet this fact is well known: Aryans deteriorate swiftly in sedentary and peaceful lives. Their proper existence is a nomadic one; when they settle down to an agricultural existence, they pave the way for their downfall; and when they pen themselves with city walls, they seal their doom. Why, I, Aryara, remember the tales of the old men – how the Sons of the Sword, on that long drift, found villages of white-skinned yellow-haired people who had drifted into the west centuries before and had quit the wandering life to dwell among the dark, garlic-eating people and gain their sustenance from the soil. And the old men told how soft and weak they were, and how easily they fell before the bronze blades of the Sword People.

Look – is not the whole history of the Sons of Aryan laid on those lines? Look – how swiftly has Persian followed Mede; Greek, Persian; Roman, Greek; and German, Roman. Aye, and the Norseman followed the Germanic tribes when they had grown flabby from a century or so of peace and idleness, and despoiled the spoils they had taken in the southland.

But let me speak of Ketrick. Ha – the short hairs at the back of my neck bristle at the very mention of his name. A reversion to type – but not to the type of some cleanly Chinaman or Mongol of recent times. The Danes drove his ancestors into the hills of Wales; and there, in what medieval century, and in what foul way did that cursed aboriginal taint creep into the clean Saxon blood of the Celtic line, there to lie dormant so long? The Celtic Welsh never mated with the Children any more than the Picts did. But there must have been survivals – vermin lurking in those grim hills, that had outlasted their time and age. In Aryara's day they were scarcely human. What must a thousand years of retrogression have done to the breed?

What foul shape stole into the Ketrick castle on some forgotten night, or rose out of the dusk to grip some woman of the line, straying in the hills?

The mind shrinks from such an image. But this I know: there must have been survivals of that foul, reptilian epoch when the Ketricks went into Wales. There still may be. But this changeling, this waif of darkness, this horror who bears the noble name of Ketrick, the brand of the serpent is upon him, and until he is destroyed there is no rest for me. Now that I know him for what he is, he pollutes the clean air and leaves the slime of the snake on the green earth. The sound of his lisping, hissing voice fills me with crawling horror and the sight of his slanted eyes inspires me with madness.

For I come of a royal race, and such as he is a continual insult and a threat, like a serpent underfoot. Mine is a regal race, though now it is become degraded and falls into decay by continual admixture with conquered races. The waves of alien blood have washed my hair black and my skin dark, but I still have the lordly stature and the blue eyes of a royal Aryan.

And as my ancestors – as I, Aryara, destroyed the scum that writhed beneath our heels, so shall I, John O'Donnel, exterminate the reptilian thing, the monster bred of the snaky taint that slumbered so long unguessed in clean Saxon veins, the vestigial serpent-things left to taunt the Sons of Aryan. They say the blow I received affected my mind; I know it but opened my eyes. Mine ancient enemy walks often on the moors alone, attracted, though he may not know it, by ancestral urgings. And on one of these lonely walks I shall meet him, and when I meet him, I will break his foul neck with my hands, as I, Aryara, broke the necks of foul night-things in the long, long ago.

Then they may take me and break my neck at the end of a rope if they will. I am not blind, if my friends are. And in the sight of the old Aryan god, if not in the blinded eyes of men, I will have kept faith with my tribe.

THE FOOTFALLS WITHIN

Weird Tales, September 1931

Solomon Kane gazed somberly at the black woman who lay dead at his feet. Little more than a girl she was, but her wasted limbs and staring eyes showed that she had suffered much before death brought her merciful relief. Kane noted the chain galls on her limbs, the deep crisscrossed scars on her back, the mark of the yoke on her neck. His cold eyes deepened strangely, showing chill glints and lights like clouds passing across depths of ice.

"Even into this lonesome land they come," he muttered. "I had not thought –"

He raised his head and gazed eastward. Black dots against the blue wheeled and circled.

"The kites mark their trail," muttered the tall Englishman. "Destruction goeth before them and death followeth after. Woe unto ye, sons of iniquity, for the wrath of God is upon ye. The cords be loosed on the iron necks of the hounds of hate and the bow of vengeance is strung. Ye are proud-stomached and strong, and the people cry out beneath your feet, but retribution cometh in the blackness of midnight and the redness of dawn."

He shifted the belt that held his heavy pistols and the keen dirk, instinctively touched the long rapier at his hip, and went stealthily but swiftly eastward. A cruel anger burned in his deep eyes like blue volcanic fires burning beneath leagues of ice, and the hand that gripped his long, cat-headed stave hardened into iron.

After some hours of steady striding, he came within hearing of the slave train that wound its laborious way through the jungle. The piteous cries of the slaves, the shouts and curses of the drivers, and the cracking of the whips came plainly to his ears. Another hour brought him even with them, and gliding along through the jungle parallel to the trail taken by the slavers, he spied upon them safely. Kane had fought Indians in Darien and had learned much of their woodcraft.

More than a hundred blacks, young men and women, staggered along the trail, stark naked and made fast together by cruel yoke-like affairs of wood. These yokes, rough and heavy, fitted over their necks and linked them together, two by two. The yokes were in turn fettered together, making one long chain. Of the drivers there were fifteen Arabs and some seventy black warriors, whose weapons and fantastic apparel showed them to be of some eastern tribe – one of those tribes subjugated and made Moslems and allies by the conquering Arabs.

Five Arabs walked ahead of the train with some thirty of their warriors, and five brought up the rear with the rest of the black Moslems. The rest marched beside the staggering slaves, urging them along with shouts and curses and with long, cruel whips which brought spurts of blood at almost every blow. These slavers were fools as well as rogues, reflected Kane – not more than half of the slaves would survive the hardships of that trek to the coast. He wondered at the presence of these raiders, for this country lay far to the south of the districts usually frequented by the Moslems. But avarice can drive men far, as the Englishman knew. He had dealt with these gentry of old. Even as he watched, old scars burned in his back – scars made by Moslem whips in a Turkish galley. And deeper still burned Kane's unquenchable hate.

He followed, shadowing his foes like a ghost, and as he stole through the jungle, he racked his brain for a plan. How might he prevail against that horde? All the Arabs and many of the blacks were armed with guns – long, clumsy firelock affairs, it is true, but guns just the same, enough to awe any tribe of natives who might oppose them. Some carried in their wide girdles long, silver-chased pistols of more effective pattern – flintlocks of Moorish and Turkish make.

Kane followed like a brooding ghost and his rage and hatred ate into his soul like a canker. Each crack of the whips was like a blow on his own shoulders. The heat and cruelty of the tropics play queer tricks with white men. Ordinary passions become monstrous things; irritation turns to a berserker rage; anger flames into unexpected madness and men kill in a red mist of passion, and wonder, aghast, afterward.

The fury Solomon Kane felt would have been enough at any time and in any place to shake a man to his foundation; now it assumed monstrous proportions, so that Kane shivered as if with a chill, iron claws scratched at his brain and he saw the slaves and the slavers through a crimson mist. Yet he might not have put his hate-born insanity into action had it not been for a mishap.

One of the slaves, a slim young girl, suddenly faltered and slipped to the earth, dragging her yoke-mate with her. A tall, hook-nosed Arab yelled savagely and lashed her viciously. Her yoke-mate staggered partly up, but the girl remained prone, writhing weakly beneath the lash, but evidently unable to rise. She whimpered pitifully between her parched lips, and the other slavers came about, their whips descending on her quivering flesh in slashes of red agony.

A half-hour of rest and a little water would have revived her, but the Arabs had no time to spare. Solomon, biting his arm until his teeth met in the flesh as he fought for control, thanked God that the lashing had ceased and steeled himself for the swift flash of the dagger that would put the child beyond torment. But the Arabs were in a mood for sport. Since the girl would fetch them no profit on the market block, they would utilize her for their pleasure – and the humor of their breed is such as to turn men's blood to icy water.

A shout from the first whipper brought the rest crowding around, their bearded faces split in grins of delighted anticipation, while the black warriors edged nearer, their brutish eyes gleaming. The wretched slaves realized their masters' intentions and a chorus of pitiful cries rose from them.

Kane, sick with horror, realized, too, that the girl's was to be no easy death. He knew what the tall Moslem intended to do, as he stooped over her with a keen dagger such as the Arabs used for skinning game. Madness overcame the Englishman. He valued his own life little; he had risked it without thought for the sake of a Negro baby or a small animal. Yet he would not have premeditatedly thrown away his one hope of succoring the wretches in the train. But he acted without conscious thought. A pistol was smoking in his hand and the tall butcher was down in the dust of the trail with his brains oozing out, before Kane realized what he had done.

He was almost as astonished as the Arabs, who stood frozen for a moment and then burst into a medley of yells. Several threw up their clumsy firelocks and sent their heavy balls crashing through the trees, and the rest, thinking no doubt that they were ambushed, led a reckless charge into the jungle. The bold suddenness of that move was Kane's undoing. Had they hesitated a moment longer he might have faded away unobserved, but as it was he saw no choice but to meet them openly and sell his life as highly as he could.

And indeed it was with a certain ferocious satisfaction that he faced his howling attackers. They halted in sudden amazement as the tall, grim Englishman stepped from behind his tree, and in that instant one of them died with a bullet from Kane's remaining pistol in his heart. Then with yells of savage rage they flung themselves on their lone defier. Kane placed his back against a huge tree and his long rapier played a shining wheel about him. Three blacks and an Arab were hacking at him with their heavy curved blades while the rest milled about, snarling like wolves, as they sought to drive in blade or ball without maiming one of their own number.

The flickering rapier parried the whistling scimitars and the Arab died on its point, which seemed to hesitate in his heart only an instant before it pierced the brain of a black swordsman. Another ebon warrior, dropping his sword and leaping in to grapple at close quarters, was disemboweled by the dirk in Kane's left hand, and the others gave back in sudden fear. A heavy ball smashed against the tree close to Kane's head and he tensed himself to spring and die in the thick of them. Then their sheikh lashed them on with his long whip and Kane heard him shouting fiercely for his warriors to take the infidel alive. Kane answered the command with a sudden cast of his dirk, which hummed so close to the sheikh's head that it slit his turban and sank deep in the shoulder of one behind him.

The sheikh drew his silver-chased pistols, threatening his own men with death if they did not take the white man, and they charged in again desperately. One of the black men ran full upon Kane's sword and an Arab behind the fellow, with the craft of his race, thrust the screaming wretch suddenly forward on the weapon, driving it hilt-deep in his writhing body, fouling the blade. Before Kane could wrench it clear, with a yell of triumph the pack rushed in on him and bore him down by sheer weight of numbers. As they grappled him from all sides, the Puritan wished in vain for the dirk he had thrown away. But even so, his taking was none too easy.

Blood spattered and faces caved in beneath his iron-hard fists that splintered teeth and shattered bone. A black warrior reeled away disabled from a vicious drive of knee to groin. Even when they had him stretched out and piled man-weight on him until he could no longer strike with fists or foot, his long lean fingers sank fiercely through a black beard to lock about a corded throat in a grip that took the power of three strong men to break and left the victim gasping and green-faced.

At last, panting from the terrific struggle, they had him bound hand and foot and the sheikh, thrusting his pistols back into his silken sash, came striding to stand and look down at his captive.

Kane glared up at the tall, lean frame, at the hawk-like face with its black curled beard and arrogant brown eyes.

"I am the sheikh Hassim ben Said," said the Arab. "Who are you?"

"My name is Solomon Kane," growled the Puritan in the sheikh's own language. "I am an Englishman, you heathen jackal."

The dark eyes of the Arab flickered with interest.

"Sulieman Kahani," said he, giving the Arabesque equivalent of the English name, "I have heard of you – you have fought the Turks betimes and the Barbary corsairs have licked their wounds because of you."

Kane deigned no reply. Hassim shrugged his shoulders.

"You will bring a fine price," said he. "Mayhap I will take you to Stamboul, where there are shahs who would desire such a man among their slaves. And I mind me now of one Kemal Bey, a man of ships, who wears a deep scar across his face of your making and who curses the name of Englishman. He will pay me a high price for you. And behold, oh Frank, I do you the honor of appointing you a separate guard. You shall not walk in the yoke-chain but free save for your hands."

Kane made no answer, and at a sign from the sheikh, he was hauled to his feet and his bonds loosened except for his hands, which they left bound firmly behind him. A stout cord was looped about his neck and the other end of this was given into the hand of a huge black warrior who bore in his free hand a great curved simitar.

"And now what think ye of my favor to you, Frank?" queried the sheikh.

"I am thinking," answered Kane in a slow, deep voice of menace, "that I would trade my soul's salvation to face you and your sword, alone and unarmed, and to tear the heart from your breast with my naked fingers."

Such was the concentrated hate in his deep resounding voice, and such primal, unconquerable fury blazed from his terrible eyes, that the hardened and fearless chieftain blanched and involuntarily recoiled as if from a maddened beast.

Then Hassim recovered his poise and with a short word to his followers, strode to the head of the cavalcade. Kane noted, with thankfulness, that the respite occasioned by his capture had given the girl who had fallen a chance to rest and revive. The skinning knife had not had time to more than touch her; she was able to reel along. Night was not far away. Soon the slavers would be forced to halt and camp.

The Englishman perforce took up the trek, his black guard remaining a few paces behind with his huge blade ever ready. Kane also noted with a touch of grim vanity, that three more blacks marched close behind, muskets ready and matches burning. They had tasted his prowess and they were taking no chances. His weapons had been recovered and Hassim had promptly appropriated all except the cat-headed ju-ju staff. This had been contemptuously cast aside by him and taken up by one of the blacks.

The Englishman was presently aware that a lean, gray-bearded Arab was walking along at his side. This Arab seemed desirous of speaking but strangely timid, and the source of his timidity seemed, curiously enough, the ju-ju stave which he had taken from the black man who had picked it up, and which he now turned uncertainly in his hands.

"I am Yussef the Hadji," said this Arab suddenly. "I have naught against you. I had no hand in attacking you and would be your friend if you would let me. Tell me, Frank, whence comes this staff and how comes it into your hands?"

Kane's first inclination was to consign his questioner to the infernal regions, but a certain sincerity of manner in the old man made him change his mind and he answered: "It was given me by my blood-brother – a black magician of the Slave Coast, named N'Longa."

The old Arab nodded and muttered in his beard and presently sent a black running forward to bid Hassim return. The tall sheikh presently came striding back along the slow-moving column, with a clank and jingle of daggers and sabers, with Kane's dirk and pistols thrust into his wide sash.

"Look, Hassim," the old Arab thrust forward the stave, "you cast it away without knowing what you did!"

"And what of it?" growled the sheikh. "I see naught but a staff – sharp-pointed and with the head of a cat on the other end – a staff with strange infidel carvings upon it."

The older man shook it at him in excitement: "This staff is older than the world! It holds mighty magic! I have read of it in the old iron-bound books and Mohammed – on whom peace! – himself hath spoken of it by allegory and parable! See the cat-head upon it? It is the head of a goddess of ancient Egypt! Ages ago, before Mohammed taught, before Jerusalem was, the priests of Bast bore this rod before the bowing, chanting worshippers! With it Musa did wonders before Pharaoh and when the Yahudi fled from Egypt they bore it with them. And for centuries it was the scepter of Israel and Judah and with it Sulieman ben Daoud drove forth the conjurers and magicians and prisoned the efreets and the evil genii! Look! Again in the hands of a Sulieman we find the ancient rod!"

Old Yussef had worked himself into a pitch of almost fanatic fervor but Hassim merely shrugged his shoulders.

"It did not save the Jews from bondage nor this Sulieman from our captivity," said he; "so I value it not as much as I esteem the long thin blade with which he loosed the souls of three of my best swordsmen."

Yussef shook his head. "Your mockery will bring you to no good end, Hassim. Some day you will meet a power that will not divide before your sword or fall to your bullets. I will keep the staff, and I warn you – abuse not the Frank. He has borne the holy and terrible staff of Sulieman and Musa and the Pharaohs, and who knows what magic he has drawn therefrom? For it is older than the world and has known the terrible hands of strange, dark pre-Adamite priests in the silent cities beneath the seas, and has drawn from an Elder World mystery and magic unguessed by human-kind. There were strange kings and stranger priests when the dawns were young, and evil was, even in their day. And with this staff they fought the evil which was ancient when their strange world was young, so many millions of years ago that a man would shudder to count them."

Hassim answered impatiently and strode away with old Yussef following him persistently and chattering away in a querulous tone. Kane shrugged his mighty shoulders. With what he knew of the strange powers of that strange staff, he was not one to question the old man's assertions, fantastic as they seemed. This much he knew – that it was made of a wood that existed nowhere on earth today. It needed but the proof of sight and touch to realize that its material had grown in some world apart. The exquisite workmanship of the head, of a pre-pyramidal age, and the hieroglyphics, symbols of a language that was forgotten when Rome was young – these, Kane sensed, were additions as modern to the antiquity of the staff itself, as would be English words carved on the stone monoliths of Stonehenge.

As for the cat-head – looking at it sometimes Kane had a peculiar feeling of alteration; a faint sensing that once the pommel of the staff was carved with a different design. The dust-ancient Egyptian who had carved the head of Bast had merely altered the original figure, and what that figure had been, Kane had never tried to guess. A close scrutiny of the staff always aroused a disquieting and almost dizzy suggestion of abysses of eons, unprovocative to further speculation.

The day wore on. The sun beat down mercilessly, then screened itself in the great trees as it slanted toward the horizon. The slaves suffered fiercely for water and a continual whimpering rose from their ranks as they staggered blindly on. Some fell and half-crawled, and were half-dragged by their reeling yoke-mates. When all were buckling from exhaustion, the sun dipped, night rushed on, and a halt was called. Camp was pitched, guards thrown out, and the slaves were fed scantily and given enough water to keep life in them – but only just enough. Their fetters were not loosened but they were allowed to sprawl about as they might. Their fearful thirst and hunger having been somewhat eased, they bore the discomforts of their shackles with characteristic stoicism.

Kane was fed without his hands being untied and he was given all the water he wished. The patient eyes of the slaves watched him drink, silently, and he was sorely ashamed to guzzle what others suffered for; he ceased before his thirst was fully quenched. A wide clearing had been selected, on all sides of which rose gigantic trees. After the Arabs had eaten and while the black Moslems were still cooking their food, old Yussef came to Kane and began to talk about the staff again. Kane answered his questions with admirable patience, considering the hatred he bore the whole race to which the Hadji belonged, and during their conversation, Hassim came striding up and looked down in contempt. Hassim, Kane ruminated, was the very symbol of militant Islam – bold, reckless, materialistic, sparing nothing, fearing nothing, as sure of his own destiny and as contemptuous of the rights of others as the most powerful Western king.

"Are you maundering about that stick again?" he gibed. "Hadji, you grow childish in your old age."

Yussef's beard quivered in anger. He shook the staff at his sheikh like a threat of evil.

"Your mockery little befits your rank, Hassim," he snapped. "We are in the heart of a dark and demon-haunted land, to which long ago were banished the devils from Arabia. If this staff, which any but a fool can tell is no rod of any world we know, has existed down to our day, who knows what other things, tangible or intangible, may have existed through the ages? This very trail we follow – know you how old it is? Men followed it before the Seljuk came out of the East or the Roman came out of the West. Over this very trail, legends say, the great Sulieman came when he drove the demons westward out of Asia and prisoned them in strange prisons. And will you say –"

A wild shout interrupted him. Out of the shadows of the jungle a black came flying as if from the hounds of Doom. With arms flinging wildly, eyes rolling to display the whites and mouth wide open so that all his gleaming teeth were visible, he made an image of stark terror not soon forgotten. The Moslem horde leaped up, snatching their weapons, and Hassim swore: "That's Ali, whom I sent to scout for meat – perchance a lion –"

But no lion followed the black man who fell at Hassim's feet, mouthing gibberish, and pointing wildly back at the black jungle whence the nerve-strung watchers expected some brain-shattering horror to burst.

"He says he found a strange mausoleum back in the jungle," said Hassim with a scowl, "but he can not tell what frightened him. He only knows a great horror overwhelmed him and sent him flying. Ali, you are a fool and a rogue."

He kicked the groveling black viciously, but the other Arabs drew about him in some uncertainty. The panic was spreading among the black warriors.

"They will bolt in spite of us," muttered a bearded Arab, uneasily watching the blacks who milled together, jabbered excitedly and flung fearsome glances over the shoulders. "Hassim, 'twere better to march on a few miles. This is an evil place after all, and though 'tis likely the fool Ali was frighted by his own shadow – still –"

"Still," jeered the sheikh, "you will all feel better when we have left it behind. Good enough; to still your fears I will move camp – but first I will have a look at this thing. Lash up the slaves; we'll swing into the jungle and pass by this mausoleum; perhaps some great king lies there. The blacks will not be afraid if we all go in a body with guns."

So the weary slaves were whipped into wakefulness and stumbled along beneath the whips again. The black warriors went silently and nervously, reluctantly obeying Hassim's implacable will but huddling close to their white masters. The moon had risen, huge, red and sullen, and the jungle was bathed in a sinister silver glow that etched the brooding trees in black shadow. The trembling Ali pointed out the way, somewhat reassured by his savage master's presence.

And so they passed through the jungle until they came to a strange clearing among the giant trees – strange because nothing grew there. The trees ringed it in a disquieting symmetrical manner and no lichen or moss grew on the earth, which seemed to have been blasted and blighted in a strange fashion. And in the midst of the glade stood the mausoleum. A great brooding mass of stone it was, pregnant with ancient evil. Dead with the death of a hundred centuries it seemed, yet Kane was aware that the air pulsed about it, as with the slow, unhuman breathing of some gigantic, invisible monster.

The black Moslems drew back, muttering, assailed by the evil atmosphere of the place. The slaves stood in a patient, silent group beneath the trees. The Arabs went forward to the frowning black mass, and Yussef, taking Kane's cord from his ebon guard, led the Englishman with him like a surly mastiff, as if for protection against the unknown.

"Some mighty sultan doubtless lies here," said Hassim, tapping the stone with his scabbard-end.

"Whence come these stones?" muttered Yussef uneasily. "They are of dark and forbidding aspect. Why should a great sultan lie in state so far from any habitation of man? If there were ruins of an old city hereabouts it would be different –"

He bent to examine the heavy metal door with its huge lock, curiously sealed and fused. He shook his head forebodingly as he made out the ancient Hebraic characters carved on the door.

"I can not read them," he quavered, "and belike it is well for me I can not. What ancient kings sealed up, is not good for men to disturb. Hassim, let us hence. This place is pregnant with evil for the sons of men."

But Hassim gave him no heed. "He who lies within is no son of Islam," said he, "and why should we not despoil him of the gems and riches that undoubtedly were laid to rest with him? Let us break open this door."

Some of the Arabs shook their heads doubtfully but Hassim's word was law. Calling to him a huge black who bore a heavy hammer, he ordered him to break open the door.

As the black swung up his sledge, Kane gave a sharp exclamation. Was he mad? The apparent antiquity of this brooding mass of stone was proof that it had stood undisturbed for thousands of years. *Yet he could have sworn that he heard the sound of footfalls within.* Back and forth they padded, as if something paced the narrow confines of that grisly prison in a never-ending monotony of movement. A cold hand touched the spine of Solomon Kane. Whether the sounds registered on his conscious ear or on some unsounded deep of soul or sub-feeling, he could not tell, but he *knew* that somewhere within his consciousness there re-echoed the tramp of monstrous feet from within that ghastly mausoleum.

"Stop!" he exclaimed. "Hassim, I may be mad, but I hear the tread of some fiend within that pile of stone."

Hassim raised his hand and checked the hovering hammer. He listened intently, and the others strained their ears in a silence that had suddenly become tense.

"I hear nothing," grunted a bearded giant.

"Nor I," came a quick chorus. "The Frank is mad!"

"Hear ye anything, Yussef?" asked Hassim sardonically.

The old Hadji shifted nervously. His face was uneasy.

"No, Hassim, no, yet –"

Kane decided he must be mad. Yet in his heart he knew he was never saner, and he knew somehow that this occult keenness of the deeper senses that set him apart from the Arabs came from long association with the ju-ju staff that old Yussef now held in his shaking hands.

Hassim laughed harshly and made a gesture to the black. The hammer fell with a crash that re-echoed deafeningly and shivered off through the black jungle in a strangely altered cachinnation. Again – again – and again the hammer fell, driven with all the power of the rippling black muscles and the mighty ebon body. And between the blows Kane still heard that lumbering tread, and he who had never known fear as men know it, felt the cold hand of terror clutching at his heart.

This fear was apart from earthly or mortal fear, as the sound of the footfalls was apart from mortal tread. Kane's fright was like a cold wind blowing on him from outer realms of unguessed Darkness, bearing him the evil and decay of an outlived epoch and an unutterably ancient period. Kane was not sure whether he heard those footfalls or by some dim instinct sensed them. But he was sure of their reality. They were not the tramp of man or beast; but inside that black, hideously ancient mausoleum some nameless *thing* moved with soul-shaking and elephantine tread.

The great black sweated and panted with the difficulty of his task. But at last, beneath the heavy blows the ancient lock shattered; the hinges snapped; the door burst inward. And Yussef screamed. From that black gaping entrance no tiger-fanged beast or demon of solid flesh and blood leaped forth. But a fearful stench flowed out in billowing, almost tangible waves and in one brain-shattering, ravening rush, whereby the gaping door seemed to gush *blood*, the Horror was upon them. It enveloped Hassim, and the fearless chieftain, hewing vainly at the almost intangible terror, screamed with sudden, unaccustomed fright as his lashing scimitar whistled only through stuff as yielding and unharmable as air, and he felt himself lapped by coils of death and destruction.

Yussef shrieked like a lost soul, dropped the ju-ju stave and joined his fellows who streamed out into the jungle in mad flight, preceded by the howling black warriors. Only the black slaves fled not, but stood shackled to their doom, wailing their terror. As in a nightmare of delirium Kane saw Hassim swayed like a reed in the wind, lapped about by a gigantic pulsing red Thing that had neither shape nor earthly substance. Then as the crack of splintering bones came to him, and the sheikh's body buckled like a straw beneath a stamping hoof, the Englishman burst his bonds with one volcanic effort and caught up the ju-ju stave.

Hassim was down, crushed and dead, sprawled like a broken toy with shattered limbs awry, and the red pulsing Thing was lurching toward Kane like a thick cloud of blood in the air, that continually changed its shape and form, and yet somehow *trod* lumberingly as if on monstrous legs!

Kane felt the cold fingers of fear claw at his brain but he braced himself, and lifting the ancient staff, struck with all his power into the center of the Horror. And he felt an unnamable, immaterial substance meet and give way before the falling staff. Then he was almost strangled by the nauseous burst of unholy stench that flooded the air, and somewhere down the dim vistas of his soul's consciousness re-echoed unbearably a hideous formless cataclysm that he knew was the death-screaming of the monster. For it was down and dying at his feet, its crimson paling in slow surges like the rise and receding of red waves on some foul coast. And as it paled, the soundless screaming dwindled away into cosmic distances as though it faded into some sphere apart and aloof beyond human ken.

Kane, dazed and incredulous, looked down on a shapeless, colorless, all but invisible mass at his feet which he knew was the corpse of the Horror, dashed back into the black realms from whence it had come, by a single blow of the staff of Solomon. Aye, the same staff, Kane knew, that in the hands of a mighty king and magician had ages ago driven the monster into that strange prison, to bide until ignorant hands loosed it again upon the world.

The old tales were true then, and King Solomon had in truth driven the demons westward and sealed them in strange places. Why had he let them live? Was human magic too weak in those dim days to more than subdue the devils? Kane shrugged his shoulders in wonderment. He knew nothing of magic, yet he had slain where that other Solomon had but imprisoned.

And Solomon Kane shuddered, for he had looked on Life that was not Life as he knew it, and had dealt and witnessed Death that was not Death as he knew it. Again the realization swept over him, as it had in the dust-haunted halls of Atlantean Negari, as it had in the abhorrent Hills of the Dead, as it had in Akaana – that human life was but one of a myriad forms of existence, that worlds existed within worlds, and that there was more than one plane of existence. The planet men call the earth spun on through the untold ages, Kane realized, and as it spun it spawned Life, and living things which wriggled about it as maggots are spawned in rot and corruption. Man was the dominant maggot now – why should he in his pride suppose that he and his adjuncts were the first maggots – or the last to rule a planet quick with unguessed life?

He shook his head, gazing in new wonder at the ancient gift of N'Longa, seeing in it at last, not merely a tool of black magic, but a sword of good and light against the powers of inhuman evil forever. And he was shaken with a strange reverence for it that was almost fear. Then he bent to the Thing at his feet, shuddering to feel its strange mass slip through his fingers like wisps of heavy fog. He thrust the staff beneath it and somehow lifted and levered the mass back into the mausoleum and shut the door.

Then he stood gazing down at the strangely mutilated body of Hassim, noting how it was smeared with foul slime and how it had already begun to decompose. He shuddered again, and suddenly a low timid voice aroused him from his somber cogitations. The slaves knelt beneath the trees and watched with great patient eyes. With a start he shook off his strange mood. He took from the moldering corpse his own pistols, dirk and rapier, making shift to wipe off the clinging foulness that was already flecking the steel with rust. He also took up a quantity of powder and shot dropped by the Arabs in their frantic flight. He knew they would return no more. They might die in their flight, or they might gain through the interminable leagues of jungle to the coast; but they would not turn back to dare the terror of that grisly glade.

Kane came to the black slaves and after some difficulty released them.

"Take up these weapons which the warriors dropped in their haste," said he, "and get you home. This is an evil place. Get ye back to your villages and when the next Arabs come, die in the ruins of your huts rather than be slaves."

Then they would have knelt and kissed his feet, but he, in much confusion, forbade them roughly. Then as they made preparations to go, one said to him: "Master, what of thee? Wilt thou not return with us? Thou shalt be our king!"

But Kane shook his head.

"I go eastward," said he. And so the tribespeople bowed to him and turned back on the long trail to their own homeland. And Kane shouldered the staff that had been the rod of the Pharaohs and of Moses and of Solomon and of nameless Atlantean kings behind them, and turned his face eastward, halting only for a single backward glance at the great mausoleum that other Solomon had built with strange arts so long ago, and which now loomed dark and forever silent against the stars.

THE GODS OF BAL–SAGOTH

Weird Tales, October 1931

1. Steel in the Storm

The play was quick and desperate; in the momentary illumination a ferocious bearded face shone before Turlogh, and his swift ax licked out, splitting it to the chin. In the brief, utter blackness that followed the flash, an unseen stroke swept Turlogh's helmet from his head and he struck back blindly, feeling his ax sink into flesh, and hearing a man howl. Again the fires of the raging skies sprang, showing the Gael the ring of savage faces, the hedge of gleaming steel that hemmed him in.

Back against the mainmast Turlogh parried and smote; then through the madness of the fray a great voice thundered, and in a flashing instant the Gael caught a glimpse of a giant form – a strangely familiar face. Then the world crashed into fire-shot blackness.

Consciousness returned slowly. Turlogh was first aware of a swaying, rocking motion of his whole body which he could not check. Then a dull throbbing in his head racked him and he sought to raise his hands to it. Then it was he realized he was bound hand and foot – not an altogether new experience. Clearing sight showed him that he was tied to the mast of the dragon ship whose warriors had struck him down. Why they had spared him, he could not understand, because if they knew him at all, they knew him to be an outlaw – an outcast from his clan, who would pay no ransom to save him from the very pits of Hell.

The wind had fallen greatly but a heavy sea was flowing, which tossed the long ship like a chip from gulf-like trough to foaming crest. A round silver moon, peering through broken clouds, lighted the tossing billows. The Gael, raised on the wild west coast of Ireland, knew that the serpent ship was crippled. He could tell it by the way she labored, plowing deep into the spume, heeling to the lift of the surge. Well, the tempest which had been raging on these southern waters had been enough to damage even such staunch craft as these Vikings built.

The same gale had caught the French vessel on which Turlogh had been a passenger, driving her off her course and far southward.

Days and nights had been a blind, howling chaos in which the ship had been hurled, flying like a wounded bird before the storm. And in the very rack of the tempest a beaked prow had loomed in the scud above the lower, broader craft, and the grappling irons had sunk in. Surely these Norsemen were wolves and the blood-lust that burned in their hearts was not human. In the terror and roar of the storm they leaped howling to the onslaught, and while the raging heavens hurled their full wrath upon them, and each shock of the frenzied waves threatened to engulf both vessels, these sea-wolves glutted their fury to the utmost – true sons of the sea, whose wildest rages found echo in their own bosoms. It had been a slaughter rather than a fight – the Celt had been the only fighting man aboard the doomed ship – and now he remembered the strange familiarity of the face he had glimpsed just before he was struck down. Who –?

"Good hail, my bold Dalcassian, it's long since we met!"

Turlogh stared at the man who stood before him, feet braced to the lifting of the deck. He was of huge stature, a good half head taller than Turlogh who stood well above six feet. His legs were like columns, his arms like oak and iron. His beard was of crisp gold, matching the massive armlets he wore. A shirt of scale-mail added to his war-like appearance as the horned helmet seemed to increase his height. But there was no wrath in the calm gray eyes which gazed tranquilly into the smoldering blue eyes of the Gael.

"Athelstane, the Saxon!"

"Aye – it's been a long day since you gave me this," the giant indicated a thin white scar on his temple. "We seem fated to meet on nights of fury – we first crossed steel the night you burned Thorfel's skalli. Then I fell before your ax and you saved me from Brogar's Picts – alone of all the folk who followed Thorfel. Tonight it was I who struck you down." He touched the great two-handed sword strapped to his shoulders and Turlogh cursed.

"Nay, revile me not," said Athelstane with a pained expression. "I could have slain you in the press – I struck with the flat, but knowing you Irish have cursed hard skulls, I struck with both hands. You have been senseless for hours. Lodbrog would have slain you with the rest of the merchant ship's crew but I claimed your life. But the Vikings would only agree to spare you on condition that you be bound to the mast. They know you of old."

"Where are we?"

"Ask me not. The storm blew us far out of our course. We were sailing to harry the coasts of Spain. When chance threw us in with your vessel, of course we seized the opportunity, but there was scant spoil. Now we are racing with the sea-flow, unknowing. The steer sweep is crippled and the whole ship lamed. We may be riding the very rim of the world for aught I know. Swear to join us and I will loose you."

"Swear to join the hosts of Hell!" snarled Turlogh. "Rather will I go down with the ship and sleep forever under the green waters, bound to this mast. My only regret is that I can not send more sea-wolves to join the hundred-odd I have already sent to purgatory!"

"Well, well," said Athelstane tolerantly, "a man must eat – here – I will loose your hands at least – now, set your teeth into this joint of meat."

Turlogh bent his head to the great joint and tore at it ravenously. The Saxon watched him a moment, then turned away. A strange man, reflected Turlogh, this renegade Saxon who hunted with the wolf-pack of the North – a savage warrior in battle, but with fibers of kindliness in his makeup which set him apart from the men with whom he consorted.

The ship reeled on blindly in the night, and Athelstane, returning with a great horn of foaming ale, remarked on the fact that the clouds were gathering again, obscuring the seething face of the sea. He left the Gael's hands unbound but Turlogh was held fast to the mast by cords about legs and body. The rovers paid no heed to their prisoner; they were too much occupied in keeping their crippled ship from going down under their feet.

At last Turlogh believed he could catch at times a deep roaring above the wash of the waves. This grew in volume, and even as the duller-eared Norsemen heard it, the ship leaped like a spurred horse, straining in every timber. As by magic the clouds, lightening for dawn, rolled away on each side, showing a wild waste of tossing gray waters, and a long line of breakers dead ahead. Beyond the frothing madness of the reefs loomed land, apparently an island. The roaring increased to deafening proportions, as the long ship, caught in the tide rip, raced headlong to her doom. Turlogh saw Lodbrog rushing about, his long beard flowing in the wind as he brandished his fists and bellowed futile commands. Athelstane came running across the deck.

"Little chance for any of us," he growled as he cut the Gael's bonds, "but you shall have as much as the rest –"

Turlogh sprang free. "Where is my ax?"

"There in that weapon-rack. But Thor's blood, man," marveled the big Saxon, "you won't burden yourself now –"

Turlogh had snatched the ax and confidence flowed like wine through his veins at the familiar feel of the slim, graceful shaft. His ax was as much a part of him as his right hand; if he must die he wished to die with it in his grip. He hastily slung it to his girdle. All armor had been stripped from him when he had been captured.

"There are sharks in these waters," said Athelstane, preparing to doff his scale-mail. "If we have to swim –"

The ship struck with a crash that snapped her masts and shivered her prow like glass. Her dragon beak shot high in the air and men tumbled like tenpins from her slanted deck. A moment she poised, shuddering like a live thing, then slid from the hidden reef and went down in a blinding smother of spray.

Turlogh had left the deck in a long dive that carried him clear. Now he rose in the turmoil, fought the waves for a mad moment, then caught a piece of wreckage that the breakers flung up. As he clambered across this, a shape bumped against him and went down again. Turlogh plunged his arm deep, caught a sword-belt and heaved the man up and on his makeshift raft. For in that instant he had recognized the Saxon, Athelstane, still burdened with the armor he had not had time to remove. The man seemed dazed. He lay limp, limbs trailing.

Turlogh remembered that ride through the breaker as a chaotic nightmare. The tide tore them through, plunging their frail craft into the depths, then flinging them into the skies. There was naught to do but hold on and trust to luck. And Turlogh held on, gripping the Saxon with one hand and their raft with the other, while it seemed his fingers would crack with the strain. Again and again they were almost swamped; then by some miracle they were through, riding in water comparatively calm and Turlogh saw a lean fin cutting the surface a yard away. It swirled in and Turlogh unslung his ax and struck. Red dyed the waters instantly and a rush of sinuous shapes made the craft rock. While the sharks tore their brother, Turlogh, paddling with his hands, urged the rude raft ashore until he could feel the bottom. He waded to the beach, half-carrying the Saxon; then, iron though he was, Turlogh O'Brien sank down, exhausted and soon slept soundly.

2. Gods from the Abyss

Turlogh did not sleep long. When he awoke the sun was just risen above the sea-rim. The Gael rose, feeling as refreshed as if he had slept the whole night through, and looked about him. The broad white beach sloped gently from the water to a waving expanse of gigantic trees. There seemed no underbrush, but so close together were the huge boles, his sight could not pierce into the jungle. Athelstane was standing some distance away on a spit of sand that ran out into the sea. The huge Saxon leaned on his great sword and gazed out toward the reefs.

Here and there on the beach lay the stiff figures that had been washed ashore. A sudden snarl of satisfaction broke from Turlogh's lips. Here at his very feet was a gift from the gods; a dead Viking lay there, fully armed in the helmet and mail shirt he had not had time to doff when the ship foundered, and Turlogh saw they were his own. Even the round light buckler strapped to the Norseman's back was his. Turlogh did pause to wonder how all his accouterments had come into the possession of one man, but stripped the dead and donned the plain round helmet and the shirt of black chain mail. Thus armed he went up the beach toward Athelstane, his eyes gleaming unpleasantly.

The Saxon turned as he approached. "Hail to you Gael," he greeted. "We be all of Lodbrog's ship-people left alive. The hungry green sea drank them all. By Thor, I owe my life to you! What with the weight of mail, and the crack my skull got on the rail, I had most certainly been food for the shark but for you. It all seems like a dream now."

"You saved my life," snarled Turlogh. "I saved yours. Now the debt is paid, the accounts are squared, so up with your sword and let us make an end."

Athelstane stared. "You wish to fight me? Why – what –?"

"I hate your breed as I hate Satan!" roared the Gael, a tinge of madness in his blazing eyes. "Your wolves have ravaged my people for five hundred years! The smoking ruins of the Southland, the seas of spilled blood call for vengeance! The screams of a thousand ravished girls are ringing in my ears, night and day! Would that the North had but a single breast for my ax to cleave!"

"But I am no Norseman," rumbled the giant in worriment.

"The more shame to you, renegade," raved the maddened Gael. "Defend yourself lest I cut you down in cold blood!"

"This is not to my liking," protested Athelstane, lifting his mighty blade, his gray eyes serious but unafraid. "Men speak truly who say there is madness in you."

Words ceased as the men prepared to go into deadly action. The Gael approached his foe, crouching panther-like, eyes ablaze. The Saxon waited the onslaught, feet braced wide apart, sword held high in both hands. It was Turlogh's ax and shield against Athelstane's two-handed sword; in a contest one stroke might end either way. Like two great jungle beasts they played their deadly, wary game then –

Even as Turlogh's muscles tensed for the death-leap, a fearful sound split the silence! Both men started and recoiled. From the depths of the forest behind them rose a ghastly and inhuman scream. Shrill, yet of great volume, it rose higher and higher until it ceased at the highest pitch, like the triumph of a demon, like the cry of some grisly ogre gloating over its human prey.

"Thor's blood!" gasped the Saxon, letting his sword-point fall. "What was that?"

Turlogh shook his head. Even his iron nerve was slightly shaken. "Some fiend of the forest. This is a strange land in a strange sea. Mayhap Satan himself reigns here and it is the gate to Hell."

Athelstane looked uncertain. He was more pagan than Christian and his devils were heathen devils. But they were none the less grim for that.

"Well," said he, "let us drop our quarrel until we see what it may be. Two blades are better than one, whether for man or devil –"

A wild shriek cut him short. This time it was a human voice, blood-chilling in its horror and despair. Simultaneously came the swift patter of feet and the lumbering rush of some heavy body among the trees. The warriors wheeled toward the sound, and out of the deep shadows a half-naked woman came flying like a white leaf blown on the wind. Her loose hair streamed like a flame of gold behind her, her white limbs flashed in the morning sun, her eyes blazed with frenzied terror. And behind her –

Even Turlogh's hair stood up. The thing that pursued the fleeing girl was neither man nor beast. In form it was like a bird, but such a bird as the rest of the world had not seen for many an age. Some twelve feet high it towered, and its evil head with the wicked red eyes and cruel curved beak was as big as a horse's head. The long arched neck was thicker than a man's thigh and the huge taloned feet could have gripped the fleeing woman as an eagle grips a sparrow.

This much Turlogh saw in one glance as he sprang between the monster and its prey who sank down with a cry on the beach. It loomed above him like a mountain of death and the evil beak darted down, denting the shield he raised and staggering him with the impact. At the same instant he struck, but the keen ax sank harmlessly into a cushioning mass of spiky feathers. Again the beak flashed at him and his sidelong leap saved his life by a hair's breadth. And then Athelstane ran in, and bracing his feet wide, swung his great sword with both hands and all his strength. The mighty blade sheared through one of the tree-like legs below the knee, and with an abhorrent screech, the monster sank on its side, flapping its short heavy wings wildly. Turlogh drove the back-spike of his ax between the glaring red eyes and the gigantic bird kicked convulsively and lay still.

"Thor's blood!" Athelstane's gray eyes were blazing with battle lust. "Truly we've come to the rim of the world –"

"Watch the forest lest another come forth," snapped Turlogh, turning to the woman who had scrambled to her feet and stood panting, eyes wide with wonder. She was a splendid young animal, tall, clean-limbed, slim and shapely. Her only garment was a sheer bit of silk hung carelessly about her hips. But though the scantiness of her dress suggested the savage, her skin was snowy white, her loose hair of purest gold and her eyes gray. Now she spoke hastily, stammeringly, in the tongue of the Norse, as if she had not so spoken in years.

"You – who are you men? When come you? What do you on the Isle of the Gods?"

"Thor's blood!" rumbled the Saxon; "she's of our own kind!"

"Not mine!" snapped Turlogh, unable even in that moment to forget his hate for the people of the North.

The girl looked curiously at the two. "The world must have changed greatly since I left it," she said, evidently in full control of herself once more, "else how is it that wolf and wild bull hunt together? By your black hair, you are a Gael, and you, big man, have a slur in your speech that can be naught but Saxon."

"We are two outcasts," answered Turlogh. "You see these dead men lining the strand? They were the crew of the dragon ship which bore us here, storm-driven. This man, Athelstane, once of Wessex, was a swordsman on that ship and I was a captive. I am

Turlogh Dubh, once a chief of Clan na O'Brien. Who are you and what land is this?"

"This is the oldest land in the world," answered the girl. "Rome, Egypt, Cathay are as but infants beside it. I am Brunhild, daughter of Rane Thorfin's son, of the Orkneys, and until a few days ago, queen of this ancient kingdom."

Turlogh looked uncertainly at Athelstane. This sounded like sorcery.

"After what we have just seen," rumbled the giant, "I am ready to believe anything. But are you in truth Rane Thorfin's son's stolen child?"

"Aye!" cried the girl, "I am that one! I was stolen when Tostig the Mad raided the Orkneys and burned Rane's steading in the absence of its master –"

"And then Tostig vanished from the face of the earth – or the sea!" interrupted Athelstane. "He was in truth a madman. I sailed with him for a ship-harrying many years ago when I was but a youth."

"And his madness cast me on this island," answered Brunhild; "for after he had harried the shores of England, the fire in his brain drove him out into unknown seas – south and south and ever south until even the fierce wolves he led murmured. Then a storm drove us on yonder reef, though at another part, rending the dragon ship even as yours was rended last night. Tostig and all his strong men perished in the waves, but I clung to pieces of wreckage and a whim of the gods cast me ashore, half-dead. I was fifteen years old. That was ten years ago.

"I found a strange terrible people dwelling here, a brown-skinned folk who knew many dark secrets of magic. They found me lying senseless on the beach and because I was the first white human they had ever seen, their priests divined that I was a goddess given them by the sea, whom they worship. So they put me in the temple with the rest of their curious gods and did reverence to me. And their high-priest, old Gothan – cursed be his name! – taught me many strange and fearful things. Soon I learned their language and much of their priests' inner mysteries. And as I grew into womanhood the desire for power stirred in me; for the people of the North are made to rule the folk of the world, and it is not for the daughter of a sea-king to sit meekly in a temple and accept the offerings of fruit and flowers and human sacrifices!"

She stopped for a moment, eyes blazing. Truly, she looked a worthy daughter of the fierce race she claimed.

"Well," she continued, "there was one who loved me – Kotar, a young chief. With him I plotted and at last I rose and flung off the yoke of old Gothan. That was a wild season of plot and counter-plot, intrigue, rebellion and red carnage! Men and women died like flies and the streets of Bal-Sagoth ran red – but in the end we triumphed, Kotar and I! The dynasty of Angar came to an end on a night of blood and fury and I reigned supreme on the Isle of the Gods, queen and goddess!"

She had drawn herself up to her full height, her beautiful face alight with fierce pride, her bosom heaving. Turlogh was at once fascinated and repelled. He had seen rulers rise and fall, and between the lines of her brief narrative he read the bloodshed and carnage, the cruelty and the treachery – sensing the basic ruthlessness of this girl-woman.

"But if you were queen," he asked, "how is it that we find you hunted through the forests of your domain by this monster, like a runaway serving wench?"

Brunhild bit her lip and an angry flush mounted to her cheeks. "What is it that brings down every woman, whatever her station? I trusted a man – Kotar, my lover, with whom I shared my rule. He betrayed me; after I had raised him to the highest power in the kingdom, next to my own, I found he secretly made love to another girl. I killed them both!"

Turlogh smiled coldly: "You are a true Brunhild! And then what?"

"Kotar was loved by the people. Old Gothan stirred them up. I made my greatest mistake when I let that old one live. Yet I dared not slay him. Well, Gothan rose against me, as I had risen against him, and the warriors rebelled, slaying those who stood faithful to me. Me they took captive but dared not kill; for after all, I was a goddess, they believed. So before dawn, fearing the people would change their minds again and restore me to power, Gothan had me taken to the lagoon which separates this part of the island from the other. The priests rowed me across the lagoon and left me, naked and helpless, to my fate."

"And that fate was – this?" Athelstane touched the huge carcass with his foot.

Brunhild shuddered. "Many ages ago there were many of these monsters on the isle, the legends say. They warred on the people of

Bal-Sagoth and devoured them by hundreds. But at last all were exterminated on the main part of the isle and on this side of the lagoon all died but this one, who had abided here for centuries. In the old times hosts of men came against him, but he was greatest of all the devil-birds and he slew all who fought him. So the priests made a god of him and left this part of the island to him. None comes here except those brought as sacrifices – as I was. He could not cross to the main island, because the lagoon swarms with great sharks which would rend even him to pieces.

"For a while I eluded him, stealing among the trees, but at last he spied me out – and you know the rest. I owe my life to you. Now what will you do with me?"

Athelstane looked at Turlogh and Turlogh shrugged. "What can we do, save starve in this forest?"

"I will tell you!" the girl cried in a ringing voice, her eyes blazing anew to the swift working of her keen brain. "There is an old legend among this people – that men of iron will come out of the sea and the city of Bal-Sagoth will fall! You, with your mail and helmets, will seem as iron men to these folk who know nothing of armor! You have slain Groth-golka the bird-god – you have come out of the sea as did I – the people will look on you as gods. Come with me and aid me to win back my kingdom! You shall be my right-hand men and I will heap honors on you! Fine garments, gorgeous palaces, fairest girls shall be yours!"

Her promises slid from Turlogh's mind without leaving an imprint, but the mad splendor of the proposal intrigued him. Strongly he desired to look on this strange city of which Brunhild spoke, and the thought of two warriors and one girl pitted against a whole nation for a crown stirred the utmost depths of his knight-errant Celtic soul.

"It is well," said he. "And what of you, Athelstane?"

"My belly is empty," growled the giant. "Lead me to where there is food and I'll hew my way to it, through a horde of priests and warriors."

"Lead us to this city!" said Turlogh to Brunhild.

"Hail!" she cried flinging her white arms high in wild exultation. "Now let Gothan and Ska and Gelka tremble! With ye at my side I'll win back the crown they tore from me, and this time I'll not spare my enemy! I'll hurl old Gothan from the highest battlement, though the bellowing of his demons shake the very bowels of the earth! And we shall see if the god Gol-goroth shall stand against the sword that cut Groth-golka's leg from under him. Now hew the head from this carcass that the people may know you have overcome the bird-god. Now follow me, for the sun mounts the sky and I would sleep in my own palace tonight!"

The three passed into the shadows of the mighty forest. The interlocking branches, hundreds of feet above their heads, made dim and strange such sunlight as filtered through. No life was seen except for an occasional gayly hued bird or a huge ape. These beasts, Brunhild said, were survivors of another age, harmless except when attacked. Presently the growth changed somewhat, the trees thinned and became smaller and fruit of many kinds was seen among the branches. Brunhild told the warriors which to pluck and eat as they walked along. Turlogh was quite satisfied with the fruit, but Athelstane, though he ate enormously, did so with scant relish. Fruit was light sustenance to a man used to such solid stuff as formed his regular diet. Even among the gluttonous Danes the Saxon's capacity for beef and ale was admired.

"Look!" cried Brunhild sharply, halting and pointing. "The spires of Bal-Sagoth!"

Through the trees the warriors caught a glimmer: white and shimmery, and apparently far away. There was an illusory impression of towering battlements, high in the air, with fleecy clouds hovering about them. The sight woke strange dreams in the mystic deeps of the Gael's soul, and even Athelstane was silent as if he too were struck by the pagan beauty and mystery of the scene.

So they progressed through the forest, now losing sight of the distant city as treetops obstructed the view, now seeing it again. And at last they came out on the low shelving banks of a broad blue lagoon and the full beauty of the landscape burst upon their eyes. From the opposite shores the country sloped upward in long gentle undulations which broke like great slow waves at the foot of a range of blue hills a few miles away. These wide swells were covered with deep grass and many groves of trees, while miles away on either hand there was seen curving away into the distance the strip of thick forest which Brunhild said belted the whole island. And among those blue dreaming hills brooded the age-old city of Bal-Sagoth, its white walls and sapphire towers clean-cut against the morning sky. The suggestion of great distance had been an illusion.

"Is that not a kingdom worth fighting for?" cried Brunhild, her voice vibrant. "Swift now – let us bind this dry wood together for a raft. We could not live an instant swimming in that shark-haunted water."

At that instant a figure leaped up from the tall grass on the other shore – a naked, brown-skinned man who stared for a moment, agape. Then as Athelstane shouted and held up the grim head of Groth-golka, the fellow gave a startled cry and raced away like an antelope.

"A slave Gothan left to see if I tried to swim the lagoon," said Brunhild with angry satisfaction. "Let him run to the city and tell them – but let us make haste and cross the lagoon before Gothan can arrive and dispute our passage."

Turlogh and Athelstane were already busy. A number of dead trees lay about and these they stripped of their branches and bound together with long vines. In a short time they had built a raft, crude and clumsy, but capable of bearing them across the lagoon. Brunhild gave a frank sigh of relief when they stepped on the other shore.

"Let us go straight to the city," said she. "The slave has reached it ere now and they will be watching us from the walls. A bold course is our only one. Thor's hammer, but I'd like to see Gothan's face when the slave tells him Brunhild is returning with two strange warriors and the head of him to whom she was given as sacrifice!"

"Why did you not kill Gothan when you had the power?" asked Athelstane.

She shook her head, her eyes clouding with something akin to fear: "Easier said than done. Half the people hate Gothan, half love him, and all fear him. The most ancient men of the city say that he was old when they were babes. The people believe him to be more god than priest, and I myself have seen him do terrible and mysterious things, beyond the power of a common man.

"Nay, when I was but a puppet in his hands, I came only to the outer fringe of his mysteries, yet I have looked on sights that froze my blood. I have seen strange shadows flit along the midnight walls, and groping along black subterranean corridors in the dead of night I have heard unhallowed sounds and have felt the presence of hideous beings. And once I heard the grisly slavering bellowings of the nameless Thing Gothan has chained deep in the bowels of the hills on which rests the city of Bal-Sagoth."

Brunhild shuddered.

"There are many gods in Bal-Sagoth, but the greatest of all is Gol-goroth, the god of darkness who sits forever in the Temple of

Shadows. When I overthrew the power of Gothan, I forbade men to worship Gol-goroth, and made the priest hail, as the one true deity, A-ala, the daughter of the sea – myself. I had strong men take heavy hammers and smite the image of Gol-goroth, but their blows only shattered the hammers and gave strange hurts to the men who wielded them. Gol-goroth was indestructible and showed no mar. So I desisted and shut the door of the Temple of Shadows which were opened only when I was overthrown and Gothan, who had been skulking in the secret places of the city, came again into his own. Then Gol-goroth reigned again in his full terror and the idols of A-ala were overthrown in the Temple of the Sea, and the priests of A-ala died howling on the red-stained altar before the black god. But now we shall see!"

"Surely you are a very Valkyrie," muttered Athelstane. "But three against a nation is great odds – especially such a people as this, who must assuredly be all witches and sorcerers."

"Bah!" cried Brunhild contemptuously. "There are many sorcerers, it is true, but though the people are strange to us, they are mere fools in their own way, as are all nations. When Gothan led me captive down the streets they spat on me. Now watch them turn on Ska, the new king Gothan has given them, when it seems my star rises again! But now we approach the city gates – be bold but wary!"

They had ascended the long swelling slopes and were not far from the walls which rose immensely upward. Surely, thought Turlogh, heathen gods built this city. The walls seemed of marble and with their fretted battlements and slim watch-towers, dwarfed the memory of such cities as Rome, Damascus, and Byzantium. A broad white winding road led up from the lower levels to the plateau before the gates and as they came up this road, the three adventurers felt hundreds of hidden eyes fixed on them with fierce intensity. The walls seemed deserted; it might have been a dead city. But the impact of those staring eyes was felt.

Now they stood before the massive gates, which to the amazed eyes of the warriors seemed to be of chased silver.

"Here is an emperor's ransom!" muttered Athelstane, eyes ablaze. "Thor's blood, if we had but a stout band of reavers and a ship to carry away the plunder!"

"Smite on the gate and then step back, lest something fall upon you," said Brunhild, and the thunder of Turlogh's ax on the portals woke the echoes in the sleeping hills.

The three then fell back a few paces and suddenly the mighty gates swung inward and a strange concourse of people stood revealed. The two white warriors looked on a pageant of barbaric grandeur. A throng of tall, slim, brown-skinned men stood in the gates. Their only garments were loincloths of silk, the fine work of which contrasted strangely with the near-nudity of the wearers. Tall waving plumes of many colors decked their heads, and armlets and leglets of gold and silver, crusted with gleaming gems, completed their ornamentation. Armor they wore none, but each carried a light shield on his left arm, made of hard wood, highly polished, and braced with silver. Their weapons were slim-bladed spears, light hatchets and slender daggers, all bladed with fine steel. Evidently these warriors depended more on speed and skill than on brute force.

At the front of this band stood three men who instantly commanded attention. One was a lean hawk-faced warrior, almost as tall as Athelstane, who wore about his neck a great golden chain from which was suspended a curious symbol in jade. One of the other men was young, evil-eyed; an impressive riot of colors in the mantle of parrot-feathers which swung from his shoulders. The third man had nothing to set him apart from the rest save his own strange personality. He wore no mantle, bore no weapons. His only garment was a plain loincloth. He was very old; he alone of all the throng was bearded, and his beard was as white as the long hair which fell about his shoulders. He was very tall and very lean, and his great dark eyes blazed as from a hidden fire. Turlogh knew without being told that this man was Gothan, priest of the Black God. The ancient exuded a very aura of age and mystery. His great eyes were like windows of some forgotten temple, behind which passed like ghosts his dark and terrible thoughts. Turlogh sensed that Gothan had delved too deep in forbidden secrets to remain altogether human. He had passed through doors that had cut him off from the dreams, desires and emotions of ordinary mortals. Looking into those unwinking orbs Turlogh felt his skin crawl, as if he had looked into the eyes of a great serpent.

Now a glance upward showed that the walls were thronged with silent dark-eyed folk. The stage was set; all was in readiness for the swift, red drama. Turlogh felt his pulse quicken with fierce exhilaration and Athelstane's eyes began to glow with ferocious light.

Brunhild stepped forward boldly, head high, her splendid figure vibrant. The white warriors naturally could not understand what passed between her and the others, except as they read from gestures and expressions, but later Brunhild narrated the conversation almost word for word.

"Well, people of Bal-Sagoth," said she, spacing her words slowly, "what words have you for your goddess whom you mocked and reviled?"

"What will you have, false one?" exclaimed the tall man, Ska, the king set up by Gothan. "You who mocked at the customs of our ancestors, defied the laws of Bal-Sagoth, which are older than the world, murdered your lover and defiled the shrine of Gol-goroth? You were doomed by law, king and god and placed in the grim forest beyond the lagoon –"

"And I, who am likewise a goddess and greater than any god," answered Brunhild mockingly, "am returned from the realm of horror with the head of Groth-golka!"

At a word from her, Athelstane held up the great beaked head, and a low whispering ran about the battlements, tense with fear and bewilderment.

"Who are these men?" Ska bent a worried frown on the two warriors.

"They are iron men who have come out of the sea!" answered Brunhild in a clear voice that carried far; "the beings who have come in response to the old prophesy, to overthrow the city of Bal-Sagoth, whose people are traitors and whose priests are false!"

At these words the fearful murmur broke out afresh all up and down the line of the walls, till Gothan lifted his vulture-head and the people fell silent and shrank before the icy stare of his terrible eyes.

Ska glared bewilderedly, his ambition struggling with his superstitious fears.

Turlogh, looking closely at Gothan, believed that he read beneath the inscrutable mask of the old priest's face. For all his inhuman wisdom, Gothan had his limitations. This sudden return of one he thought well disposed of, and the appearance of the white-skinned giants accompanying her, had caught Gothan off his guard, Turlogh believed, rightly. There had been no time to properly prepare for their reception. The people had already begun to murmur in the streets against the severity of Ska's brief rule. They had always believed in Brunhild's divinity; now that she returned with two tall men of her own hue, bearing the grim trophy that marked the conquest of another of their gods, the people were wavering. Any small thing might turn the tide either way.

"People of Bal-Sagoth!" shouted Brunhild suddenly, springing back and flinging her arms high, gazing full into the faces that looked down at her. "I bid you avert your doom before it is too late! You cast me out and spat on me; you turned to darker gods than I! Yet all this will I forgive if you return and do obeisance to me! Once you reviled me – you called me bloody and cruel! True, I was a hard mistress – but has Ska been an easy master? You said I lashed the people with whips of rawhide – has Ska stroked you with parrot feathers?

"A virgin died on my altar at the full tide of each moon – but youths and maidens die at the waxing and the waning, the rising and the setting of each moon, before Gol-goroth, on whose altar a fresh human heart forever throbs! Ska is but a shadow! Your real lord is Gothan, who sits above the city like a vulture! Once you were a mighty people; your galleys filled the seas. Now you are a remnant and that is dwindling fast! Fools! You will all die on the altar of Gol-goroth ere Gothan is done and he will stalk alone among the silent ruins of Bal-Sagoth!

"Look at him!" her voice rose to a scream as she lashed herself to an inspired frenzy, and even Turlogh, to whom the words were meaningless, shivered. "Look at him where he stands there like an evil spirit out of the past! He is not even human! I tell you, he is a foul ghost, whose beard is dabbled with the blood of a million butcheries – an incarnate fiend out of the mist of the ages come to destroy the people of Bal-Sagoth!

"Choose now! Rise up against the ancient devil and his blasphemous gods, receive your rightful queen and deity again and you shall regain some of your former greatness. Refuse, and the ancient prophesy shall be fulfilled and the sun will set on the silent and crumbled ruins of Bal-Sagoth!"

Fired by her dynamic words, a young warrior with the insignia of a chief sprang to the parapet and shouted: "Hail to A-ala! Down with the bloody gods!"

Among the multitude many took up the shout and steel clashed as a score of fights started. The crowd on the battlements and in the streets surged and eddied, while Ska glared, bewildered. Brunhild, forcing back her companions who quivered with eagerness for action of some kind, shouted: "Hold! Let no man strike a blow yet! People of Bal-Sagoth, it has been a tradition since the beginning of time that a king must fight for his crown! Let Ska cross steel with one of these warriors! If Ska wins, I will kneel before him and let him strike off my head! If Ska loses, then you shall accept me as your rightful queen and goddess!"

A great roar of approval went up from the walls as the people ceased their brawls, glad enough to shift the responsibility to their rulers.

"Will you fight, Ska?" asked Brunhild, turning to the king mockingly. "Or will you give me your head without further argument?"

"Slut!" howled Ska, driven to madness. "I will take the skulls of these fools for drinking cups, and then I will rend you between two bent trees!"

Gothan laid a hand on his arm and whispered in his ear, but Ska had reached the point where he was deaf to all but his fury. His achieved ambition, he had found, had faded to the mere part of a puppet dancing on Gothan's string; now even the hollow bauble of his kingship was slipping from him and this wench mocked him to his face before his people. Ska went, to all practical effects, stark mad.

Brunhild turned to her two allies. "One of you must fight Ska."

"Let me be the one!" urged Turlogh, eyes dancing with eager battle-lust. "He has the look of a man quick as a wildcat, and Athelstane, while a very bull for strength, is a thought slow for such work –"

"Slow!" broke in Athelstane reproachfully. "Why, Turlogh, for a man my weight –"

"Enough," Brunhild interrupted. "He must choose for himself."

She spoke to Ska, who glared red-eyed for an instant, then indicated Athelstane, who grinned joyfully, cast aside the bird's head and unslung his sword. Turlogh swore and stepped back. The king had decided that he would have a better chance against this huge buffalo of a man who looked slow, than against the black-haired tigerish warrior, whose cat-like quickness was evident.

"This Ska is without armor," rumbled the Saxon. "Let me likewise doff my mail and helmet so that we fight on equal terms –"

"No!" cried Brunhild. "Your armor is your only chance! I tell you, this false king fights like the play of summer lightning! You will be hard put to hold your own as it is. Keep on your armor, I say!"

"Well, well," grumbled Athelstane, "I will – I will. Though I say it is scarcely fair. But let him come on and make an end of it."

The huge Saxon strode ponderously toward his foe, who warily crouched and circled away. Athelstane held his great sword in both hands before him, pointed upward, the hilt somewhat below the level of his chin, in position to strike a blow to right or left, or to parry a sudden attack.

Ska had flung away his light shield, his fighting-sense telling him that it would be useless before the stroke of that heavy blade. In his right hand he held his slim spear as a man holds a throwing-dart, in his left a light, keen-edged hatchet. He meant to make a fast, shifty fight of it, and his tactics were good. But Ska, having never encountered armor before, made his fatal mistake in supposing it to be apparel or ornament through which his weapons would pierce.

Now he sprang in, thrusting at Athelstane's face with his spear. The Saxon parried with ease and instantly cut tremendously at Ska's legs. The king bounded high, clearing the whistling blade, and in midair he hacked down at Athelstane's bent head. The light hatchet shivered to bits on the Viking's helmet and Ska sprang back out of reach with a blood-lusting howl.

And now it was Athelstane who rushed with unexpected quickness, like a charging bull, and before that terrible onslaught Ska, bewildered by the breaking of his hatchet, was caught off his guard – flat-footed. He caught a fleeting glimpse of the giant looming over him like an overwhelming wave and he sprang in, instead of out, stabbing ferociously. That mistake was his last. The thrusting spear glanced harmlessly from the Saxon's mail, and in that instant the great sword sang down in a stroke the king could not evade. The force of that stroke tossed him as a man is tossed by a plunging bull. A dozen feet away fell Ska, king of Bal-Sagoth, to lie shattered and dead in a ghastly welter of blood and entrails. The throng gaped, struck silent by the prowess of that deed.

"Hew off his head!" cried Brunhild, her eyes flaming as she clenched her hands so that the nails bit into her palms. "Impale that carrion's head on your sword-point so that we may carry it through the city gates with us as token of victory!"

But Athelstane shook his head, cleansing his blade: "Nay, he was a brave man and I will not mutilate his corpse. It is no great feat I have done, for he was naked and I full-armed. Else it is in my mind, the brawl had gone differently."

Turlogh glanced at the people on the walls. They had recovered from their astonishment and now a vast roar went up: "A-ala! Hail to the true goddess!" And the warriors in the gateway dropped to their knees and bowed their foreheads in the dust before Brunhild, who stood proudly erect, bosom heaving with fierce triumph. Truly, thought Turlogh, she is more than a queen – she is a shield woman, a Valkyrie, as Athelstane said.

Now she stepped aside and tearing the golden chain with its jade symbol from the dead neck of Ska, held it on high and shouted: "People of Bal-Sagoth, you have seen how your false king died before this golden-bearded giant, who being of iron, shows no single cut! Choose now – do you receive me of your own free will?"

"Aye, we do!" the multitude answered in a great shout. "Return to your people, oh mighty and all-powerful queen!"

Brunhild smiled sardonically. "Come," said she to the warriors; "they are lashing themselves into a very frenzy of love and loyalty, having already forgotten their treachery. The memory of the mob is short!"

Aye, thought Turlogh, as at Brunhild's side he and the Saxon passed through the mighty gates between files of prostrate chieftains; aye, the memory of the mob is very short. But a few days have passed since they were yelling as wildly for Ska the liberator – scant hours had passed since Ska sat enthroned, master of life and death, and the people bowed before his feet. Now – Turlogh glanced at the mangled corpse which lay deserted and forgotten before the silver gates. The shadow of a circling vulture fell across it. The clamor of the multitude filled Turlogh's ears and he smiled a bitter smile.

The great gates closed behind the three adventurers and Turlogh saw a broad white street stretching away in front of him. Other lesser streets radiated from this one. The two warriors caught a jumbled and chaotic impression of great white stone buildings shouldering each other; of sky-lifting towers and broad stair-fronted palaces. Turlogh knew there must be an ordered system by which the city was laid out, but to him all seemed a waste of stone and metal and polished wood, without rhyme or reason. His baffled eyes sought the street again.

Far up the street extended a mass of humanity, from which rose a rhythmic thunder of sound. Thousands of naked, gayly plumed men and women knelt there, bending forward to touch the marble flags with their foreheads, then swaying back with an upward flinging of their arms, all moving in perfect unison like the bending and rising of tall grass before the wind. And in time to their bowing they lifted a monotoned chant that sank and swelled in a frenzy of ecstasy. So her wayward people welcomed back the goddess A-ala.

Just within the gates Brunhild stopped and there came to her the young chief who had first raised the shout of revolt upon the walls. He knelt and kissed her bare feet, saying: "Oh great queen and goddess, thou knowest Zomar was ever faithful to thee! Thou knowest how I fought for thee and barely escaped the altar of Gol-goroth for thy sake!"

"Thou hast indeed been faithful, Zomar," answered Brunhild in the stilted language required for such occasions. "Nor shall thy fidelity go unrewarded. Henceforth thou art commander of my own bodyguard." Then in a lower voice she added: "Gather a band from your own retainers and from those who have espoused my cause all along, and bring them to the palace. I do not trust the people any more than I have to!"

Suddenly Athelstane, not understanding the conversation, broke in: "Where is the old one with the beard?"

Turlogh started and glanced around. He had almost forgotten the wizard. He had not seen him go – yet he was gone! Brunhild laughed ruefully.

"He's stolen away to breed more trouble in the shadows. He and Gelka vanished when Ska fell. He has secret ways of coming and going and none may stay him. Forget him for the time being; heed ye well – we shall have plenty of him anon!"

Now the chiefs brought a finely carved and highly ornamented palanquin carried by two strong slaves and Brunhild stepped into this, saying to her companions: "They are fearful of touching you, but ask if you would be carried. I think it better that you walk, one on each side of me."

"Thor's blood!" rumbled Athelstane, shouldering the huge sword he had never sheathed. "I'm no infant! I'll split the skull of the man who seeks to carry me!"

And so up the long white street went Brunhild, daughter of Rane Thorfin's son in the Orkneys, goddess of the sea, queen of age-old Bal-Sagoth. Borne by two great slaves she went, with a white giant striding on each side with bared steel, and a concourse of chiefs following, while the multitude gave way to right and left, leaving a wide lane down which she passed. Golden trumpets sounded a fanfare of triumph, drums thundered, chants of worship echoed to the ringing skies. Surely in this riot of glory, this barbaric pageant of splendor, the proud soul of the North-born girl drank deep and grew drunken with imperial pride.

Athelstane's eyes glowed with simple delight at this flame of pagan magnificence, but to the black haired fighting-man of the West, it seemed that even in the loudest clamor of triumph, the trumpet, the drum and shouting faded away into the forgotten dust and silence of eternity. Kingdoms and empires pass away like mist from the sea, thought Turlogh; the people shout and triumph and even in the revelry of Belshazzar's feast, the Medes break the gates of Babylon. Even now the shadow of doom is over this city and the slow tides of oblivion lap the feet of this unheeding race. So in a strange mood Turlogh O'Brien strode beside the palanquin, and it seemed to him that he and Athelstane walked in a dead city, through throngs of dim ghosts, cheering a ghost queen.

3. The Fall of the Gods

Night had fallen on the ancient city of Bal-Sagoth. Turlogh, Athelstane and Brunhild sat alone in a room of the inner palace. The queen half-reclined on a silken couch, while the men sat on mahogany chairs, engaged in the viands that slave-girls had served on golden dishes. The walls of this room, as of all the palace, were of marble, with golden scrollwork. The ceiling was of lapis-lazuli and the floor of silver-inlaid marble tiles. Heavy velvet hangings decorated the walls and silken cushions; richly-made divans and mahogany chairs and tables littered the room in careless profusion.

"I would give much for a horn of ale, but this wine is not sour to the palate," said Athelstane, emptying a golden flagon with relish. "Brunhild, you have deceived us. You let us understand it would take hard fighting to win back your crown – yet I have struck but one blow and my sword is thirsty as Turlogh's ax which has not drunk at all. We hammered on the gates and the people fell down and worshipped with no more ado. And until a while ago, we but stood by your throne in the great palace room, while you spoke to the throngs that came and knocked their heads on the floor before you – by Thor, never have I heard such clattering and jabbering!

My ears ring till now – what were they saying? And where is that old conjurer Gothan?"

"Your steel will drink deep yet, Saxon," answered the girl grimly, resting her chin on her hands and eyeing the warriors with deep moody eyes. "Had you gambled with cities and crowns as I have done, you would know that seizing a throne may be easier than keeping it. Our sudden appearance with the bird-god's head, your killing of Ska, swept the people off their feet. As for the rest – I held audience in the palace as you saw, even if you did not understand and the people who came in bowing droves were assuring me of their unswerving loyalty – ha! I graciously pardoned them all, but I am no fool. When they have time to think, they will begin to grumble again. Gothan is lurking in the shadows somewhere, plotting evil to us all, you may be sure. This city is honeycombed with secret corridors and subterranean passages of which only the priests know. Even I, who have traversed some of them when I was Gothan's puppet, know not where to look for the secret doors, since Gothan always led me through them blindfolded.

"Just now, I think I hold the upper hand. The people look on you with more awe than they regard me. They think your armor and helmets are part of your bodies and that you are invulnerable. Did you not note them timidly touching your mail as we passed through the crowd, and the amazement on their faces as they felt the iron of it?"

"For a people so wise in some ways they are very foolish in others," said Turlogh. "Who are they and whence came they?"

"They are so old," answered Brunhild, "that their most ancient legends give no hint of their origin. Ages ago they were a part of a great empire which spread out over the many isles of this sea. But some of the islands sank and vanished with their cities and people. Then the red-skinned savages assailed them and isle after isle fell before them. At last only this island was left unconquered, and the people have become weaker and forgotten many ancient arts. For lack of ports to sail to, the galleys rotted by the wharves which themselves crumbled into decay. Not in the memory of man has any son of Bal-Sagoth sailed the seas. At irregular intervals the red people descend upon the Isle of the Gods, traversing the seas in their long war-canoes which bear grinning skulls on the prows. Not far away as a Viking would reckon a sea-voyage, but out of sight over the sea rim lie the islands inhabited by those red men who centuries ago slaughtered the folk who dwelt there. We have always beaten them off; they can not scale the walls, but still they come and the fear of their raid is always hovering over the isle.

"But it is not them I fear; it is Gothan, who is at this moment either slipping like a loathly serpent through his black tunnels or else brewing abominations in one of his hidden chambers. In the caves deep in the hills to which his tunnels lead, he works fearful and unholy magic. His subjects are beasts – serpents, spiders, and great apes; and men – red captives and wretches of his own race. Deep in his grisly caverns he makes beasts of men and half-men of beasts, mingling bestial with human in ghastly creation. No man dares guess at the horrors that have spawned in the darkness, or what shapes of terror and blasphemy have come into being during the ages Gothan has wrought his abominations; for he is not as other men, and has discovered the secret of life everlasting. He has at least brought into foul life one creature that even he fears, the gibbering, mowing, nameless Thing he keeps chained in the farthest cavern that no human foot save his has trod. He would loose it against me if he dared. . . .

"But it grows late and I would sleep. I will sleep in the room next to this, which has no other opening than this door. Not even a slave-girl will I keep with me, for I trust none of these people fully. You shall keep this room, and though the outer door is bolted, one had better watch while the other sleeps. Zomar and his guardsmen patrol the corridors outside, but I shall feel safer with two men of my own blood between me and the rest of the city."

She rose, and with a strangely lingering glance at Turlogh, entered her chamber and closed the door behind her.

Athelstane stretched and yawned. "Well, Turlogh," said he lazily, "men's fortunes are unstable as the sea. Last night I was the picked swordsman of a band of reavers and you a captive. This dawn we were lost outcasts springing at each other's throats. Now we are sword brothers and right-hand men to a queen. And you, I think, are destined to become a king."

"How so?"

"Why, have you not noticed the Orkney girl's eyes on you? Faith there's more than friendship in her glances that rest on those black locks and that brown face of yours. I tell you –"

"Enough," Turlogh's voice was harsh as an old wound stung him. "Women in power are white-fanged wolves. It was the spite of a woman that –" He stopped.

"Well, well," returned Athelstane tolerantly, "there are more good women than bad ones. I know – it was the intrigues of a woman that made you an outcast. Well, we should be good comrades. I am an outlaw, too. If I should show my face in Wessex I would soon be looking down on the countryside from a stout oak limb."

"What drove you out on the Viking path? So far have the Saxons forgotten the ocean-ways that King Alfred was obliged to hire Frisian rovers to build and man his fleet when he fought the Danes."

Athelstane shrugged his mighty shoulders and began whetting his dirk.

"So England – was – again – barred – to – me. I – took – the – Viking – path – again –"

Athelstane's words trailed off. His hands slid limply from his lap and the whetstone and dirk dropped to the floor. His head fell forward on his broad chest and his eyes closed.

"Too much wine," muttered Turlogh. "But let him slumber; I'll keep watch."

Yet even as he spoke, the Gael was aware of a strange lassitude stealing over him. He lay back in the broad chair. His eyes felt heavy and sleep veiled his brain despite himself. And as he lay there, a strange nightmare vision came to him. One of the heavy hangings on the wall opposite the door swayed violently and from behind it slunk a fearful shape that crept slavering across the room. Turlogh watched it apathetically, aware that he was dreaming and at the same time wondering at the strangeness of the dream. The thing was grotesquely like a crooked gnarled man in shape, but its face was bestial. It bared yellow fangs as it lurched silently toward him, and from under penthouse brows small reddened eyes gleamed demoniacally. Yet there was something of the human in its countenance; it was neither ape nor man, but an unnatural creature horribly compounded of both.

Now the foul apparition halted before him, and as the gnarled fingers clutched his throat, Turlogh was suddenly and fearfully aware that this was no dream but a fiendish reality. With a burst of desperate effort he broke the unseen chains that held him and hurled himself from the chair. The grasping fingers missed his throat, but quick as he was, he could not elude the swift lunge of those hairy arms, and the next moment he was tumbling about the floor in a death grip with the monster, whose sinews felt like pliant steel.

That fearful battle was fought in silence save for the hissing of hard-drawn breath. Turlogh's left forearm was thrust under the apish chin, holding back the grisly fangs from his throat, about which the monster's fingers had locked. Athelstane still slept in his chair, head fallen forward. Turlogh tried to call to him, but those throttling hands had shut off his voice – were fast choking out his life. The room swam in a red haze before his distended eyes. His right hand, clenched into an iron mallet, battered desperately at the fearful face bent toward his; the beast-like teeth shattered under his blows and blood splattered, but still the red eyes gloated and the taloned fingers sank deeper and deeper until a ringing in Turlogh's ears knelled his soul's departure.

Even as he sank into semi-unconsciousness, his falling hand struck something his numbed fighting-brain recognized as the dirk Athelstane had dropped on the floor. Blindly, with a dying gesture, Turlogh struck and felt the fingers loosen suddenly. Feeling the return of life and power, he heaved up and over, with his assailant beneath him. Through red mists that slowly lightened, Turlogh Dubh saw the ape-man, now encrimsoned, writhing beneath him, and he drove the dirk home until the dumb horror lay still with wide staring eyes.

The Gael staggered to his feet, dizzy and panting, trembling in every limb. He drew in great gulps of air and his giddiness slowly cleared. Blood trickled plentifully from the wounds in his throat. He noted with amazement that the Saxon still slumbered. And suddenly he began to feel again the tides of unnatural weariness and lassitude that had rendered him helpless before. Picking up his ax, he shook off the feeling with difficulty and stepped toward the curtain from behind which the ape-man had come. Like an invisible wave a subtle power emanating from those hangings struck him, and with weighted limbs he forced his way across the room. Now he stood before the curtain and felt the power of a terrific evil will beating upon his own, menacing his very soul, threatening to enslave him, brain and body. Twice he raised his hand and twice it dropped limply to his side. Now for the third time he made a mighty effort and tore the hangings bodily from the wall. For a flashing instant he caught a glimpse of a bizarre, half-naked figure in a mantle of parrot-feathers and a head-gear of waving plumes. Then as he felt the full hypnotic blast of those blazing eyes, he closed his own eyes and struck blind. He felt his ax sink deep; then he opened his eyes and gazed at the silent figure which lay at his feet, cleft head in a widening crimson pool.

And now Athelstane suddenly heaved erect, eyes flaring bewilderedly, sword out. "What –?" he stammered, glaring wildly. "Turlogh, what in Thor's name's happened? Thor's blood! That is a priest there, but what is this dead thing?"

"One of the devils of this foul city," answered Turlogh, wrenching his ax free. "I think Gothan has failed again. This one stood behind the hangings and bewitched us unawares. He put the spell of sleep on us –"

"Aye, I slept," the Saxon nodded dazedly. "But how came they here –"

"There must be a secret door behind those hangings, though I can not find it –"

"Hark!" From the room where the queen slept there came a vague scuffling sound, that in its very faintness seemed fraught with grisly potentialities.

"Brunhild!" Turlogh shouted. A strange gurgle answered him. He thrust against the door. It was locked. As he heaved up his ax to hew it open, Athelstane brushed him aside and hurled his full weight against it. The panels crashed and through their ruins Athelstane plunged into the room. A roar burst from his lips. Over the Saxon's shoulder Turlogh saw a vision of delirium. Brunhild, queen of Bal-Sagoth, writhed helpless in midair, gripped by the black shadow of a nightmare. Then as the great black shape turned cold flaming eyes on them Turlogh saw it was a living creature. It stood, man-like, upon two tree-like legs, but its outline and face were not of a man, beast or devil. This, Turlogh felt, was the horror that even Gothan had hesitated to loose upon his foes; the archfiend that the demoniac priest had brought into life in his hidden caves of horror. What ghastly knowledge had been necessary, what hideous blending of human and bestial things with nameless shapes from outer voids of darkness?

Held like a babe in arms Brunhild writhed, eyes flaring with horror, and as the Thing took a misshapen hand from her white throat to defend itself, a scream of heart-shaking fright burst from her pale lips. Athelstane, first in the room, was ahead of the Gael. The black shape loomed over the giant Saxon, dwarfing and overshadowing him, but Athelstane, gripping the hilt with both hands, lunged upward. The great sword sank over half its length into the black body and came out crimson as the monster reeled back.

A hellish pandemonium of sound burst forth, and the echoes of that hideous yell thundered through the palace and deafened the hearers. Turlogh was springing in, ax high, when the fiend dropped the girl and fled reeling across the room, vanishing in a dark opening that now gaped in the wall. Athelstane, clean berserk, plunged after it.

Turlogh made to follow, but Brunhild, reeling up, threw her white arms around him in a grip even he could hardly break. "No!" she screamed, eyes ablaze with terror. "Do not follow them into that fearful corridor! It must lead to Hell itself! The Saxon will never return! Let you not share his fate!"

"Loose me, woman!" roared Turlogh in a frenzy, striving to disengage himself without hurting her. "My comrade may be fighting for his life!"

"Wait till I summon the guard!" she cried, but Turlogh flung her from him, and as he sprang through the secret doorway, Brunhild smote on the jade gong until the palace re-echoed. A loud pounding began in the corridor and Zomar's voice shouted: "Oh, queen, are you in peril? Shall we burst the door?"

"Hasten!" she screamed, as she rushed to the outer door and flung it open.

Turlogh, leaping recklessly into the corridor, raced along in darkness for a few moments, hearing ahead of him the agonized bellowing of the wounded monster and the deep fierce shouts of the Viking. Then these noises faded away in the distance as he came into the narrow passageway faintly lighted with torches stuck into niches. Face down on the floor lay a brown man, clad in gray feathers, his skull crushed like an eggshell.

How long Turlogh O'Brien followed the dizzy windings of the shadowy corridor he never knew. Other smaller passages led off to each side but he kept to the main corridor. At last he passed under an arched doorway and came out into a strange vasty room.

Somber massive columns upheld a shadowy ceiling so high it seemed like a brooding cloud arched against a midnight sky. Turlogh saw that he was in a temple. Behind a black red-stained stone altar loomed a mighty form, sinister and abhorrent. The god Golgoroth! Surely it must be he. But Turlogh spared only a single glance for the colossal figure that brooded there in the shadows. Before him was a strange tableau. Athelstane leaned on his great sword and gazed at the two shapes which sprawled in a red welter at his feet. Whatever foul magic had brought the Black Thing into life, it had taken but a thrust of English steel to hurl it back into a limbo from whence it came. The monster lay half-across its last victim – a gaunt white-bearded man whose eyes were starkly evil, even in death.

"Gothan!" ejaculated the startled Gael.

"Aye, the priest – I was close behind this troll or whatever it is, all the way along the corridor, but for all its size it fled like a deer. Once one in a feather mantle tried to halt it, and it smashed his skull and paused not an instant. At last we burst into this temple, I closed upon the monster's heels with my sword raised for the death-cut. But Thor's blood! When it saw the old one standing by that altar, it gave one fearful howl and tore him to pieces and died itself, all in an instant, before I could reach it and strike."

Turlogh gazed at the huge formless thing. Looking directly at it, he could form no estimate of its nature. He got only a chaotic impression of great size and inhuman evil. Now it lay like a vast shadow blotched out on the marble floor. Surely black wings beating from moonless gulfs had hovered over its birth, and the grisly souls of nameless demons had gone into its being.

And now Brunhild rushed from the dark corridor with Zomar and the guardsmen. And from outer doors and secret nooks came others silently – warriors, and priests in feathered mantles, until a great throng stood in the Temple of Darkness.

A fierce cry broke from the queen as she saw what had happened. Her eyes blazed terribly and she was gripped by a strange madness.

"At last!" she screamed, spurning the corpse of her arch-foe with her heel. "At last I am true mistress of Bal-Sagoth! The secrets of the hidden ways are mine now, and old Gothan's beard is dabbled in his own blood!"

She flung her arms high in fearful triumph, and ran toward the grim idol, screaming exultant insults like a mad-woman. And at that instant the temple rocked! The colossal image swayed outward, and then pitched suddenly forward as a tall tower falls. Turlogh shouted and leaped forward, but even as he did, with a thunder like the bursting of a world, the god Gol-goroth crashed down upon the doomed woman, who stood frozen. The mighty image splintered into a thousand great fragments, blotting from the sight of men forever Brunhild, daughter of Rane Thorfin's son, queen of Bal-Sagoth. From under the ruins there oozed a wide crimson stream.

Warriors and priests stood frozen, deafened by the crash of that fall, stunned by the weird catastrophe. An icy hand touched Turlogh's spine. Had that vast bulk been thrust over by the hand of a dead man? As it had rushed downward it had seemed to the Gael that the inhuman features had for an instant taken on the likeness of the dead Gothan!

Now as all stood speechless, the acolyte Gelka saw and seized his opportunity.

"Gol-goroth has spoken!" he screamed. "He has crushed the false goddess! She was but a wicked mortal! And these strangers, too, are mortal! See – he bleeds!"

The priest's finger stabbed at the dried blood on Turlogh's throat and a wild roar went up from the throng. Dazed and bewildered by the swiftness and magnitude of the late events, they were like crazed wolves, ready to wipe out doubts and fear in a burst of bloodshed. Gelka bounded at Turlogh, hatchet flashing, and a knife in the hand of a satellite licked into Zomar's back. Turlogh had not understood the shout, but he realized the air was tense with danger for Athelstane and himself. He met the leaping Gelka with a stroke that sheared through the waving plumes and the skull beneath, then half a dozen lances broke on his buckler and a rush of bodies swept him back against a great pillar. Then Athelstane, slow of thought, who had stood gaping for the flashing second it had taken this to transpire, awoke in a blast of awesome fury. With a deafening roar he swung his heavy sword in a mighty arc. The whistling blade whipped off a head, sheared through a torso and sank deep into a spinal column. The three corpses fell across each other and even in the madness of the strife, men cried out at the marvel of that single stroke.

But like a brown, blind tide of fury the maddened people of Bal-Sagoth rolled on their foes. The guardsmen of the dead queen, trapped in the press, died to a man without a chance to strike a blow. But the overthrow of the two white warriors was no such easy task. Back to back they smashed and smote; Athelstane's sword was a thunderbolt of death; Turlogh's ax was lightning. Hedged close by a sea of snarling brown faces and flashing steel they hacked their way slowly toward a doorway. The very mass of the attackers hindered the warriors of Bal-Sagoth, for they had no space to guide their strokes, while the weapons of the seafarers kept a bloody ring clear in front of them.

Heaping a ghastly row of corpses as they went, the comrades

slowly cut their way through the snarling press. The Temple of Shadows, witness of many a bloody deed, was flooded with gore spilled like a red sacrifice to her broken gods. The heavy weapons of the white fighters wrought fearful havoc among their naked, lighter-limbed foes, while their armor guarded their own lives. But their arms, legs and faces were cut and gashed by the frantically flying steel and it seemed the sheer number of their foes would overwhelm them ere they could reach the door.

Then they had reached it, and made desperate play until the brown warriors, no longer able to come upon them from all sides, drew back for a breathing-space, leaving a torn red heap before the threshold. And in that instant the two sprang back into the corridor and seizing the great brazen door, slammed it in the very faces of the warriors who leaped howling to prevent it. Athelstane, bracing his mighty legs, held it against their combined efforts until Turlogh had time to find and slip the bolt.

"Thor!" gasped the Saxon, shaking the blood in a red shower from his face. "This is close play! What now, Turlogh?"

"Down the corridor, quick!" snapped the Gael, "before they come on us from this way and trap us like rats against this door. By Satan, the whole city must be roused! Hark to that roaring!"

In truth, as they raced down the shadowed corridor, it seemed to them that all Bal-Sagoth had burst into rebellion and civil war. From all sides came the clashing of steel, the shouts of men, and the screams of women, overshadowed by a hideous howling. A lurid glow became apparent down the corridor and then even as Turlogh, in the lead, rounded a corner and came out into an open courtyard, a vague figure leaped at him and a heavy weapon fell with unexpected force on his shield, almost felling him. But even as he staggered he struck back and the upper-spike on his ax sank under the heart of his attacker, who fell at his feet. In the glare that illumined all, Turlogh saw his victim differed from the brown warriors he had been fighting. This man was naked, powerfully muscled and of a copperish red rather than brown. The heavy animal-like jaw, the slanting low forehead showed none of the intelligence and refinement of the brown people, but only a brute ferocity. A heavy war-club, rudely carved, lay beside him.

"By Thor!" exclaimed Athelstane. "The city burns!"

Turlogh looked up. They were standing on a sort of raised courtyard from which broad steps led down into the streets and from this vantage point they had a plain view of the terrific end of Bal-

Sagoth. Flames leaped madly higher and higher, paling the moon, and in the red glare pigmy figures ran to and fro, falling and dying like puppets dancing to the tune of the Black Gods. Through the roar of the flames and the crashing of falling walls cut screams of death and shrieks of ghastly triumph. The city was swarming with naked, copper-skinned devils who burned and ravished and butchered in one red carnival of madness.

The red men of the isles! By the thousands they had descended on the Isle of the Gods in the night, and whether stealth or treachery let them through the walls, the comrades never knew, but now they ravened through the corpse-strewn streets, glutting their blood-lust in holocaust and massacre wholesale. Not all the gashed forms that lay in the crimson-running streets were brown; the people of the doomed city fought with desperate courage, but outnumbered and caught off guard, their courage was futile. The red men were like blood-hungry tigers.

"What ho, Turlogh!" shouted Athelstane, beard a-bristle, eyes ablaze as the madness of the scene fired a like passion in his own fierce soul. "The world ends! Let us into the thick of it and glut our steel before we die! Who shall we strike for – the red or the brown?"

"Steady!" snapped the Gael. "Either people would cut our throats. We must hack our way through to the gates, and the Devil take them all. We have no friends here. This way – down these stairs. Across the roofs in yonder direction I see the arch of a gate."

The comrades sprang down the stairs, gained the narrow street below and ran swiftly in the way Turlogh indicated. About them washed a red inundation of slaughter. A thick smoke veiled all now, and in the murk chaotic groups merged, writhed and scattered, littering the shattered flags with gory shapes. It was like a nightmare in which demoniac figures leaped and capered, looming suddenly in the fire-shot mist, vanishing as suddenly. The flames from each side of the streets shouldered each other, singeing the hair of the warriors as they ran. Roofs fell in with an awesome thunder and walls crashing into ruin filled the air with flying death. Men struck blindly from the smoke and the seafarers cut them down and never knew whether their skins were brown or red.

Now a new note rose in the cataclysmic horror. Blinded by the smoke, confused by the winding streets, the red men were trapped in the snare of their own making. Fire is impartial; it can burn the lighter as well as the intended victim; and a falling wall is blind. The red men abandoned their prey and ran howling to and fro like beasts, seeking escape; many, finding this futile, turned back in a last unreasoning storm of madness as a blinded tiger turns, and made their last moments of life a crimson burst of slaughter.

Turlogh, with the unerring sense of direction that comes to men who live the life of the wolf, ran toward the point where he knew an outer gate to be; yet in the windings of the streets and the screen of smoke, doubt assailed him. From the flame-shot murk in front of him a fearful scream rang out. A naked girl reeled blindly into view and fell at Turlogh's feet, blood gushing from her mutilated breast. A howling, red-stained devil, close on her heels, jerked back her head and cut her throat, a fraction of a second before Turlogh's ax ripped the head from its shoulders and spun it grinning into the street. And at that second a sudden wind shifted the writhing smoke and the comrades saw the open gateway ahead of them, a-swarm with red warriors. A fierce shout, a blasting rush, a mad instant of volcanic ferocity that littered the gateway with corpses, and they were through and racing down the slopes toward the distant forest and the beach beyond. Before them the sky was reddening for dawn; behind them rose the soul-shaking tumult of the doomed city.

Like hunted things they fled, seeking brief shelter among the many groves from time to time, to avoid groups of savages who ran toward the city. The whole island seemed to be swarming with them; the chiefs must have drawn on all the isles within hundreds of miles for a raid of such magnitude. And at last the comrades reached the strip of forest, and breathed deeply as they came to the beach and found it abandoned save for a number of long skull-decorated war canoes.

Athelstane sat down and gasped for breath. "Thor's blood! What now? What may we do but hide in these woods until those red devils hunt us out?"

"Help me launch this boat," snapped Turlogh. We'll take our chance on the open main –"

"Ho!" Athelstane leaped erect, pointing. "Thor's blood, a ship!"

The sun was just up, gleaming like a great golden coin on the sea-rim. And limned in the sun swam a tall, high-pooped craft. The comrades leaped into the nearest canoe, shoved off and rowed like mad, shouting and waving their oars to attract the attention of the crew. Powerful muscles drove the long slim craft along at an incredible clip, and it was not long before the ship stood about and allowed them to come alongside. Dark-faced men, clad in mail, looked over the rail.

"Spaniards," muttered Athelstane. "If they recognize me, I had better stayed on the island!"

But he clambered up the chain without hesitation, and the two wanderers fronted the lean somber-faced man whose armor was that of a knight of Asturias. He spoke to them in Spanish and Turlogh answered him, for the Gael, like many of his race, was a natural linguist and had wandered far and spoken many tongues. In a few words the Dalcassian told their story and explained the great pillar of smoke which now rolled upward in the morning air from the isle.

"Tell him there is a king's ransom for the taking," put in Athelstane. "Tell of the silver gates, Turlogh."

But when the Gael spoke of the vast loot in the doomed city, the commander shook his head.

"Good sir, we have not time to secure it, nor men to waste in the taking. Those red fiends you describe would hardly give up anything – though useless to them – without a fierce battle and neither my time nor my force is mine. I am Don Roderigo del Cortez of Castile and this ship, the Gray Friar, is one of a fleet that sailed to harry the Moorish Corsairs. Some days agone we were separated from the rest of the fleet in a sea skirmish and the tempest blew us far off our course. We are even now beating back to rejoin the fleet if we can find it; if not, to harry the infidel as well as we may. We serve God and the king and we can not halt for mere dross as you suggest. But you are welcome aboard this ship and we have need of such fighting men as you appear to be. You will not regret it, should you wish to join us and strike a blow for Christendom against the Moslems."

In the narrow-bridged nose and deep dark eyes, in the lean ascetic face, Turlogh read the fanatic, the stainless cavalier, the knight errant. He spoke to Athelstane: "This man is mad, but there are good blows to be struck and strange lands to see; anyway, we have no other choice."

"One place is as good as another to masterless men and wanderers," quoth the huge Saxon. "Tell him we will follow him to Hell and singe the tail of the Devil if there be any chance of loot."

4. Empire

Turlogh and Athelstane leaned on the rail, gazing back at the swiftly receding Island of the Gods, from which rose a pillar of smoke, laden with the ghosts of a thousand centuries and the shadows and mysteries of forgotten empire, and Athelstane cursed as only a Saxon can.

"A king's ransom – and after all that blood-letting – no loot!"

Turlogh shook his head. "We have seen an ancient kingdom fall – we have seen the last remnant of the world's oldest empire sink into flames and the abyss of oblivion, and barbarism rear its brute head above the ruins. So pass the glory and the splendor and the imperial purple – in red flames and yellow smoke."

"But not one bit of plunder –" persisted the Viking.

Again Turlogh shook his head. "I brought away with me the rarest gem upon the island – something for which men and women have died and the gutters run with blood."

He drew from his girdle a small object – a curiously carved symbol of jade.

"The emblem of kingship!" exclaimed Athelstane.

"Aye – as Brunhild struggled with me to keep me from following you into the corridor, this thing caught in my mail and was torn from the golden chain that held it."

"He who bears it is king of Bal-Sagoth," ruminated the mighty Saxon. "As I predicted, Turlogh, you are a king!"

Turlogh laughed with bitter mirth and pointed to the great billowing column of smoke which floated in the sky away on the sea-rim.

"Aye – a kingdom of the dead – an empire of ghosts and smoke. I am Ard-Righ of a phantom city – I am King Turlogh of Bal-Sagoth and my kingdom is fading in the morning sky. And therein it is like all other empires in the world – dreams and ghosts and smoke."

THE BLACK STONE

Weird Tales, November 1931

"They say foul things of Old Times still lurk
In dark forgotten corners of the world,
And Gates still gape to loose, on certain nights,
Shapes pent in Hell."
– Justin Geoffrey

I read of it first in the strange book of Von Junzt, the German eccentric who lived so curiously and died in such grisly and mysterious fashion. It was my fortune to have access to his *Nameless Cults* in the original edition, the so-called Black Book, published in Dusseldorf in 1839, shortly before a hounding doom overtook the author. Collectors of rare literature were familiar with *Nameless Cults* mainly through the cheap and faulty translation which was pirated in London by Bridewall in 1845, and the carefully expurgated edition put out by the Golden Goblin Press of New York, 1909. But the volume I stumbled upon was one of the unexpurgated German copies, with heavy black leather covers and rusty iron hasps. I doubt if there are more than half a dozen such volumes in the entire world today, for the quantity issued was not great, and when the manner of the author's demise was bruited about, many possessors of the book burned their volumes in panic.

Von Junzt spent his entire life (1795-1840) delving into forbidden subjects; he traveled in all parts of the world, gained entrance into innumerable secret societies, and read countless little-known and esoteric books and manuscripts in the original; and in the chapters of the Black Book, which range from startling clarity of exposition to murky ambiguity, there are statements and hints to freeze the blood of a thinking man. Reading what Von Junzt *dared* put in print arouses uneasy speculations as to what it was that he dared *not* tell. What dark matters, for instance, were contained in those closely written pages that formed the unpublished manuscript on which he worked unceasingly for months before his death, and which lay torn and scattered all over the floor of the locked and bolted chamber in which Von Junzt was found dead with the marks of taloned fingers on his throat? It will never be known, for the author's closest friend, the Frenchman Alexis Ladeau, after having spent a whole night piecing the fragments together and reading what was written, burnt them to ashes and cut his own throat with a razor.

But the contents of the published matter are shuddersome enough, even if one accepts the general view that they but represent the ravings of a madman. There among many strange things I found mention of the Black Stone, that curious, sinister monolith that broods among the mountains of Hungary, and about which so many dark legends cluster. Van Junzt did not devote much space to it – the bulk of his grim work concerns cults and objects of dark worship which he maintained existed in his day, and it would seem that the Black Stone represents some order or being lost and forgotten centuries ago. But he spoke of it as one of the *keys* – a phrase used many times by him, in various relations, and constituting one of the obscurities of his work. And he hinted briefly at curious sights to be seen about the monolith on Midsummer's Night. He mentioned Otto Dostmann's theory that this monolith was a remnant of the Hunnish invasion and had been erected to commemorate a victory of Attila over the Goths. Von Junzt contradicted this assertion without giving any refutory facts, merely remarking that to attribute the origin of the Black Stone to the Huns was as logical as assuming that William the Conqueror reared Stonehenge.

This implication of enormous antiquity piqued my interest immensely and after some difficulty I succeeded in locating a rat-eaten and moldering copy of Dostmann's *Remnants of Lost Empires* (Berlin, 1809, "Der Drachenhaus" Press). I was disappointed to find that Dostmann referred to the Black Stone even more briefly than had Von Junzt, dismissing it with a few lines as an artifact comparatively modern in contrast with the Greco-Roman ruins of Asia Minor which were his pet theme. He admitted his inability to make out the defaced characters on the monolith but pronounced them unmistakably Mongoloid. However, little as I learned from Dostmann, he did mention the name of the village adjacent to the Black Stone – Stregoicavar – an ominous name, meaning something like Witch-Town.

A close scrutiny of guidebooks and travel articles gave me no further information – Stregoicavar, not on any map that I could find, lay in a wild, little-frequented region, out of the path of casual tourists. But I did find subject for thought in Dornly's *Magyar Folklore*. In his chapter on *Dream Myths* he mentions the Black

Stone and tells of some curious superstitions regarding it – especially the belief that if anyone sleeps in the vicinity of the monolith, that person will be haunted by monstrous nightmares forever after; and he cited tales of the peasants regarding too-curious people who ventured to visit the Stone on Midsummer Night and who died raving mad because of *something* they saw there.

That was all I could gleam from Dornly, but my interest was even more intensely roused as I sensed a distinctly sinister aura about the Stone. The suggestion of dark antiquity, the recurrent hint of unnatural events on Midsummer Night, touched some slumbering instinct in my being, as one senses, rather than hears, the flowing of some dark subterraneous river in the night.

And I suddenly saw a connection between this Stone and a certain weird and fantastic poem written by the mad poet, Justin Geoffrey: *The People of the Monolith*. Inquiries led to the information that Geoffrey had indeed written that poem while traveling in Hungary, and I could not doubt that the Black Stone was the very monolith to which he referred in his strange verse. Reading his stanzas again, I felt once more the strange dim stirrings of subconscious promptings that I had noticed when first reading of the Stone.

I had been casting about for a place to spend a short vacation and I made up my mind. I went to Stregoicavar. A train of obsolete style carried me from Temesvar to within striking distance, at least, of my objective, and a three days' ride in a jouncing coach brought me to the little village which lay in a fertile valley high up in the fir-clad mountains. The journey itself was uneventful, but during the first day we passed the old battlefield of Schomvaal where the brave Polish-Hungarian knight, Count Boris Vladinoff, made his gallant and futile stand against the victorious hosts of Suleiman the Magnificent, when the Grand Turk swept over eastern Europe in 1526.

The driver of the coach pointed out to me a great heap of crumbling stones on a hill nearby, under which, he said, the bones of the brave Count lay. I remembered a passage from Larson's *Turkish Wars*. "After the skirmish" (in which the Count with his small army had beaten back the Turkish advance-guard) "the Count was standing beneath the half-ruined walls of the old castle on the hill, giving orders as to the disposition of his forces, when an aide brought to him a small lacquered case which had been taken from the body of the famous Turkish scribe and historian, Selim Bahadur, who had fallen in the fight. The Count took therefrom a roll of parchment and began to read, but he had not read far before he turned very pale and, without saying a word, replaced the parchment in the case and thrust the case into his cloak. At that very instant a hidden Turkish battery suddenly opened fire, and the balls striking the old castle, the Hungarians were horrified to see the walls crash down in ruin, completely covering the brave Count. Without a leader the gallant little army was cut to pieces, and in the war-swept years which followed, the bones of the noblemen were never recovered. Today the natives point out a huge and moldering pile of ruins near Schomvaal beneath which, they say, still rests all that the centuries have left of Count Boris Vladinoff."

I found the village of Stregoicavar a dreamy, drowsy little village that apparently belied its sinister cognomen – a forgotten back-eddy that Progress had passed by. The quaint houses and the quainter dress and manners of the people were those of an earlier century. They were friendly, mildly curious but not inquisitive, though visitors from the outside world were extremely rare.

"Ten years ago another American came here and stayed a few days in the village," said the owner of the tavern where I had put up, "a young fellow and queer-acting – mumbled to himself – a poet, I think."

I knew he must mean Justin Geoffrey.

"Yes, he was a poet," I answered, "and he wrote a poem about a bit of scenery near this very village."

"Indeed?" Mine host's interest was aroused. "Then, since all great poets are strange in their speech and actions, he must have achieved great fame, for his actions and conversations were the strangest of any man I ever I knew."

"As is usual with artists," I answered, "most of his recognition has come since his death."

"He is dead, then?"

"He died screaming in a madhouse five years ago."

"Too bad, too bad," sighed mine host sympathetically. "Poor lad – he looked too long at the Black Stone."

My heart gave a leap, but I masked my keen interest and said casually. "I have heard something of this Black Stone; somewhere near this village, is it not?"

"Nearer than Christian folk wish," he responded. "Look!" He drew me to a latticed window and pointed up at the fir-clad slopes of the brooding blue mountains. "There beyond where you see the bare face of that jutting cliff stands that accursed Stone. Would that it were ground to powder and the powder flung into the Danube to be carried to the deepest ocean! Once men tried to destroy the thing, but each man who laid hammer or maul against it came to an evil end. So now the people shun it."

"What is there so evil about it?" I asked curiously.

"It is a demon-haunted thing," he answered uneasily and with the suggestion of a shudder. "In my childhood I knew a young man who came up from below and laughed at our traditions – in his foolhardiness he went to the Stone one Midsummer Night and at dawn stumbled into the village again, stricken dumb and mad. Something had shattered his brain and sealed his lips, for until the day of his death, which came soon after, he spoke only to utter terrible blasphemies or to slaver gibberish.

"My own nephew when very small was lost in the mountains and slept in the woods near the Stone, and now in his manhood he is tortured by foul dreams, so that at times he makes the night hideous with his screams and wakes with cold sweat upon him.

"But let us talk of something else, *Herr*; it is not good to dwell upon such things."

I remarked on the evident age of the tavern and he answered with pride. "The foundations are more than four hundred years old; the original house was the only one in the village which was not burned to the ground when Suleiman's devil swept through the mountains. Here, in the house that then stood on these same foundations, it is said, the scribe Selim Bahadur had his headquarters while ravaging the country hereabouts."

I learned then that the present inhabitants of Stregoicavar are not descendants of the people who dwelt there before the Turkish raid of 1526. The victorious Moslems left no living human in the village or the vicinity thereabouts when they passed over. Men, women and children they wiped out in one red holocaust of murder, leaving a vast stretch of country silent and utterly deserted. The present people of Stregoicavar are descended from hardy settlers from the lower valleys who came into the ruined village after the Turk was thrust back.

Mine host did not speak of the extermination of the original inhabitants with any great resentment and I learned that his ancestors in the lower levels had looked on the mountaineers with even more hatred and aversion than they regarded the Turks. He was rather vague regarding the causes of this feud, but said that the original inhabitants of Stregoicavar had been in the habit of making stealthy raids on the lowlands and stealing girls and children. Moreover, he said that they were not exactly of the same blood as his own people; the sturdy, original Magyar-Slavic stock had mixed and intermarried with a degraded aboriginal race until the breeds had blended, producing an unsavory amalgamation. Who these aborigines were, he had not the slightest idea, but maintained that they were "pagans" and had dwelt in the mountains since time immemorial, before the coming of the conquering peoples.

I attached little importance to this tale; seeing in it merely a parallel to the amalgamation of Celtic tribes with Mediterranean aborigines in the Galloway hills, with the resultant mixed race which, as Picts, has such an extensive part in Scotch legendary. Time has a curious foreshortening effect on folklore, and just as tales of the Picts became intertwined with legends of an older Mongoloid race, so that eventually the Picts were ascribed the repulsive appearance of the squat primitives, whose individuality merged, in the telling, into Pictish tales, and was forgotten; so, I felt, the supposed inhuman attributes of the first villagers of Stregoicavar could be traced to older, outworn myths with invading Huns and Mongols.

The morning after my arrival I received directions from mine host, who gave them worriedly, and set out to find the Black Stone. A few hours' tramp up the fir-covered slopes brought me to the face of the rugged, solid stone cliff which jutted boldly from the mountainside. A narrow trail wound up it, and mounting this, I looked out over the peaceful valley of Stregoicavar, which seemed to drowse, guarded on either hand by the great blue mountains. No huts or any sign of human tenancy showed between the cliff whereon I stood and the village. I saw numbers of scattering farms in the valley but all lay on the other side of Stregoicavar, which itself seemed to shrink from the brooding slopes which masked the Black Stone.

The summit of the cliffs proved to be a sort of thickly wooded plateau. I made my way through the dense growth for a short distance and came into a wide glade; and in the center of the glade reared a gaunt figure of black stone.

It was octagonal in shape, some sixteen feet in height and about a foot and a half thick. It had once evidently been highly polished, but now the surface was thickly dinted as if savage efforts had been made to demolish it; but the hammers had done little more than to flake off small bits of stone and mutilate the characters which once had evidently marched up in a spiraling line round and round the shaft to the top. Up to ten feet from the base these characters were almost completely blotted out, so that it was very difficult to trace their direction. Higher up they were plainer, and I managed to squirm part of the way up the shaft and scan them at close range. All were more or less defaced, but I was positive that they symbolized no language now remembered on the face of the earth. I am fairly familiar with all hieroglyphics known to researchers and philologists and I can say, with certainty that those characters were like nothing of which I have ever read or heard. The nearest approach to them that I ever saw were some crude scratches on a gigantic and strangely symmetrical rock in a lost valley of Yucatan. I remember that when I pointed out these marks to the archeologist who was my companion, he maintained that they either represented natural weathering or the idle scratching of some Indian. To my theory that the rock was really the base of a long-vanished column, he merely laughed, calling my attention to the dimensions of it, which suggested, if it were built with any natural rules of architectural symmetry, a column a thousand feet high. But I was not convinced.

I will not say that the characters on the Black Stone were similar to those on that colossal rock in Yucatan; but one suggested the other. As to the substance of the monolith, again I was baffled. The stone of which it was composed was a dully gleaming black, whose surface, where it was not dinted and roughened, created a curious illusion of semi-transparency.

I spent most of the morning there and came away baffled. No connection of the Stone with any other artifact in the world suggested itself to me. It was as if the monolith had been reared by alien hands, in an age distant and apart from human ken.

I returned to the village with my interest in no way abated. Now that I had seen the curious thing, my desire was still more keenly whetted to investigate the matter further and seek to learn by what strange hands and for what strange purpose the Black Stone had been reared in the long ago.

I sought out the tavern-keeper's nephew and questioned him in regard to his dreams, but he was vague, though willing to oblige. He did not mind discussing them, but was unable to describe them with any clarity. Though he dreamed the same dreams repeatedly, and though they were hideously vivid at the time, they left no distinct impression on his waking mind. He remembered them only as chaotic nightmares through which huge whirling fires shot lurid tongues of flame and a black drum bellowed incessantly. One thing only he remembered clearly – in one dream he had seen the Black Stone, not on a mountain slope but set like a spire on a colossal black castle.

As for the rest of the villagers I found them not inclined to talk about the Stone, with the exception of the schoolmaster, a man of surprizing education, who spent much more of his time out in the world than any of the rest.

He was much interested in what I told him of Von Junzt's remarks about the Stone, and warmly agreed with the German author in the alleged age of the monolith. He believed that a coven had once existed in the vicinity and that possibly all of the original villagers had been members of that fertility cult which once threatened to undermine European civilization and gave rise to the tales of witchcraft. He cited the very name of the village to prove his point; it had not been originally named Stregoicavar, he said; according to legends the builders had called it Xuthltan, which was the aboriginal name of the site on which the village had been built many centuries ago.

This fact roused again an indescribable feeling of uneasiness. The barbarous name did not suggest connection with any Scythic, Slavic or Mongolian race to which an aboriginal people of these mountains would, under natural circumstances, have belonged.

That the Magyars and Slavs of the lower valleys believed the original inhabitants of the village to be members of the witchcraft cult was evident, the schoolmaster said, by the name they gave it, which name continued to be used even after the older settlers had been massacred by the Turks, and the village rebuilt by a cleaner and more wholesome breed.

He did not believe that the members of the cult erected the monolith but he did believe that they used it as a center of their activities, and repeating vague legends which had been handed down since before the Turkish invasion, he advanced the theory that the degenerate villagers had used it as a sort of altar on which they offered human sacrifices, using as victims the girls and babies stolen from his own ancestors in the lower valleys.

He discounted the myths of weird events on Midsummer Night, as well as a curious legend of a strange deity which the witch-people of Xuthltan were said to have invoked with chants and wild rituals of flagellation and slaughter.

He had never visited the Stone on Midsummer Night, he said, but he would not fear to do so; whatever *had* existed or taken place there in the past, had been long engulfed in the mists of time and oblivion. The Black Stone had lost its meaning save as a link to a dead and dusty past.

It was while returning from a visit with this schoolmaster one night about a week after my arrival at Stregoicavar that a sudden recollection struck me – it was Midsummer Night! The very time that the legends linked with grisly implications to the Black Stone. I turned away from the tavern and strode swiftly through the village. Stregoicavar lay silent; the villagers retired early. I saw no one as I passed rapidly out of the village and up into the firs which masked the mountain's slopes with whispering darkness. A broad silver moon hung above the valley, flooding the crags and slopes in a weird light and etching the shadows blackly. No wind blew through the firs, but a mysterious, intangible rustling and whispering was abroad. Surely on such nights in past centuries, my whimsical imagination told me, naked witches astride magic broomsticks had flown across the valley, pursued by jeering demoniac familiars.

I came to the cliffs and was somewhat disquieted to note that the illusive moonlight lent them a subtle appearance I had not noticed before – in the weird light they appeared less like natural cliffs and more like the ruins of cyclopean and Titan-reared battlements jutting from the mountain-slope.

Shaking off this hallucination with difficulty I came upon the plateau and hesitated a moment before I plunged into the brooding darkness of the woods. A sort of breathless tenseness hung over the shadows, like an unseen monster holding its breath lest it scare away its prey.

I shook off the sensation – a natural one, considering the eeriness of the place and its evil reputation – and made my way through the wood, experiencing a most unpleasant sensation that I was being followed, and halting once, sure that something clammy and unstable had brushed against my face in the darkness.

I came out into the glade and saw the tall monolith rearing its gaunt height above the sward. At the edge of the woods on the side toward the cliffs was a stone which formed a sort of natural seat. I sat down, reflecting that it was probably while there that the mad poet, Justin Geoffrey, had written his fantastic *People of the Monolith*. Mine host thought that it was the Stone which had caused Geoffrey's insanity, but the seeds of madness had been sown in the poet's brain long before he ever came to Stregoicavar.

A glance at my watch showed that the hour of midnight was close at hand. I leaned back, waiting whatever ghostly demonstration might appear. A thin night wind started up among the branches of the firs, with an uncanny suggestion of faint, unseen pipes whispering an eerie and evil tune. The monotony of the sound and my steady gazing at the monolith produced a sort of self-hypnosis upon me; I grew drowsy. I fought this feeling, but sleep stole on me in spite of myself; the monolith seemed to sway and dance, strangely distorted to my gaze, and then I slept.

I opened my eyes and sought to rise, but lay still, as if an icy hand gripped me helpless. Cold terror stole over me. The glade was no longer deserted. It was thronged by a silent crowd of strange people, and my distended eyes took in strange barbaric details of costume which my reason told me were archaic and forgotten even in this backward land. Surely, I thought, these are villagers who have come here to hold some fantastic conclave – but another glance told me that these people were not the folk of Stregoicavar. They were a shorter, more squat race, whose brows were lower, whose faces were broader and duller. Some had Slavic and Magyar features, but those features were degraded as from a mixture of some baser, alien strain I could not classify. Many wore the hides of wild beasts, and their whole appearance, both men and women, was one of sensual brutishness. They terrified and repelled me, but they gave me no heed. They formed in a vast half-circle in front of the monolith and began a sort of chant, flinging their arms in unison and weaving their bodies rhythmically from the waist upward. All eyes were fixed on the top of the Stone which they seemed to be invoking. But the strangest of all was the dimness of their voices; not fifty yards from me hundreds of men and women were unmistakably lifting their voices in a wild chant, yet those voices came to me as a faint indistinguishable murmur as if from across vast leagues of Space – or *time*.

Before the monolith stood a sort of brazier from which a vile, nauseous yellow smoke billowed upward, curling curiously in a swaying spiral around the black shaft, like a vast unstable snake.

On one side of this brazier lay two figures – a young girl, stark naked and bound hand and foot, and an infant, apparently only a few months old. On the other side of the brazier squatted a hideous old hag with a queer sort of black drum on her lap; this drum she beat with slow light blows of her open palms, but I could not hear the sound.

The rhythm of the swaying bodies grew faster and into the space between the people and the monolith sprang a naked young woman, her eyes blazing, her long black hair flying loose. Spinning dizzily on her toes, she whirled across the open space and fell prostrate before the Stone, where she lay motionless. The next instant a fantastic figure followed her – a man from whose waist hung a goatskin, and whose features were entirely hidden by a sort of mask made from a huge wolf's head, so that he looked like a monstrous, nightmare being, horribly compounded of elements both human and bestial. In his hand he held a bunch of long fir switches bound together at the larger ends, and the moonlight glinted on a chain of heavy gold looped about his neck. A smaller chain depending from it suggested a pendant of some sort, but this was missing.

The people tossed their arms violently and seemed to redouble their shouts as this grotesque creature loped across the open space with many a fantastic leap and caper. Coming to the woman who lay before the monolith, he began to lash her with the switches he bore, and she leaped up and spun into the wild mazes of the most incredible dance I have ever seen. And her tormentor danced with her, keeping the wild rhythm, matching her every whirl and bound, while incessantly raining cruel blows on her naked body. And at every blow he shouted a single word, over and over, and all the people shouted it back. I could see the working of their lips, and now the faint far-off murmur of their voices merged and blended into one distant shout, repeated over and over with slobbering ecstasy. But what the one word was, I could not make out.

In dizzy whirls spun the wild dancers, while the lookers-on, standing still in their tracks, followed the rhythm of their dance with swaying bodies and weaving arms. Madness grew in the eyes of the capering votaress and was reflected in the eyes of the watchers. Wilder and more extravagant grew the whirling frenzy of that mad dance – it became a bestial and obscene thing, while the old hag howled and battered the drum like a crazy woman, and the switches cracked out a devil's tune.

Blood trickled down the dancer's limbs but she seemed not to feel the lashing save as a stimulus for further enormities of outrageous motion; bounding into the midst of the yellow smoke which now spread out tenuous tentacles to embrace both flying figures, she seemed to merge with that foul fog and veil herself with it. Then emerging into plain view, closely followed by the beast-thing that flogged her, she shot into an indescribable, explosive burst of dynamic mad motion, and on the very crest of that mad wave, she dropped suddenly to the sward, quivering and panting as if completely overcome by her frenzied exertions. The lashing continued with unabated violence and intensity and she began to wriggle toward the monolith on her belly. The priest – or such I will call him – followed, lashing her unprotected body with all the power of his arm as she writhed along, leaving a heavy track of blood on the trampled earth. She reached the monolith, and gasping and panting, flung both arms about it and covered the cold stone with fierce hot kisses, as in frenzied and unholy adoration.

The fantastic priest bounded high in the air, flinging away the red-dabbled switches, and the worshippers, howling and foaming at the mouths, turned on each other with tooth and nail, rending one another's garments and flesh in a blind passion of bestiality. The priest swept up the infant with a long arm, and shouting again that Name, whirled the wailing babe high in the air and dashed its brains out against the monolith, leaving a ghastly stain on the black surface. Cold with horror I saw him rip the tiny body open with his bare brutish fingers and fling handfuls of blood on the shaft, then toss the red and torn shape into the brazier, extinguishing flame and smoke in a crimson rain, while the maddened brutes behind him howled over and over the Name. Then suddenly they all fell prostrate, writhing like snakes, while the priest flung wide his gory hands as in triumph. I opened my mouth to scream my horror and loathing, but only a dry rattle sounded; a huge monstrous toad-like thing squatted on the top of the monolith!

I saw its bloated, repulsive and unstable outline against the moonlight and set in what would have been the face of a natural creature, its huge, blinking eyes which reflected all the lust, abysmal greed, obscene cruelty and monstrous evil that has stalked the sons of men since their ancestors moved blind and hairless in the treetops. In those grisly eyes were mirrored all the unholy things and vile secrets that sleep in the cities under the sea, and that skulk from the light of day in the blackness of primordial caverns. And so that ghastly thing that the unhallowed ritual of cruelty and sadism and blood had evoked from the silence of the hills, leered and blinked down on its bestial worshippers, who groveled in abhorrent abasement before it.

Now the beast-masked priest lifted the bound and weakly writhing girl in his brutish hands and held her up toward that horror on the monolith. And as that monstrosity sucked in its breath, lustfully and slobberingly, something snapped in my brain and I fell into a merciful faint.

I opened my eyes on a still white dawn. All the events of the night rushed back on me and I sprang up, then stared about me in amazement. The monolith brooded gaunt and silent above the sward which waved, green and untrampled, in the morning breeze. A few quick strides took me across the glade; here had the dancers leaped and bounded until the ground should have been trampled bare, and here had the votaress wriggled her painful way to the Stone, streaming blood on the earth. But no drop of crimson showed on the uncrushed sward. I looked, shudderingly, at the side of the monolith against which the bestial priest had brained the stolen baby – but no dark stain nor grisly clot showed there.

A dream! It had been a wild nightmare – or else – I shrugged my shoulders. What vivid clarity for a dream!

I returned quietly to the village and entered the inn without being seen. And there I sat meditating over the strange events of the night. More and more was I prone to discard the dream-theory. That what I had seen was illusion and without material substance, was evident. But I believed that I had looked on the mirrored shadow of a deed perpetrated in ghastly actuality in bygone days. But how was I to know? What proof to show that my vision had been a gathering of foul specters rather than a nightmare originating in my brain?

As if for answer a name flashed into my mind – Selim Bahadur! According to legend this man, who had been a soldier as well as a scribe, had commanded that part of Suleiman's army which had devastated Stregoicavar; it seemed logical enough; and if so, he had gone straight from the blotted-out countryside to the bloody field of Schomvaal, and his doom. I sprang up with a sudden shout – that manuscript which was taken from the Turk's body, and which Count Boris shuddered over – might it not contain some narration of what the conquering Turks found in Stregoicavar? What else could have shaken the iron nerves of the Polish adventurer?

And since the bones of the Count had never been recovered, what more certain than that the lacquered case, with its mysterious contents, still lay hidden beneath the ruins that covered Boris Vladinoff? I began packing my bag with fierce haste.

Three days later found me ensconced in a little village a few miles from the old battlefield, and when the moon rose I was working with savage intensity on the great pile of crumbling stone that crowned the hill. It was back-breaking toil – looking back now I can not see how I accomplished it, though I labored without a pause from moonrise to dawn. Just as the sun was coming up I tore aside the last tangle of stones and looked on all that was mortal of Count Boris Vladinoff – only a few pitiful fragments of crumbling bone – and among them, crushed out of all original shape, lay a case whose lacquered surface had kept it from complete decay through the centuries.

I seized it with frenzied eagerness, and piling back some of the stones on the bones I hurried away; for I did not care to be discovered by the suspicious peasants in an act of apparent desecration.

Back in my tavern chamber I opened the case and found the parchment comparatively intact; and there was something else in the case – a small squat object wrapped in silk. I was wild to plumb the secrets of those yellowed pages, but weariness forbade me. Since leaving Stregoicavar I had hardly slept at all, and the terrific exertions of the previous night combined to overcome me. In spite of myself I was forced to stretch myself on my bed, nor did I awake until sundown.

I snatched a hasty supper, and then in the light of a flickering candle, I set myself to read the neat Turkish characters that covered the parchment. It was difficult work, for I am not deeply versed in the language and the archaic style of the narrative baffled me. But as I toiled through it a word or a phrase here and there leaped at me and a dimly growing horror shook me in its grip. I bent my energies fiercely to the task, and as the tale grew clearer and took more tangible form my blood chilled in my veins, my hair stood up and my tongue clove to my mouth. All external things partook of the grisly madness of that infernal manuscript until the night sounds of insects and creatures in the woods took the form of ghastly murmurings and stealthy treadings of ghoulish horrors and the sighing of the night wind changed to tittering obscene gloating of evil over the souls of men.

At last when gray dawn was stealing through the latticed window, I laid down the manuscript and took up and unwrapped the thing in the bit of silk. Staring at it with haggard eyes I knew the truth of the matter was clinched, even had it been possible to doubt the veracity of that terrible manuscript.

And I replaced both obscene things in the case, nor did I rest nor sleep nor eat until that case containing them had been weighted with stones and flung into the deepest current of the Danube which, God grant, carried them back into the Hell from which they came.

It was no dream I dreamed on Midsummer Midnight in the hills above Stregoicavar. Well for Justin Geoffrey that he tarried there only in the sunlight and went his way, for had he gazed upon that ghastly conclave, his mad brain would have snapped before it did. How my own reason held, I do not know.

No – it was no dream – I gazed upon a foul rout of votaries long dead, come up from Hell to worship as of old; ghosts that bowed before a ghost. For Hell has long claimed their hideous god. Long, long he dwelt among the hills, a brain-shattering vestige of an outworn age, but no longer his obscene talons clutch for the souls of living men, and his kingdom is a dead kingdom, peopled only by the ghosts of those who served him in his lifetime and theirs.

By what foul alchemy or godless sorcery the Gates of Hell are opened on that one eerie night I do not know, but mine own eyes have seen. And I know I looked on no living thing that night, for the manuscript written in the careful hand of Selim Bahadur narrated at length what he and his raiders found in the valley of Stregoicavar; and I read, set down in detail, the blasphemous obscenities that torture wrung from the lips of screaming worshippers; and I read, too, of the lost, grim black cavern high in the hills where the horrified Turks hemmed a monstrous, bloated, wallowing toad-like being and slew it with flame and ancient steel blessed in old times by Muhammad, and with incantations that were old when Arabia was young. And even staunch old Selim's hand shook as he recorded the cataclysmic, earth-shaking death-howls of the monstrosity, which died not alone; for half-score of his slayers perished with him, in ways that Selim would not or could not describe.

And that squat idol carved of gold and wrapped in silk was an image of *himself*, and Selim tore it from the golden chain that looped the neck of the slain high priest of the mask.

Well that the Turks swept out that foul valley with torch and cleanly steel! Such sights as those brooding mountains have looked on belong to the darkness and abysses of lost eons. No – it is not fear of the toad-thing that makes me shudder in the night. He is made fast in Hell with his nauseous horde, freed only for an hour on the most weird night of the year, as I have seen. And of his worshippers, none remains.

But it is the realization that such things once crouched beast-like above the souls of men which brings cold sweat to my brow; and I fear to peer again into the leaves of Von Junzt's abomination. For now I understand his repeated phrase of *keys*! – aye! Keys to Outer Doors – links with an abhorrent past and – who knows? – of abhorrent spheres of the *present*. And I understand why the cliffs look like battlements in the moonlight and why the tavern-keeper's nightmare-haunted nephew saw in his dream, the Black Stone like a spire on a cyclopean black castle. If men ever excavate among those mountains they may find incredible things below those masking slopes. For the cave wherein the Turks trapped the – *thing* – was not truly a cavern, and I shudder to contemplate the gigantic gulf of eons which must stretch between this age and the time when the earth shook herself and reared up, like a wave, those blue mountains that, rising, enveloped unthinkable things. May no man ever seek to uproot that ghastly spire men call the Black Stone!

A Key! Aye, it is a Key, symbol of a forgotten horror. That horror has faded into the limbo from which it crawled, loathsomely, in the black dawn of the earth. But what of the other fiendish possibilities hinted at by Von Junzt – what of the monstrous hand which strangled out his life? Since reading what Selim Bahadur wrote, I can no longer doubt anything in the Black Book. Man was not always master of the earth – *and is he now?*

And the thought recurs to me – if such a monstrous entity as the Master of the Monolith somehow survived its own unspeakably distant epoch so long – *what nameless shapes may even now lurk in the dark places of the world?*

THE DARK MAN

Weird Tales, December 1931

"For this is the night of the drawing of swords,
And the painted tower of the heathen hordes
Leans to our hammers, fires and cords,
Leans a little and falls."
– Chesterton

A biting wind drifted the snow as it fell. The surf snarled along the rugged shore and farther out the long leaden combers moaned ceaselessly. Through the gray dawn that was stealing over the coast of Connacht a fisherman came trudging, a man rugged as the land that bore him. His feet were wrapped in rough cured leather; a single garment of deerskin scantily outlined his body. He wore no other clothing. As he strode stolidly along the shore, as heedless of the bitter cold as if he were the shaggy beast he appeared at first glance, he halted. Another man loomed up out of the veil of falling snow and drifting sea-mist. Turlogh Dubh stood before him.

This man was nearly a head taller than the stocky fisherman, and he had the bearing of a fighting man. No single glance would suffice, but any man or woman whose eyes fell on Turlogh Dubh would look long. Six feet and one inch he stood, and the first impression of slimness faded on closer inspection. He was big but trimly molded; a magnificent sweep of shoulder and depth of chest. Rangy he was, but compact, combining the strength of a bull with the lithe quickness of a panther. The slightest movement he made showed that steel-trap coordination that makes the super-fighter. Turlogh Dubh – Black Turlogh, once of the Clan na O'Brien.[1] And black he was as to hair, and dark of complexion. From under heavy black brows gleamed eyes of a hot volcanic blue. And in his clean-shaven face there was something of the somber-

1 To avoid confusion I have used the modern terms for places and clans. —REH.

ness of dark mountains, of the ocean at midnight. Like the fisherman, he was a part of this fierce land.

On his head he wore a plain vizorless helmet without crest or symbol. From neck to mid-thigh he was protected by a close-fitting shirt of black chain mail. The kilt he wore below his armor and which reached to his knees was of plain drab material. His legs were wrapped with hard leather that might turn a sword edge, and the shoes on his feet were worn with much traveling.

A broad belt encircled his lean waist, holding a long dirk in a leather sheath. On his left arm he carried a small round shield of hide-covered wood, hard as iron, braced and reinforced with steel, and having a short, heavy spike in the center. An ax hung from his right wrist, and it was to this feature that the fisherman's eyes wandered. The weapon with its three-foot handle and graceful lines looked slim and light when the fisherman mentally compared it to the great axes carried by the Norsemen. Yet scarcely three years had passed, as the fisherman knew, since such axes as these had shattered the northern hosts into red defeat and broken the pagan power forever.

There was individuality about the ax as about its owner. It was not like any other the fisherman had ever seen. Single-edged it was, with a short three-edged spike on the back and another on the top of the head. Like the wielder, it was heavier than it looked. With its slightly curved shaft and the graceful artistry of the blade, it looked like the weapon of an expert – swift, lethal, deadly, cobra-like. The head was of finest Irish workmanship, which meant, at that day, the finest in the world. The handle, cut from the head of a century-old oak, specially fire-hardened and braced with steel, was as unbreakable as an iron bar.

"Who are you?" asked the fisherman, with the bluntness of the west.

"Who are you to ask?" answered the other.

The fisherman's eyes roved to the single ornament the warrior wore – a heavy golden armlet on his left arm.

"Clean-shaven and close-cropped in the Norman fashion," he muttered. "And dark – you'd be Black Turlogh, the outlaw of Clan na O'Brien. You range far; I heard of you last in the Wicklow hills preying off the O'Reillys and the Oastmen alike."

"A man must eat, outcast or not," growled the Dalcassian.

The fisherman shrugged his shoulders. A masterless man – it was a hard road. In those days of clans, when a man's own kin cast him out he became a son of Ishmael with a vengeance. All men's hands were against him. The fisherman had heard of Turlogh Dubh – a strange, bitter man, a terrible warrior and a crafty strategist, but one whom sudden bursts of strange madness made a marked man even in that land and age of madmen.

"It's a bitter day," said the fisherman, apropos of nothing.

Turlogh stared somberly at his tangled beard and wild matted hair. "Have you a boat?"

The other nodded toward a small sheltered cove where lay snugly anchored a trim craft built with the skill of a hundred generations of men who had torn their livelihood from the stubborn sea.

"It scarce looks seaworthy," said Turlogh.

"Seaworthy? You who were born and bred on the western coast should know better. I've sailed her alone to Drumcliff Bay and back, and all the devils in the wind ripping at her."

"You can't take fish in such a sea."

"Do ye think it's only you chiefs that take sport in risking your hides? By the saints, I've sailed to Ballinskellings in a storm – and back too – just for the fun of the thing."

"Good enough," said Turlogh. "I'll take your boat."

"Ye'll take the devil! What kind of talk is this? If you want to leave Erin, go to Dublin and take the ship with your Dane friends."

A black scowl made Turlogh's face a mask of menace. "Men have died for less than that."

"Did you not intrigue with the Danes? And is that not why your clan drove you out to starve in the heather?"

"The jealousy of a cousin and the spite of a woman," growled Turlogh. "Lies – all lies. But enough. Have you seen a long serpent beating up from the south in the last few days?"

"Aye – three days ago we sighted a dragon-beaked galley before the scud. But she didn't put in – faith, the pirates get naught from the western fishers but hard blows."

"That would be Thorfel the Fair," muttered Turlogh, swaying his ax by its wrist-strap. "I knew it."

"There has been a ship-harrying in the south?"

"A band of reavers fell by night on the castle on Kilbaha. There was a sword-quenching – and the pirates took Moira, daughter of Murtagh, a chief of the Dalcassians."

"I've heard of her," muttered the fisherman. "There'll be a wetting of swords in the south – a red sea-plowing, eh, my black jewel?"

"Her brother Dermod lies helpless from a sword-cut in the foot. The lands of her clan are harried by the MacMurroughs in the east and the O'Connors from the north. Not many men can be spared from the defense of the tribe, even to seek for Moira – the clan is fighting for its life. All Erin is rocking under the Dalcassian throne since great Brian fell. Even so, Cormac O'Brien has taken ship to hunt down her ravishers – but he follows the trail of a wild goose, for it is thought the riders were Danes from Coningbeg. Well – we outcasts have ways of knowledge – it was Thorfel the Fair who holds the Isle of Slyne, that the Norse call Helni, in the Hebrides. There he has taken her – there I follow him. Lend me your boat."

"You are mad!" cried the fisherman sharply. "What are you saying. From Connacht to the Hebrides in an open boat? In this weather? I say you are mad."

"I will essay it," answered Turlogh absently. "Will you lend me your boat?"

"No."

"I might slay you and take it," said Turlogh.

"You might," returned the fisherman stolidly.

"You crawling swine," snarled the outlaw in swift passion, "a princess of Erin languishes in the grip of a red-bearded reaver of the north and you haggle like a Saxon."

"Man, I must live!" cried the fisherman as passionately. "Take my boat and I shall starve! Where can I get another like it? It is the cream of its kind!"

Turlogh reached for the armlet on his left arm. "I will pay you. Here is a torc that Brian Boru put on my arm with his own hand before Clontarf. Take it; it would buy a hundred boats. I have starved with it on my arm, but now the need is desperate."

But the fisherman shook his head, the strange illogic of the Gael burning in his eyes. "No! My hut is no place for a torc that King Brian's hands have touched. Keep it – and take the boat, in the name of the saints, if it means that much to you."

"You shall have it back when I return," promised Turlogh, "and mayhap a golden chain that now decks the bull neck of some northern reaver."

The day was sad and leaden. The wind moaned and the everlasting monotone of the sea was like the sorrow that is born in the heart of man. The fisherman stood on the rocks and watched the frail craft glide and twist serpent-like among the rocks until the blast of the open sea smote it and tossed it like a feather. The wind caught sail and the slim boat leaped and staggered, then righted herself and raced before the gale, dwindling until it was but a dancing speck in the eyes of the watcher. And then a flurry of snow hid it from his sight.

Turlogh realized something of the madness of his pilgrimage. But he was bred to hardships and peril. Cold and ice and driving sleet that would have frozen a weaker man, only spurred him to greater efforts. He was as hard and supple as a wolf. Among a race of men whose hardiness astounded even the toughest Norsemen, Turlogh Dubh stood out alone. At birth he had been tossed into a snow-drift to test his right to survive. His childhood and boyhood had been spent on the mountains, coasts and moors of the west. Until manhood he had never worn woven cloth upon his body; a wolf-skin had formed the apparel of this son of a Dalcassian chief. Before his outlawry he could out-tire a horse, running all day long beside it. He had never wearied at swimming. Now, since the intrigues of jealous clansmen had driven him into the wastelands and the life of the wolf, his ruggedness was such as cannot be conceived by a civilized man.

The snow ceased, the weather cleared, the wind held. Turlogh necessarily hugged the coastline, avoiding the reefs against which it seemed again and again he would be dashed. With tiller, sail and oar he worked tirelessly. Not one man out of a thousand of seafarers could have accomplished it, but Turlogh did. He needed no sleep; as he steered he ate from the rude provisions the fisherman had provided him. By the time he sighted Malin Head the weather had calmed wonderfully. There was still a heavy sea, but the gale had slackened to a sharp breeze that sent the little boat skipping along. Days and nights merged into each other; Turlogh drove eastward. Once he put into shore for fresh water and to snatch a few hours' sleep.

As he steered he thought of the fisherman's last words: "Why should you risk your life for a clan that's put a price on your head?"

Turlogh shrugged his shoulders. Blood was thicker than water. The mere fact that his people had booted him out to die like a hunted wolf on the moors did not alter the fact that they *were* his people. Little Moira, daughter of Murtagh na Kilbaha, had nothing to do with it. He remembered her – he had played with her when he was a boy and she a babe – he remembered the deep grayness of her eyes and the burnished sheen of her black hair, the fairness of her skin. Even as a child she had been remarkably beautiful – why, she was only a child now, for he, Turlogh, was young and he was many years her senior. Now she was speeding north to become the unwilling bride of a Norse reaver. Thorfel the Fair – the Handsome – Turlogh swore by gods that knew not the cross. A red mist waved across his eyes so that the rolling sea swam crimson all around him. An Irish girl a captive in a skalli of a Norse pirate – with a vicious wrench Turlogh turned his bows straight for the open sea. There was a tinge of madness in his eyes.

It is a long slant from Malin Head to Helni straight out across the foaming billows, as Turlogh took it. He was aiming for a small island that lay, with many other small islands, between Mull and the Hebrides. A modern seaman with charts and compass might have difficulty in finding it. Turlogh had neither. He sailed by instinct and through knowledge. He knew these seas as a man knows his house. He had sailed them as a raider and as an avenger, and once he had sailed them as a captive lashed to the deck of a Danish dragon ship. And he followed a red trail. Smoke drifting from headlands, floating pieces of wreckage, charred timbers showed that Thorfel was ravaging as he went. Turlogh growled in savage satisfaction; he was close behind the Viking, in spite of the long lead. For Thorfel was burning and pillaging the shores as he went, and Turlogh's course was like an arrow's.

He was still a long way from Helni when he sighted a small island slightly off his course. He knew it of old as one uninhabited, but there he could get fresh water. So he steered for it. The Isle of Swords it was called, no man knew why. And as he neared the beach he saw a sight which he rightly interpreted. Two boats were drawn up on the shelving shore. One was a crude affair, something like the one Turlogh had, but considerably larger. The other was a long, low craft – undeniably Viking. Both were deserted. Turlogh listened for the clash of arms, the cry of battle, but silence reigned. Fishers, he thought, from the Scotch isles; they had been sighted by some band of rovers on ship or on some other island, and had been pursued in the long rowboat. But it had been a longer chase than they had anticipated, he was sure; else they would not have started out in an open boat. But inflamed with the murder lust, the reavers would have followed their prey across a hundred miles of rough water, in an open boat, if necessary.

Turlogh drew inshore, tossed over the stone that served for anchor and leaped upon the beach, ax ready. Then up the shore a short distance he saw a strange red huddle of forms. A few swift strides brought him face to face with mystery. Fifteen red-bearded Danes lay in their own gore in a rough circle. Not one breathed. Within this circle, mingling with the bodies of their slayers, lay other men, such as Turlogh had never seen. Short of stature they were, and very dark; their staring dead eyes were the blackest Turlogh had ever seen. They were scantily armored, and their stiff hands still gripped broken swords and daggers. Here and there lay arrows that had shattered on the corselets of Danes, and Turlogh observed with surprize that many of them were tipped with flint.

"This was a grim fight," he muttered. "Aye, this was a rare sword-quenching. Who are these people? In all the isles I have never seen their like before. Seven – is that all? Where are their comrades who helped them slay these Danes?"

No tracks led away from the bloody spot. Turlogh's brow darkened.

"These were all – seven against fifteen – yet the slayers died with the slain. What manner of men are these who slay twice their number of Vikings? They are small men – their armor is mean. Yet –"

Another thought struck him. Why did not the strangers scatter and flee, hide themselves in the woods? He believed he knew the answer. There, at the very center of the silent circle, lay a strange thing. A statue it was, of some dark substance and it was in the form of a man. Some five feet long – or high – it was, carved in a semblance of life that made Turlogh start. Half over it lay the corpse of an ancient man, hacked almost beyond human semblance. One lean arm was locked about the figure; the other was outstretched, the hand gripping a flint dagger which was sheathed to the hilt in the breast of a Dane. Turlogh noted the fearful wounds that disfigured all the dark men. They had been hard to kill – they had fought until literally hacked to pieces, and dying, they had dealt death to their slayers. So much Turlogh's eyes showed him. In the dead faces of the dark strangers was a terrible desperation. He noted how their dead hands were still locked in the beards of their foes. One lay beneath the body of a huge Dane, and on this Dane Turlogh could see no wound; until he looked closer and saw the dark man's teeth were sunk, beast-like, into the bull throat of the other.

He bent and dragged the figure from among the bodies. The ancient's arm was locked about it, and he was forced to tear it away with all his strength. It was as if, even in death, the old one clung to his treasure; for Turlogh felt that it was for this image that the small dark men had died. They might have scattered and eluded their foes, but that would have meant giving up their image. They chose to die beside it. Turlogh shook his head; his hatred of the Norse, a heritage of wrongs and outrages, was a burning, living thing, almost an obsession, that at times drove him to the point of insanity. There was, in his fierce heart, no room for mercy; the sight of these Danes, lying dead at his feet, filled him with savage satisfaction. Yet he sensed here, in these silent dead men, a passion stronger than his. Here was some driving impulse deeper than his hate. Aye – and older. These little men seemed very ancient to him, not old as individuals are old, but old as a race is old. Even their corpses exuded an intangible aura of the primeval. And the image –

The Gael bent and grasped it, to lift it. He expected to encounter great weight and was astonished. It was no heavier than if it had been made of light wood. He tapped it, and the sound was solid. At first he thought it was of iron; then he decided it was of stone, but such stone as he had never seen; and he felt that no such stone was to be found in the British Isles or anywhere in the world that he knew. For like the little dead men, it looked *old*. It was smooth and free from corrosion, as if carved yesterday, but for all that, it was a symbol of antiquity, Turlogh knew. It was the figure of a man who much resembled the small dark men who lay about it. But it differed subtly. Turlogh felt somehow that this was the image of a man who had lived long ago, for surely the unknown sculptor had had a living model. And he had contrived to bring a touch of life into his work. There was the sweep of the shoulders, the depth of the chest, the powerfully molded arms; the strength of the features was evident. The firm jaw, the regular nose, the high forehead, all indicated a powerful intellect, a high courage, an inflexible will. Surely, thought Turlogh, this man was a king – or a god. Yet he wore no crown; his only garment was a sort of loincloth, wrought so cunningly that every wrinkle and fold was carved as in reality.

"This was their god," mused Turlogh, looking about him. "They fled before the Danes – but died for their god at last. Who are these people? Whence come they? Whither were they bound?"

He stood, leaning on his ax, and a strange tide rose in his soul. A sense of mighty abysses of time and space opened before him; of the, strange, endless tides of mankind that drift forever; of the waves of humanity that wax and wane with the waxing and waning of the sea-tides. Life was a door opening upon two black, unknown worlds – and how many races of men with their hopes and fears, their loves and their hates, had passed through that door – on their pilgrimage from the dark to the dark? Turlogh sighed. Deep in his soul stirred the mystic sadness of the Gael.

"You were a king once, Dark Man," he said to the silent image. "Mayhap you were a god and reigned over all the world. Your people passed – as mine are passing. Surely you were a king of the Flint People, the race whom my Celtic ancestors destroyed. Well – we have had our day, and we, too, are passing. These Danes who lie at your feet – they are the conquerors now. They must have their day – but they too will pass. But you shall go with me, Dark Man, king, god, or devil though you be. Aye, for it is in my mind that you will bring me luck, and luck is what I shall need when I sight Helni, Dark Man."

Turlogh bound the image securely in the bows. Again he set out for his sea-plowing. Now the skies grew gray and the snow fell in driving lances that stung and cut. The waves were gray-grained with ice and the winds bellowed and beat on the open boat. But Turlogh feared not. And his boat rode as it had never ridden before. Through the roaring gale and the driving snow it sped, and to the mind of the Dalcassian it seemed that the Dark Man lent him aid. Surely he had been lost a hundred times without supernatural assistance. With all his skill at boat-handling he wrought, and it seemed to him that there was an unseen hand on the tiller, and at the oar; that more than human skill aided him when he trimmed his sail.

And when all the world was a driving white veil in which even the Gael's sense of direction was lost, it seemed to him that he was steering in compliance with a silent voice that spoke in the dim reaches of his consciousness. Nor was he surprized when, at last, when the snow had ceased and the clouds had rolled away beneath a cold silvery moon, he saw land loom up ahead and recognized it as the isle of Helni. More, he knew that just around a point of land was the bay where Thorfel's dragon ship was moored when not ranging the seas, and a hundred yards back from the bay lay Thorfel's skalli. He grinned fiercely. All the skill in the world could not have brought him to this exact spot – it was pure luck – no, it was more than luck. Here was the best possible place for him to make an approach – within half a mile of his foe's hold, yet hidden from sight of any watchers by this jutting promontory. He glanced at the Dark Man in the bows – brooding, inscrutable as the sphinx. A strange feeling stole over the Gael – that all this was his work; that he, Turlogh, was only a pawn in the game. What was this fetish? What grim secret did those carven eyes hold? Why did the dark little men fight so terribly for him?

Turlogh ran his boat inshore, into a small creek. A few yards up this he anchored and stepped out onshore. A last glance at the brooding Dark Man in the bows, and he turned and went hurriedly up the slope of the promontory, keeping to cover as much as possible. At the top of the slope he gazed down on the other side. Less than half a mile away Thorfel's dragon ship lay at anchor. And there lay Thorfel's skalli, also the long low building of rough-hewn log emitting the gleams that betokened the roaring fires within. Shouts of wassail came clearly to the listener through the sharp still air. He ground his teeth. Wassail! Aye, they were celebrating the ruin and destruction they had committed – the homes left in smoking embers – the slain men – the ravished girls. They were lords of the world, these Vikings – all the southland lay helpless beneath their swords. The southland folk lived only to furnish them sport – and slaves – Turlogh shuddered violently and shook as if in a chill. The blood-sickness was on him like a physical pain, but he fought back the mists of passion that clouded his brain. He was here, not to fight but to steal away the girl they had stolen.

He took careful note of the ground, like a general going over the plan of his campaign. He noted where the trees grew thick close behind the skalli; that the smaller houses, the storehouses and servants' huts were between the main building and the bay. A huge fire was blazing down by the shore and a few carles were roaring and drinking about it, but the fierce cold had driven most of them into the drinking-hall of the main building.

Turlogh crept down the thickly wooded slope, entering the forest which swept about in a wide curve away from the shore. He kept to the fringe of its shadows, approaching the skalli in a rather indirect route, but afraid to strike out boldly in the open lest he be seen by the watchers that Thorfel surely had out. Gods, if he only had the warriors of Clare at his back as he had of old! Then there would be no skulking like a wolf among the trees! His hand locked like iron on his ax-shaft as he visualized the scene – the charge, the shouting, the blood-letting, the play of the Dalcassian axes – he sighed. He was a lone outcast; never again would he lead the swordsmen of his clan to battle.

He dropped suddenly in the snow behind a low shrub and lay still. Men were approaching from the same direction in which he had come – men who grumbled loudly and walked heavily. They came into sight – two of them, huge Norse warriors, their silver-scaled armor flashing in the moonlight. They were carrying something between them with difficulty and to Turlogh's amazement he saw it was the Dark Man. His consternation at the realization that they had found his boat was gulfed in a greater astonishment. These men were giants; their arms bulged with iron muscles. Yet they were staggering under what seemed a stupendous weight. In their hands the Dark Man seemed to weigh hundreds of pounds; yet Turlogh had lifted it as lightly as a feather! He almost swore in his amazement. Surely these men were drunk. One of them spoke, and Turlogh's short neck hairs bristled at the sound of the guttural accents, as a dog will bristle at the sight of a foe.

"Let it down; Thor's death, the thing weighs a ton. Let's rest."

The other grunted a reply, and they began to ease the image to the earth. Then one of them lost his hold on it; his hand slipped and the Dark Man crashed heavily into the snow. The first speaker howled.

"You clumsy fool, you dropped it on my foot! Curse you, my ankle's broken!"

"It twisted out of my hand!" cried the other. "The thing's alive, I tell you!"

"Then I'll slay it," snarled the lame Viking, and drawing his sword, he struck savagely at the prostrate figure. Fire flashed as the blade shivered into a hundred pieces, and the other Norseman howled as a flying sliver of steel gashed his cheek.

"The devil's in it!" shouted the other, throwing his hilt away. "I've not even scratched it! Here, take hold – let's get it into the ale-hall and let Thorfel deal with it."

"Let it lie," growled the second man, wiping the blood from his face. "I'm bleeding like a butchered hog. Let's go back and tell Thorfel that there's no ship stealing on the island. That's what he sent us to the point to see."

"What of the boat where we found this?" snapped the other. "Some Scotch fisher driven out of his course by the storm and hiding like a rat in the woods now, I guess. Here, bear a hand; idol or devil, we'll carry this to Thorfel."

Grunting with the effort, they lifted the image once more and went on slowly, one groaning and cursing as he limped along, the other shaking his head from time to time as the blood got into his eyes.

Turlogh rose stealthily and watched them. A touch of chilliness traveled up and down his spine. Either of these men was as strong as he, yet it was taxing their powers to the utmost to carry what he had handled easily. He shook his head and took up his way again.

At last he reached a point in the woods nearest the skalli. Now was the crucial test. Somehow he must reach that building and hide himself, unperceived. Clouds were gathering. He waited until one obscured the moon and in the gloom that followed, ran swiftly and silently across the snow, crouching. A shadow out of the shadows he seemed. The shouts and songs from within the long building were deafening. Now he was close to its side, flattening himself against the rough-hewn logs. Vigilance was most certainly relaxed now – yet what foe should Thorfel expect, when he was friends with all northern reavers, and none else could be expected to fare forth on a night such as this had been?

A shadow among the shadows, Turlogh stole about the house. He noted a side door and slid cautiously to it. Then he drew back close against the wall. Someone within was fumbling at the latch. Then a door was flung open and a big warrior lurched out, slamming the door to behind him. Then he saw Turlogh. His bearded lips parted, but in that instant the Gael's hands shot to his throat and locked there like a wolf-trap. The threatened yell died in a gasp. One hand flew to Turlogh's wrist, the other drew a dagger and stabbed upward. But already the man was senseless; the dagger rattled feebly against the outlaw's corselet and dropped into the snow. The Norseman sagged in his slayer's grasp, his throat literally crushed by that iron grip. Turlogh flung him contemptuously into the snow and spat on his dead face before he turned again to the door.

The latch had not fastened within. The door sagged a trifle. Turlogh peered in and saw an empty room, piled with ale barrels. He entered noiselessly, shutting the door but not latching it. He thought of hiding his victim's body, but he did not know how he could do it. He must trust to luck that no one saw it in the deep snow where it lay. He crossed the room and found it led into another parallel with the outer wall. This was also a storeroom, and was empty. From this a doorway, without a door but furnished with a curtain of skins, let into the main hall, as Turlogh could tell from the sounds on the other side. He peered out cautiously.

He was looking into the drinking-hall – the great hall which served as a banquet, council, and living-hall of the master of the skalli. This hall, with its smoke-blackened rafters, great roaring fire-places, and heavily laden boards, was a scene of terrific revelry tonight. Huge warriors with golden beards and savage eyes sat or lounged on the rude benches, strode about the hall or sprawled full length on the floor. They drank mightily from foaming horns and leathern jacks, and gorged themselves on great pieces of rye bread and huge chunks of meat they cut with their daggers from whole roasted joints. It was a scene of strange incongruity, for in contrast with these barbaric men and their rough songs and shouts, the walls were hung with rare spoils that betokened civilized workmanship. Fine tapestries that Norman women had worked; richly chased weapons that princes of France and Spain had wielded; armor and silken garments from Byzantium and the Orient – for the dragon ships ranged far. With these were placed the spoils of the hunt, to show the Viking's mastery of beasts as well as men.

The modern man can scarcely conceive of Turlogh O'Brien's feeling toward these men. To him they were devils – ogres who dwelt in the north only to descend on the peaceful people of the south. All the world was their prey to pick and choose, to take and spare as it pleased their barbaric whims. His brain throbbed and burned as he gazed. As only a Gael can hate, he hated them – their magnificent arrogance, their pride and their power, their contempt for all other races, their stern, forbidding eyes – above all else he hated the eyes that looked scorn and menace on the world. The Gaels were cruel but they had strange moments of sentiment and kindness. There was no sentiment in the Norse make-up.

The sight of this revelry was like a slap in Black Turlogh's face, and only one thing was needed to make his madness complete. This was furnished. At the head of the board sat Thorfel the Fair, young, handsome, arrogant, flushed with wine and pride. He *was* handsome, was young Thorfel. In build he much resembled Turlogh himself, except that he was larger in every way, but there the resemblance ceased. As Turlogh was exceptionally dark among a dark people, Thorfel was exceptionally blond among a people essentially fair. His hair and mustache were like fine-spun gold and his light gray eyes flashed scintillant lights. By his side – Turlogh's nails bit into his palms, Moira of the O'Briens seemed greatly out of place among these huge blond men and strapping yellow-haired women. She was small, almost frail, and her hair was black with glossy bronze tints. But her skin was fair as theirs, with a delicate rose tint their most beautiful women could not boast. Her full lips were white now with fear and she shrank from the clamor and uproar. Turlogh saw her tremble as Thorfel insolently put his arm about her. The hall waved redly before Turlogh's eyes and he fought doggedly for control.

"Thorfel's brother, Osric, to his right," he muttered to himself; "on the other side Tostig, the Dane, who can cleave an ox in half with that great sword of his – they say. And there is Halfgar, and Sweyn, and Oswick, and Athelstane, the Saxon – the one *man* of a pack of sea-wolves. And name of the devil – what is this? A priest?"

A priest it was, sitting white and still in the rout, silently counting his beads, while his eyes wandered pitying toward the slender Irish girl at the head of the board. Then Turlogh saw something else. On a smaller table to one side, a table of mahogany whose rich scrollwork showed that it was loot from the southland, stood the Dark Man. The two crippled Norsemen had brought it to the hall, after all. The sight of it brought a strange shock to Turlogh and cooled his seething brain. Only five feet tall? It seemed much larger now, somehow. It loomed above the revelry, as a god that broods on deep dark matters beyond the ken of the human insects who howl at his feet. As always when looking at the Dark Man, Turlogh felt as if a door had suddenly opened on outer space and the wind that blows among the stars. Waiting – waiting – for whom? Perhaps the carven eyes of the Dark Man looked through the skalli walls, across the snowy waste, and over the promontory. Perhaps those sightless eyes saw the five boats that even now slid silently with muffled oars, through the calm dark waters. But of this Turlogh Dubh knew nothing; nothing of the boats or their silent rowers; small, dark men with inscrutable eyes.

Thorfel's voice cut through the din: "Ho, friends!" They fell silent and turned as the young sea-king rose to his feet. "Tonight," he thundered, "I am taking a bride!"

A thunder of applause shook the noisy rafters. Turlogh cursed with sick fury.

Thorfel caught up the girl with rough gentleness and set her on the board.

"Is she not a fit bride for a Viking?" he shouted. "True, she's a bit shy, but that's only natural."

"All Irish are cowards!" shouted Oswick.

"As proved by Clontarf and the scar on your jaw!" rumbled Athelstane, which gentle thrust made Oswick wince and brought a roar of rough mirth from the throng.

"'Ware her temper, Thorfel," called a bold-eyed young Juno who sat with the warriors. "Irish girls have claws like cats."

Thorfel laughed with the confidence of a man used to mastery. "I'll teach her her lessons with a stout birch switch. But enough. It grows late. Priest, marry us."

"Daughter," said the priest unsteadily, rising, "these pagan men have brought me here by violence to perform Christian nuptials in an ungodly house. Do you marry this man willingly?"

"No! No! Oh God, No!" Moira screamed with a wild despair that brought the sweat to Turlogh's forehead. "Oh most holy master, save me from this fate! They tore me from my home – struck down my brother that would have saved me! This man bore me off as if I were a chattel – a soulless beast!"

"Be silent!" thundered Thorfel, slapping her across the mouth, lightly but with enough force to bring a trickle of blood from her delicate lips. "By Thor, you grow independent. I am determined to have a wife, and all the squeals of a puling little wench will not stop me. Why, you graceless hussy, am I not wedding you in the Christian manner, simply because of your foolish superstitions? Take care that I do not dispense with the nuptials, and take you as slave, not wife!"

"Daughter," quavered the priest, afraid, not for himself, but for her, "bethink you! This man offers you more than many a man would offer. It is at least an honorable married state."

"Aye," rumbled Athelstane, "marry him like a good wench and make the best of it. There's more than one southland woman on the cross benches of the north."

What can I do? The question tore through Turlogh's brain. There was but one thing to do – wait – until the ceremony was over and Thorfel had retired with his bride. Then steal her away as best he could. After that – but he dared not look ahead. He had done and would do his best. What he did, he of necessity did alone; a masterless man had no friends, even among masterless men. There was no way to reach Moira to tell her of his presence. She must go through with the wedding without even the slim hope of deliverance that knowledge of his presence might have lent. Instinctively, his eyes flashed to the Dark Man standing somber and aloof from the rout. At his feet the old quarreled with the new – the pagan with the Christian – and Turlogh even in that moment felt that the old and new were alike young to the Dark Man.

Did the carven ears of the Dark Man hear strange prows grating on the beach, the stroke of a stealthy knife in the night, the gurgle that marks the severed throat? Those in the skalli heard only their own noise and those who revelled by the fire outside sang on, unaware of the silent coils of death closing about them.

"Enough!" shouted Thorfel. "Count your beads and mutter your mummery, priest! Come here, wench, and marry!" He jerked the girl off the board and plumped her down on her feet before him. She tore loose from him with flaming eyes. All the hot Gaelic blood was roused in her.

"You yellow-haired swine!" she cried. "Do you think that a princess of Clare, with Brian Boru's blood in her veins, would sit at the cross bench of a barbarian and bear the tow-headed cubs of a northern thief? No – I'll never marry you!

"Then I'll take you as a slave!" he roared, snatching at her wrist.

"Nor that way either, swine!" she exclaimed, her fear forgotten in fierce triumph. With the speed of light she snatched a dagger from his girdle, and before he could seize her she drove the keen blade under her heart. The priest cried out as though he had received the wound, and springing forward, caught her in his arms as she fell.

"The curse of Almighty God on you, Thorfel!" he cried, with a voice that rang like a clarion, as he bore her to a couch nearby.

Thorfel stood nonplussed. Silence reigned for an instant, and in that instant Turlogh O'Brien went mad.

"Lamh Laidir Abu!" the war cry of the O'Briens ripped through the stillness like the scream of a wounded panther, and as men whirled toward the shriek, the frenzied Gael came through the doorway like the blast of a wind from Hell. He was in the grip of the Celtic black fury beside which the berserk rage of the Viking pales. Eyes glaring and a tinge of froth on his writhing lips, he crashed among the men who sprawled, off guard, in his path. Those terrible eyes were fixed on Thorfel at the other end of the hall, but as Turlogh rushed he smote to right and left. His charge was the rush of a whirlwind that left a litter of dead and dying men in his wake.

Benches crashed to the floor, men yelled, ale flooded from upset casks. Swift as was the Celt's attack, two men blocked his way with drawn swords before he could reach Thorfel – Halfgar and Oswick. The scarred-faced Viking went down with a cleft skull before he could lift his weapon, and Turlogh, catching Halfgar's blade on his shield, struck again like lightning and the clean ax sheared through hauberk, ribs and spine.

The hall was in a terrific uproar. Men were seizing weapons and pressing forward from all sides, and in the midst the lone Gael raged silently and terribly. Like a wounded tiger was Turlogh Dubh in his madness. His eerie movement was a blur of speed, an explosion of dynamic force. Scarce had Halfgar fallen when the Gael leaped across his crumpling form at Thorfel, who had drawn his sword and stood as if bewildered. But a rush of carles swept between them. Swords rose and fell and the Dalcassian ax flashed among them like the play of summer lightning. On either hand and from before and behind a warrior drove at him. From one side Osric rushed, swinging a two-handed sword; from the other a house-carle drove in with a spear. Turlogh stooped beneath the swing of the sword and struck a double blow, forehand and back. Thorfel's brother dropped, hewed through the knee, and the carle died on his feet as the back-lash return drove the ax's back-spike through his skull. Turlogh straightened, dashing his shield into the face of the swordsman who rushed him from the front. The spike in the center of the shield made a ghastly ruin of his features; then even as the Gael wheeled cat-like to guard his rear, he felt the shadow of Death loom over him. From the corner of his eye he saw the Dane Tostig swinging his great two-handed sword, and jammed against the table, off balance, he knew that even his superhuman quickness could not save him. Then the whistling sword struck the Dark Man on the table and with a clash like thunder, shivered to a thousand blue sparks. Tostig staggered, dazedly, still holding the useless hilt, and Turlogh thrust as with a sword; the upper spike of his ax struck the Dane over the eye and crashed through to the brain.

And even at that instant, the air was filled with a strange singing and men howled. A huge carle, ax still lifted, pitched forward clumsily against the Gael, who split his skull before he saw that a flint-pointed arrow transfixed his throat. The hall seemed full of glancing beams of light that hummed like bees and carried quick death in their humming. Turlogh risked his life for a glance toward the great doorway at the other end of the hall. Through it was pouring a strange horde. Small, dark men they were, with beady black eyes and immobile faces. They were scantily armored, but they bore swords, spears, and bows. Now at close range they drove their long black arrows point-blank and the carles went down in windrows.

Now a red wave of combat swept the skalli hall, a storm of strife that shattered tables, smashed the benches, tore the hangings and trophies from the walls, and stained the floors with a red lake. There had been less of the black strangers than Vikings, but in the surprize of the attack, the first flight of arrows had evened the odds, and now at hand-grips the strange warriors showed themselves in no way inferior to their huge foes. Dazed with surprize and the ale they had drunk, with no time to arm themselves fully, the Norsemen yet fought back with all the reckless ferocity of their race. But the primitive fury of the attackers matched their own valor, and at the head of the hall, where a white-faced priest shielded a dying girl, Black Turlogh tore and ripped with a frenzy that made valor and fury alike futile.

And over all towered the Dark Man. To Turlogh's shifting glances, caught between the flash of sword and ax, it seemed that the image had grown – expanded – heightened; that it loomed giant-like over the battle; that its head rose into smoke-filled rafters of the great hall – that it brooded like a dark cloud of death over these insects who cut each other's throats at its feet. Turlogh sensed in the lightning sword-play and the slaughter that this was the proper element for the Dark Man. Violence and fury were exuded by him. The raw scent of fresh-spilled blood was good to his nostrils and these yellow-haired corpses that rattled at his feet were as sacrifices to him.

The storm of battle rocked the mighty hall. The skalli became a shambles where men slipped in pools of blood, and slipping, died. Heads spun grinning from slumping shoulders. Barbed spears tore the heart, still beating, from the gory breast. Brains splashed and clotted the madly driving axes. Daggers lunged upward, ripping bellies and spilling entrails upon the floor. The clash and clangor of steel rose deafeningly. No quarter was asked or given. A wounded Norseman had dragged down one of the dark men, and doggedly strangled him regardless of the dagger his victim plunged again and again into his body.

One of the dark men seized a child who ran howling from an

inner room, and dashed its brains out against the wall. Another gripped a Norse woman by her golden hair and hurling her to her knees, cut her throat, while she spat in his face. One listening for cries of fear or pleas of mercy would have heard none; men, women or children, they died slashing and clawing, their last gasp a sob of fury, or a snarl of quenchless hatred.

And about the table where stood the Dark Man, immovable as a mountain, washed the red waves of slaughter. Norsemen and tribesmen died at his feet. How many red infernos of slaughter and madness have your strange carved eyes gazed upon, Dark Man?

Shoulder to shoulder Sweyn and Thorfel fought. The Saxon Athelstane, his golden beard a-bristle with the battle-joy, had placed his back against the wall and a man fell at each sweep of his two-handed ax. Now Turlogh came in like a wave, avoiding, with a lithe twist of his upper body, the first ponderous stroke. Now the superiority of the light Irish ax was proved, for before the Saxon could shift his heavy weapon, the Dalcassian ax lit out like a striking cobra and Athelstane reeled as the edge bit through the corselet into the ribs beneath. Another stroke and he crumpled, blood gushing from his temple.

Now none barred Turlogh's way to Thorfel except Sweyn, and even as the Gael leaped like a panther toward the slashing pair, one was ahead of him. The chief of the Dark Men glided like a shadow under the slash of Sweyn's sword, and his own short blade thrust upward under the mail. Thorfel faced Turlogh alone. Thorfel was no coward; he even laughed with pure battle-joy as he thrust, but there was no mirth in Black Turlogh's face, only a frantic rage that writhed his lips and made his eyes coals of blue fire.

In the first swirl of steel Thorfel's sword broke. The young sea-king leaped like a tiger at his foe, thrusting with the shards of the blade. Turlogh laughed fiercely as the jagged remnant gashed his cheek, and at the same instant he cut Thorfel's left foot from under him. The Norseman fell with a heavy crash, then struggled to his knees, clawing for his dagger. His eyes were clouded.

"Make an end, curse you!" he snarled.

Turlogh laughed. "Where is your power and your glory now?" he taunted. "You who would have for unwilling wife an Irish princess – you –"

Suddenly his hate strangled him, and with a howl like a maddened panther he swung his ax in a whistling arc that cleft the Norseman from shoulder to breastbone. Another stroke severed the head, and with the grisly trophy in his hand he approached the couch where lay Moira O'Brien. The priest had lifted her head and held a goblet of wine to her pale lips. Her cloudy gray eyes rested with slight recognition of Turlogh – but it seemed at last she knew him and she tried to smile.

"Moira, blood of my heart," said the outlaw heavily, "you die in a strange land. But the birds in the Culland hills will weep for you, and the heather will sigh in vain for the tread of your little feet. But you shall not be forgotten; axes shall drip for you and for you shall galleys crash and walled cities go up in flames. And that your ghost go not unassuaged into the realms of Tir-na-n-Oge, behold this token of vengeance!"

And he held forth the dripping head of Thorfel.

"In God's name, my son," said the priest, his voice husky with horror, "have done – have done. Will you do your ghastly deeds in the very presence of – see, she is dead. May God in His infinite justice have mercy on her soul, for though she took her own life, yet she died as she lived, in innocence and purity."

Turlogh dropped his ax-head to the floor and his head was bowed. All the fire of his madness had left him and there remained only a dark sadness, a deep sense of futility and weariness. Over all the hall there was no sound. No groans of the wounded were raised, for the knives of the little dark men had been at work, and save their own, there were no wounded. Turlogh sensed that the survivors had gathered about the statue on the table and now stood looking at him with inscrutable eyes. The priest mumbled over the body of the girl, telling his beads. Flames ate at the farther wall of the building, but none heeded it. Then from among the dead on the floor a huge form heaved up unsteadily. Athelstane the Saxon, overlooked by the killers, leaned against the wall and stared about dazedly. Blood flowed from a wound in his ribs and another in his scalp where Turlogh's ax had struck glancingly.

The Gael walked over to him. "I have no hatred for you, Saxon," said he, heavily, "but blood calls for blood and you must die."

Athelstane looked at him without an answer. His large gray eyes were serious, but without fear. He too was a barbarian – more pagan than Christian; he too realized the rights of the blood-feud. But as Turlogh raised his ax, the priest sprang between, his thin hands outstretched, his eyes haggard.

"Have done! In God's name I command you! Almighty Powers,

has not enough blood been shed this fearful night? In the name of the Most High, I claim this man."

Turlogh dropped his ax. "He is yours; not for your oath or your curse, not for your creed but for that you too are a man and did your best for Moira."

A touch on his arm made Turlogh turn. The chief of the strangers stood regarding him with inscrutable eyes.

"Who are you?" asked the Gael idly. He did not care; he felt only weariness.

"I am Brogar, chief of the Picts, Friend of the Dark Man."

"Why do you call me that?" asked Turlogh.

"He rode in the bows of your boat and guided you to Helni through wind and snow. He saved your life when he broke the great sword of the Dane."

Turlogh glanced at the brooding Dark One. It seemed there must be human or superhuman intelligence behind those strange stone eyes. Was it chance alone that caused Tostig's sword to strike the image as he swung it in a death blow?

"What is this thing?" asked the Gael

"It is the only God we have left," answered the other somberly. "It is the image of our greatest king, Bran Mak Morn, he who gathered the broken lines of the Pictish tribes into a single mighty nation, he who drove forth the Norseman and Briton and shattered the legions of Rome, centuries ago. A wizard made this statue while the great Morni yet lived and reigned, and when he died in the last great battle, his spirit entered into it. It is our god.

"Ages ago we ruled. Before the Dane, before the Gael, before the Briton, before the Roman, we reigned in the western isles. Our stone circles rose to the sun. We worked in flint and hides and were happy. Then came the Celts and drove us into the wilderness. They held the southland. But we throve in the north and were strong. Rome broke the Britons and came against us. But there rose among us Bran Mak Morn, of the blood of Brule the Spear-slayer, the friend of King Kull of Valusia who reigned thousands of years ago before Atlantis sank. Bran became king of all Caledon. He broke the iron ranks of Rome and sent the legions cowering south behind their Wall.

"Bran Mak Morn fell in battle; the nation fell apart. Civil wars rocked it. The Gaels came and reared the kingdom of Dalriadia above the ruins of the Cruithni. When the Scot Kenneth McAlpine broke the kingdom of Galloway, the last remnant of the

Pictish empire faded like snow on the mountains. Like wolves we live now among the scattered islands, among the crags of the highlands and the dim hills of Galloway. We are a fading people. We pass. But the Dark Man remains – the Dark One, the great king, Bran Mak Morn, whose ghost dwells forever in the stone likeness of his living self."

As in a dream Turlogh saw an ancient Pict who looked much like the one in whose dead arms he had found the Dark Man, lift the image from the table. The old man's arms were thin as withered branches and his skin clung to his skull like a mummy's, but he handled with ease the image that two strong Vikings had had trouble in carrying.

As if reading his thoughts, Brogar spoke softly: "Only a friend may with safety touch the Dark One. We knew you to be a friend, for he rode in your boat and did you no harm."

"How know you this?"

"The Old One," pointing to the white-bearded ancient, "Gonar, high priest of the Dark One – the ghost of Bran comes to him in dreams. It was Grok, the lesser priest and his people who stole the image and took to sea in a long boat. In dreams Gonar followed; aye, as he slept he sent his spirit with the ghost of the Morni, and he saw the pursuit by the Danes, the battle and slaughter on the Isle of Swords. He saw you come and find the Dark One, and he saw that the ghost of the great king was pleased with you. Woe to the foes of Mak Morn! But good luck shall fare the friends of him."

Turlogh came to himself as from a trance. The heat of the burning hall was in his face and the flickering flames lit and shadowed the carven face of the Dark Man as his worshippers bore him from the building, lending it a strange life. Was it, in truth, that the spirit of a long-dead king lived in that cold stone? Bran Mak Morn loved his people with a savage love; he hated their foes with a terrible hate. Was it possible to breathe into inanimate blind stone a pulsating love and hate that should outlast the centuries?

Turlogh lifted the still, slight form of the dead girl and bore her out of the flaming hall. Five long open boats lay at anchor, and scattered about the embers of the fires the carles had lit, lay the reddened corpses of the revelers who had died silently.

"How stole ye upon these undiscovered?" asked Turlogh. "And whence came you in those open boats?"

"The stealth of the panther is theirs who live by stealth," answered the Pict. "And these were drunken. We followed the path of the Dark One and we came hither from the Isle of Altar, near the Scottish mainland, from whence Grok stole the Dark Man."

Turlogh knew no island of that name but he did realize the courage of these men in daring the seas in boats such as these. He thought of his own boat and requested Brogar to send some of his men for it. The Pict did so. While he waited for them to bring it around the point, he watched the priest bandaging the wounds of the survivors. Silent, immobile, they spoke no word either of complaint or thanks.

The fisherman's boat came scudding around the point just as the first hint of sunrise reddened the waters. The Picts were getting into their boats, lifting in the dead and wounded. Turlogh stepped into his boat and gently eased his pitiful burden down.

"She shall sleep in her own land," he said somberly. "She shall not lie in this cold foreign isle. Brogar, whither go you?"

"We take the Dark One back to his isle and his altar," said the Pict. "Through the mouth of his people he thanks you. The tie of blood is between us, Gael, and mayhap we shall come to you again in your need, as Bran Mak Morn, great king of Pictdom, shall come again to his people some day in the days to come."

"And you, good Jerome? You will come with me?"

The priest shook his head and pointed to Athelstane. The wounded Saxon reposed on a rude couch made of skins piled on the snow.

"I stay here to attend this man. He is sorely wounded."

Turlogh looked about. The walls of the skalli had crashed into a mass of glowing embers. Brogar's men had set fire to the storehouses and the long galley, and the smoke and flame vied luridly with the growing morning light.

"You will freeze or starve. Come with me."

"I will find sustenance for us both. Persuade me not, my son."

"He is a pagan and a reaver."

"No matter. He is a human – a living creature. I will not leave him to die."

"So be it."

Turlogh prepared to cast off. The boats of the Picts were already rounding the point. The rhythmic clacks of their oar-locks came clearly to him. They looked not back, bending stolidly to their work.

He glanced at the stiff corpses about the beach, at the charred embers of the skalli and the glowing timbers of the galley. In the glare the priest seemed unearthly in his thinness and whiteness, like a saint from some old illuminated manuscript. In his worn pallid face was a more than human sadness, a greater than human weariness.

"Look!" he cried suddenly, pointing seaward. "The ocean is of blood! See how it swims red in the rising sun! Oh my people, my people, the blood you have spilt in anger turns the very seas to scarlet! How can you win through?"

"I came in the snow and sleet," said Turlogh, not understanding at first. "I go as I came."

The priest shook his head. "It is more than a mortal sea. Your hands are red with blood and you follow a red sea-path, yet the fault is not wholly with you. Almighty God, when will the reign of blood cease?"

Turlogh shook his head. "Not so long as the race lasts."

The morning wind caught and filled his sail. Into the west he raced like a shadow fleeing the dawn. And so passed Turlogh Dubh O'Brien from the sight of the priest Jerome, who stood watching, shading his weary brow with his thin hand, until the boat was a tiny speck far out on the tossing wastes of the blue ocean.

THE THING ON THE ROOF

Weird Tales, February 1932

They lumber through the night
With their elephantine tread;
I shudder in affright
As I cower in my bed.
They lift colossal wings
On the high gable roofs
Which tremble to the trample
Of their mastodonic hoofs.

– Justin Geoffrey: *Out of the Old Land.*

Let me begin by saying that I was surprized when Tussmann called on me. We had never been close friends; the man's mercenary instincts repelled me; and since our bitter controversy of three years before, when he attempted to discredit my *Evidences of Nahua Culture in Yucatan*, which was the result of years of careful research, our relations had been anything but cordial. However, I received him and found his manner hasty and abrupt, but rather abstracted, as if his dislike for me had been thrust aside in some driving passion that had hold of him.

His errand was quickly stated. He wished my aid in obtaining a volume in the first edition of Von Junzt's *Nameless Cults* – the edition known as the Black Book, not from its color, but because of its dark contents. He might almost as well have asked me for the original Greek translation of the *Necronomicon*. Though since my return from Yucatan I had devoted practically all my time to my avocation of book collecting, I had not stumbled onto any hint that the book in the Dusseldorf edition was still in existence.

A word as to this rare work. Its extreme ambiguity in spots, coupled with its incredible subject matter, has caused it long to be regarded as the ravings of a maniac and the author was damned with the brand of insanity. But the fact remains that much of his assertions are unanswerable, and that he spent the full forty-five years of his life prying into strange places and discovering secret and abysmal things. Not a great many volumes were printed in the first edition and many of these were burned by their frightened owners when Von Junzt was found strangled in a mysterious manner, in his barred and bolted chamber one night in 1840, six months after he had returned from a mysterious journey to Mongolia.

Five years later a London printer, one Bridewall, pirated the work, and issued a cheap translation for sensational effect, full of grotesque woodcuts, and riddled with misspellings, faulty translations and the usual errors of a cheap and unscholarly printing. This still further discredited the original work, and publishers and public forgot about the book until 1909 when the Golden Goblin Press of New York brought out an edition.

Their production was so carefully expurgated that fully a fourth of the original matter was cut out; the book was handsomely bound and decorated with the exquisite and weirdly imaginative illustrations of Diego Vasquez. The edition was intended for popular consumption but the artistic instinct of the publishers defeated that end, since the cost of issuing the book was so great that they were forced to cite it at a prohibitive price.

I was explaining all this to Tussmann when he interrupted brusquely to say that he was not utterly ignorant in such matters. One of the Golden Goblin books ornamented his library, he said, and it was in it that he found a certain line which aroused his interest. If I could procure him a copy of the original 1839 edition, he would make it worth my while; knowing, he added, that it would be useless to offer me money, he would, instead, in return for my trouble on his behalf, make a full retraction of his former accusations in regard to my Yucatan researches, and offer a complete apology in *The Scientific News*.

I will admit that I was astounded at this, and realized that if the matter meant so much to Tussmann that he was willing to make such concessions, it must indeed be of the utmost importance. I answered that I considered that I had sufficiently refuted his charges in the eyes of the world and had no desire to put him in a humiliating position, but that I would make the utmost efforts to procure him what he wanted.

He thanked me abruptly and took his leave, saying rather vaguely that he hoped to find a complete exposition of something in the Black Book which had evidently been slighted in the later edition.

I set to work, writing letters to friends, colleagues and book dealers all over the world, and soon discovered that I had assumed a task of no small magnitude. Three months elapsed before my efforts were crowned with success, but at last, through the aid of Professor James Clement of Richmond, Virginia, I was able to obtain what I wished.

I notified Tussmann and he came to London by the next train. His eyes burned avidly as he gazed at the thick, dusty volume with its heavy leather covers and rusty iron hasps, and his fingers quivered with eagerness as he thumbed the time-yellowed pages.

And when he cried out fiercely and smashed his clenched fist down on the table I knew that he had found what he hunted.

"Listen!" he commanded, and he read to me a passage that spoke of an old, old temple in a Honduras jungle where a strange god was worshipped by an ancient tribe which became extinct before the coming of the Spaniards. And Tussmann read aloud of the mummy that had been, in life, the last high priest of that vanished people, and which now lay in a chamber hewn in the solid rock of the cliff against which the temple was built. About that mummy's withered neck was a copper chain, and on that chain a great red jewel carved in the form of a toad. This jewel was a key, Von Junzt went on to say, to the treasure of the temple which lay hidden in a subterranean crypt far below the temple's altar.

Tussmann's eyes blazed.

"I have seen that temple! I have stood before the altar. I have seen the sealed-up entrance of the chamber in which, the natives say, lies the mummy of the priest. It is a very curious temple, no more like the ruins of the prehistoric Indians than it is like the buildings of the modern Latin-Americans. The Indians in the vicinity disclaim any former connection with the place; they say that the people who built that temple were a different race from themselves, and were there when their own ancestors came into the country. I believe it to be a remnant of some long-vanished civilization which began to decay thousands of years before the Spaniards came.

"I would have liked to have broken into the sealed-up chamber, but I had neither the time nor the tools for the task. I was hurrying to the coast, having been wounded by an accidental gunshot in the foot, and I stumbled onto the place purely by chance.

"I have been planning to have another look at it, but circumstances have prevented – now I intend to let nothing stand in my way! By chance I came upon a passage in the Golden Goblin edition of this book, describing the temple. But that was all; the mummy was only briefly mentioned. Interested, I obtained one of Bridewall's translations but ran up against a blank wall of baffling blunders. By some irritating mischance the translator had even mistaken the location of the Temple of the Toad, as Von Junzt calls it, and has it in Guatemala instead of Honduras. The general description is faulty, the jewel is mentioned and the fact that it is a 'key'. But a key to what, Bridewall's book does not state. I now felt that I was on the track of a real discovery, unless Von Junzt was, as many maintain, a madman. But that the man was actually in Honduras at one time is well attested, and no one could so vividly describe the temple – as he does in the Black Book – unless he had seen it himself. How he learned of the jewel is more than I can say. The Indians who told me of the mummy said nothing of any jewel. I can only believe that Von Junzt found his way into the sealed crypt somehow – the man had uncanny ways of learning hidden things.

"To the best of my knowledge only one other white man has seen the Temple of the Toad besides Von Junzt and myself – the Spanish traveler Juan Gonzales, who made a partial exploration of that country in 1793. He mentioned, briefly, a curious fane that differed from most Indian ruins, and spoke skeptically of a legend current among the natives that there was 'something unusual' hidden under the temple. I feel certain that he was referring to the Temple of the Toad.

"Tomorrow I sail for Central America. Keep the book; I have no more use for it. This time I am going fully prepared and I intend to find what is hidden in that temple, if I have to demolish it. It can be nothing less than a great store of gold! The Spaniards missed it, somehow; when they arrived in Central America, the Temple of the Toad was deserted; they were searching for living Indians from whom torture could wring gold; not for mummies of lost peoples. But I mean to have that treasure."

So saying Tussman took his departure. I sat down and opened the book at the place where he had left off reading, and I sat until midnight, wrapt in Von Junzt's curious, wild and at times utterly vague expoundings. And I found pertaining to the Temple of the Toad certain things which disquieted me so much that the next morning I attempted to get in touch with Tussmann, only to find that he had already sailed.

Several months passed and then I received a letter from Tussmann, asking me to come and spend a few days with him at his estate in Sussex; he also requested me to bring the Black Book with me.

I arrived at Tussmann's rather isolated estate just after nightfall. He lived in almost feudal state, his great ivy-grown house and broad lawns surrounded by high stone walls. As I went up the hedge-bordered way from the gate to the house, I noted that the place had not been well kept in its master's absence. Weeds grew rank among the trees, almost choking out the grass. Among some unkempt bushes over against the outer wall, I heard what appeared to be a horse or an ox blundering and lumbering about. I distinctly heard the clink of its hoof on a stone.

A servant who eyed me suspiciously admitted me and I found Tussmann pacing to and fro in his study like a caged lion. His giant frame was leaner, harder than when I had last seen him; his face was bronzed by a tropic sun. There were more and harsher lines in his strong face and his eyes burned more intensely than ever. A smoldering, baffled anger seemed to underlie his manner.

"Well, Tussmann," I greeted him, "what success? Did you find the gold?"

"I found not an ounce of gold," he growled. "The whole thing was a hoax – well, not all of it. I broke into the sealed chamber and found the mummy –"

"And the jewel?" I exclaimed.

He drew something from his pocket and handed it to me.

I gazed curiously at the thing I held. It was a great jewel, clear and transparent as crystal, but of a sinister crimson, carved, as Von Junzt had declared, in the shape of a toad. I shuddered involuntarily; the image was peculiarly repulsive. I turned my attention to the heavy and curiously wrought copper chain which supported it.

"What are these characters carved on the chain?" I asked curiously.

"I can not say," Tussmann replied. "I had thought perhaps you might know. I find a faint resemblance between them and certain partly defaced hieroglyphics on a monolith known as the Black Stone in the mountains of Hungary. I have been unable to decipher them."

"Tell me of your trip," I urged, and over our whiskey-and-sodas he began, as if with a strange reluctance.

"I found the temple again with no great difficulty, though it lies in a lonely and little-frequented region. The temple is built against a sheer stone cliff in a deserted valley unknown to maps and explorers. I would not endeavor to make an estimate of its antiquity, but it is built of a sort of unusually hard basalt, such as I have never seen anywhere else, and its extreme weathering suggests incredible age.

"Most of the columns which form its facade are in ruins, thrusting up shattered stumps from worn bases, like the scattered and broken teeth of some grinning hag. The outer walls are crumbling, but the inner walls and the columns which support such of the roof as remains intact, seem good for another thousand years, as well as the walls of the inner chamber.

"The main chamber is a large circular affair with a floor composed of great squares of stone. In the center stands the altar, merely a huge, round, curiously carved block of the same material. Directly behind the altar, in the solid stone cliff which forms the rear wall of the chamber, is the sealed and hewn-out chamber wherein lay the mummy of the temple's last priest.

"I broke into the crypt with not too much difficulty and found the mummy exactly as is stated in the Black Book. Though it was in a remarkable state of preservation, I was unable to classify it. The withered features and general contour of the skull suggested certain degraded and mongrel peoples of Lower Egypt, and I feel certain that the priest was a member of a race more akin to the Caucasian than the Indian. Beyond this, I can not make any positive statement.

"But the jewel was there, the chain looped about the dried-up neck."

From this point Tussmann's narrative became so vague that I had some difficulty in following him and wondered if the tropic sun had affected his mind. He had opened a hidden door in the altar somehow with the jewel – just how, he did not plainly say, and it struck me that he did not clearly understand himself the action of the jewel-key. But the opening of the secret door had had a bad effect on the hardy rogues in his employ. They had refused point-blank to follow him through that gaping black opening which had appeared so mysteriously when the gem was touched to the altar.

Tussmann entered alone with his pistol and electric torch, finding a narrow stone stair that wound down into the bowels of the earth, apparently. He followed this and presently came into a broad corridor, in the blackness of which his tiny beam of light was almost engulfed. As he told this he spoke with strange annoyance of a toad which hopped ahead of him, just beyond the circle of light, all the time he was below ground.

Making his way along dank tunnels and stairways that were wells of solid blackness, he at last came to a heavy door fantastically carved, which he felt must be the crypt wherein was secreted the gold of the ancient worshippers. He pressed the toad-jewel against it at several places and finally the door gaped wide.

"And the treasure?" I broke in eagerly.

He laughed in savage self-mockery.

"There was no gold there, no precious gems – nothing" – he hesitated – "nothing that I could bring away."

Again his tale lapsed into vagueness. I gathered that he had left the temple rather hurriedly without searching any further for the supposed treasure. He had intended bringing the mummy away with him, he said, to present to some museum, but when he came up out of the pits, it could not be found and he believed that his men, in superstitious aversion to having such a companion on their road to the coast, had thrown it into some well or cavern.

"And so," he concluded, "I am in England again no richer than when I left."

"You have the jewel," I reminded him. "Surely it is valuable."

He eyed it without favor, but with a sort of fierce avidness almost obsessional.

"Would you say that it is a ruby?" he asked.

I shook my head. "I am unable to classify it."

"And I. But let me see the book."

He slowly turned the heavy pages, his lips moving as he read. Sometimes he shook his head as if puzzled, and I noticed him dwell long over a certain line.

"This man dipped so deeply into forbidden things," said he, "I can not wonder that his fate was so strange and mysterious. He must have had some foreboding of his end – here he warns men not to disturb sleeping things."

Tussmann seemed lost in thought for some moments.

"Aye, sleeping things," he muttered, "that seem dead, but only lie waiting for some blind fool to awake them – I should have read further in the Black Book – and I should have shut the door when I left the crypt – but I have the key and I'll keep it in spite of Hell."

He roused himself from his reveries and was about to speak when he stopped short. From somewhere upstairs had come a peculiar sound.

"What was that?" he glared at me. I shook my head and he ran to the door and shouted for a servant. The man entered a few moments later and he was rather pale.

"You were upstairs?" growled Tussmann.

"Yes, sir."

"Did you hear anything?" asked Tussmann harshly and in a manner almost threatening and accusing.

"I did, sir," the man answered with a puzzled look on his face.

"What did you hear?" The question was fairly snarled.

"Well, sir," the man laughed apologetically, "you'll say I'm a bit off, I fear, but to tell you the truth, sir, it sounded like a horse stamping around on the roof!"

A blaze of absolute madness leaped into Tussmann's eyes.

"You fool!" he screamed. "Get out of here!" The man shrank back in amazement and Tussmann snatched up the gleaming toad-carved jewel.

"I've been a fool!" he raved. "I didn't read far enough – and I should have shut the door – but by heaven, the key is mine and I'll keep it in spite of man or devil."

And with these strange words he turned and fled upstairs. A moment later his door slammed heavily and a servant, knocking timidly, brought forth only a blasphemous order to retire and a luridly worded threat to shoot anyone who tried to obtain entrance into the room.

Had it not been so late I would have left the house, for I was certain that Tussmann was stark mad. As it was, I retired to the room a frightened servant showed me, but I did not go to bed. I opened the pages of the Black Book at the place where Tussmann had been reading.

This much was evident, unless the man was utterly insane: he had stumbled upon something unexpected in the Temple of the Toad. Something unnatural about the opening of the altar door had frightened his men, and in the subterraneous crypt Tussmann had found *something* that he had not thought to find. And I believed that he had been followed from Central America, and that the reason for his persecution was the jewel he called the Key.

Seeking some clue in Von Junzt's volume, I read again of the Temple of the Toad, of the strange pre-Indian people who worshipped there, and of the huge, tittering, tentacled, hoofed monstrosity that they worshipped.

Tussmann had said that he had not read far enough when he had first seen the book. Puzzling over this cryptic phrase I came upon the line he had pored over – marked by his thumb nail. It seemed to me to be another of Von Junzt's many ambiguities, for it merely stated that a temple's god was the temple's treasure. Then the dark implication of the hint struck me and cold sweat beaded my forehead.

The Key to the Treasure! And the temple's treasure was the temple's god! And sleeping Things might awaken on the opening of their prison door! I sprang up, unnerved by the intolerable suggestion, and at that moment something crashed in the stillness and the death-scream of a human being burst upon my ears.

In an instant I was out of the room, and as I dashed up the stairs I heard sounds that have made me doubt my sanity ever since. At Tussmann's door I halted, essaying with shaking hand to turn the knob. The door was locked, and as I hesitated I heard from within a hideous high-pitched tittering and then the disgusting squashy sound as if a great, jelly-like bulk was being forced through the window. The sound ceased and I could have sworn I heard a faint swish of gigantic wings. Then silence.

Gathering my shattered nerves, I broke down the door. A foul and overpowering stench billowed out like a yellow mist. Gasping in nausea I entered. The room was in ruins, but nothing was missing except that crimson toad-carved jewel Tussmann called the Key, and that was never found. A foul, unspeakable slime smeared the windowsill, and in the center of the room lay Tussmann, his head crushed and flattened; and on the red ruin of skull and face, the plain print of an enormous hoof.

THE LAST DAY

Weird Tales, March 1932

Hinged in the brooding west a black sun hung,
And Titan shadows barred the dying world.
The blind black oceans groped – their tendrils curled,
And writhed and fell in feathered spray and clung,
Climbing the granite ladders, rung by rung,
Which held them from the tribes whose death-cries skirled.
Above unholy fires red wings unfurled –
Gray ashes floated down from where they swung.

A demon crouched, chin propped on brutish fist,
Gripping a crystal ball between his knees.
His skull-mouth gaped and icy shone his eye.
Down crashed the crystal globe – a fire-shot mist
Masked the dark lands which sank below the seas –
A painted sun hung in the starless sky.

HORROR FROM THE MOUND

Weird Tales, May 1932

Steve Brill did not believe in ghosts or demons. Juan Lopez did. But neither the caution of the one nor the sturdy skepticism of the other was shield against the horror that fell upon them – the horror forgotten by men for more than three hundred years – a screaming fear monstrously resurrected from the black lost ages.

Yet as Steve Brill sat on his sagging stoop that last evening, his thoughts were as far from uncanny menaces as the thoughts of man can be. His ruminations were bitter but materialistic. He surveyed his farmland and he swore. Brill was tall, rangy and tough as boot-leather – true son of the iron-bodied pioneers who wrenched West Texas from the wilderness. He was browned by the sun and strong as a long-horned steer. His lean legs and the boots on them showed his cowboy instincts, and now he cursed himself that he had ever climbed off the hurricane deck of his crank-eyed mustang and turned to farming. He was no farmer, the young puncher admitted profanely.

Yet his failure had not all been his fault. Plentiful rain in the winter – so rare in West Texas – had given promise of good crops. But as usual, things had happened. A late blizzard had destroyed all the budding fruit. The grain which had looked so promising was ripped to shreds ands battered into the ground by terrific hailstorms just as it was turning yellow. A period of intense dryness, followed by another hailstorm, finished the corn.

Then the cotton, which had somehow struggled through, fell before a swarm of grasshoppers which stripped Brill's field almost overnight. So Brill sat and swore that he would not renew his lease – he gave fervent thanks that he did not own the land on which he had wasted his sweat, and that there were still broad rolling ranges to the west where a strong young man could make his living riding and roping.

Now as Brill sat glumly, he was aware of the approaching form of his nearest neighbor, Juan Lopez, a taciturn old Mexican who lived in a hut just out of sight over the hill across the creek, and grubbed for a living. At present he was clearing a strip of land on an adjoining farm, and in returning to his hut he crossed a corner of Brill's pasture.

Brill idly watched him climb through the barbed-wire fence and trudge along the path he had worn in the short dry grass. He had been working at his present job for over a month now, chopping down tough gnarly mesquite trees and digging up their incredibly long roots, and Brill knew that he always followed the same path home. And watching, Brill noted him swerving far aside, seemingly to avoid a low rounded hillock which jutted above the level of the pasture. Lopez went far around this knoll and Brill remembered that the old Mexican always circled it at a distance. And another thing came into Brill's idle mind – Lopez always increased his gait when he was passing the knoll, and he always managed to get by it before sundown – yet Mexican laborers generally worked from the first light of dawn to the last glint of twilight, especially at these grubbing jobs, when they were paid by the acre and not by the day. Brill's curiosity was aroused.

He rose, and sauntering down the slight slope on the crown of which his shack sat, hailed the plodding Mexican.

"Hey, Lopez, wait a minute."

Lopez halted, looked about, and remained motionless but unenthusiastic as the white man approached.

"Lopez," said Brill lazily, "it ain't none of my business, but I just wanted to ask you – how come you always go so far around that old Indian mound?"

"No sabe," grunted Lopez shortly.

"You're a liar," responded Brill genially. "You savvy all right; you speak English as good as me. What's the matter – you think that mound's ha'nted or somethin'?"

Brill could speak Spanish himself and read it, too, but like most Anglo-Saxons he much preferred to speak his own language.

Lopez shrugged his shoulders.

"It is not a good place, *no bueno*," he muttered, avoiding Brill's eye. "Let hidden things rest."

"I reckon you're scared of ghosts," Brill bantered. "Shucks, if that is an Indian mound, them Indians been dead so long their ghosts 'ud be plumb wore out by now."

Brill knew that the illiterate Mexicans looked with superstitious aversion on the mounds that are found here and there through the Southwest – relics of a past and forgotten age, containing the moldering bones of chiefs and warriors of a lost race.

"Best not to disturb what is hidden in the earth," grunted Lopez.

"Bosh," said Brill. "Me and some boys busted into one of them mounds over in the Palo Pinto country and dug up pieces of skeleton with some beads and flint arrowheads and the like. I kept some of the teeth a long time till I lost 'em, and I ain't never been ha'nted."

"Indians?" snorted Lopez unexpectedly. "Who spoke of Indians? There have been more than Indians in this country. In the old times strange things happened here. I have heard the tales of my people, handed down from generation to generation. And my people were here long before yours, Señor Brill."

"Yeah, you're right," admitted Steve. "First white men in this country was Spaniards, of course. Coronado passed along not very far from here, I hear-tell, and Hernando de Estrada's expedition came through here – away back yonder – I dunno how long ago."

"In 1545," said Lopez. "They pitched camp yonder where your corral stands now."

Brill turned to glance at his rail-fenced corral, inhabited now by his saddle-horse, a pair of work-horses and a scrawny cow.

"How come you know so much about it?" he asked curiously.

"One of my ancestors marched with de Estrada," answered Lopez. "A soldier, Porfirio Lopez; he told his son of that expedition, and he told *his* son, and so down the family line to me, who have no son to whom I can tell the tale."

"I didn't know you were so well connected," said Brill. "Maybe you know somethin' about the gold de Estrada was supposed to have hid around here somewhere."

"There was no gold," growled Lopez. "De Estrada's soldiers bore only their arms, and they fought their way through hostile country – many left their bones along the trail. Later – many years later – a mule train from Sante Fe was attacked not many miles from here by Comanches and they hid their gold and escaped; so the legends got mixed up. But even their gold is not there now, because Gringo buffalo-hunters found it and dug it up."

Brill nodded abstractedly, hardly heeding. Of all the continent of North America there is no section so haunted by tales of lost or hidden treasure as is the Southwest. Uncounted wealth passed back and forth over the hills and plains of Texas and New Mexico in the old days when Spain owned the gold and silver mines of the New World and controlled the rich fur trade of the West, and echoes of that wealth linger on in tales of golden caches. Some such vagrant dream, born of failure and pressing poverty, rose in Brill's mind.

Aloud he spoke: "Well, anyway, I got nothin' else to do and I believe I'll dig into that old mound and see what I can find."

The effect of that simple statement on Lopez was nothing short of shocking. He recoiled and his swarthy brown face went ashy; his black eyes flared and he threw up his arms in a gesture of intense expostulation.

"Dios, no!" he cried. "Don't do that, Señor Brill! There is a curse – my grandfather told me –"

"Told you what?" asked Brill.

"I can not speak," he muttered. "I am sworn to silence. Only to an eldest son could I open my heart. But believe me when I say better had you cut your throat than to break into that accursed mound."

"Well," said Brill, impatient of Mexican superstitions, "if it's so bad why don't you tell me about it? Gimme a logical reason for not bustin' into it."

"I can not speak!" cried the Mexican desperately. "I *know!* – but I swore to silence on the Holy Crucifix, just as every man of my family has sworn. It is a thing so dark, it is to risk damnation even to speak of it! Were I to tell you, I would blast the soul from your body. But I have sworn – and I have no son, so my lips are sealed forever."

"Aw, well," said Brill sarcastically, "why don't you write it out?"

Lopez started, stared, and to Steve's surprize, caught at the suggestion.

"I will! *Dios* be thanked the good priest taught me to write when I was a child. My oath said nothing of writing. I only swore not to speak. I will write out the whole thing for you, if you will swear not to speak of it afterward, and to destroy the paper as soon as you have read it."

"Sure," said Brill, to humor him, and the old Mexican seemed much relieved.

"*Bueno!* I will go at once and write. Tomorrow as I go to work I will bring you the paper and you will understand why no one must open that accursed mound!"

And Lopez hurried along his homeward path, his stooped shoulders swaying with the effort of his unwonted haste. Steve grinned after him, shrugged his shoulders and turned back toward his own shack. Then he halted, gazing back at the low rounded mound with its grass-grown sides. It must be an Indian tomb, he decided, what of its symmetry and its similarity to other Indian mounds he had seen. He scowled as he tried to figure out the seeming connection between the mysterious knoll and the martial ancestor of Juan Lopez.

Brill gazed after the receding figure of the old Mexican. A shallow valley, cut by a half-dry creek, bordered with trees and underbrush, lay between Brill's pasture and the low sloping hill beyond which lay Lopez's shack. Among the trees along the creek bank the old Mexican was disappearing. And Brill came to a sudden decision.

Hurrying up the slight slope, he took a pick and a shovel from the tool shed built onto the back of his shack. The sun had not yet set and Brill believed he could open the mound deep enough to determine its nature before dark. If not, he could work by lantern-light. Steve, like most of his breed, lived mostly by impulse, and his present urge was to tear into that mysterious hillock and find what, if anything, was concealed therein. The thought of treasure came again to his mind, piqued by the evasive attitude of Lopez.

What if, after all, that grassy heap of brown earth hid riches – virgin ore from forgotten mines, or the minted coinage of old Spain? Was it not possible that the musketeers of de Estrada had themselves reared that pile above a treasure they could not bear away, molding it in the likeness of an Indian mound to fool seekers? Did old Lopez know that? It would not be strange if, knowing of treasure there, the old Mexican refrained from disturbing it. Ridden with grisly superstitious fears, he might well live out a life of barren toil rather than risk the wrath of lurking ghosts or devils – for the Mexicans say that hidden gold is always accursed, and surely there was supposed to be some especial doom resting on this mound. Well, Brill meditated, Latin-Indian devils had no terrors for the Anglo-Saxon, tormented by the demons of drought and storm and crop failure.

Steve set to work with the savage energy characteristic of his breed. The task was no light one; the soil, baked by the fierce sun, was iron-hard, and mixed with rocks and pebbles. Brill sweated profusely and grunted with his efforts, but the fire of the treasure-hunter was on him. He shook the sweat out of his eyes and drove in the pick with mighty strokes that ripped and crumbled the close-packed dirt.

The sun went down, and in the long dreamy summer twilight he worked on, almost oblivious of time or space. He began to be convinced that the mound was a genuine Indian tomb, as he found traces of charcoal in the soil. The ancient people which reared these sepulchers had kept fires burning upon them for days, at some point in the building. All the mounds Steve had ever opened had contained a solid stratum of charcoal a short distance below the surface. But the charcoal traces he found now were scattered about through the soil.

His idea of a Spanish-built treasure trove faded, but he persisted. Who knows? Perhaps that strange folk men now called Mound-Builders had treasure of their own which they laid away with the dead.

Then Steve yelped in exultation as his pick rang on a bit of metal. He snatched it up and held it close to his eyes, straining in the waning light. It was caked and corroded with rust, worn almost paper-thin, but he knew it for what it was – a spur-rowel, unmistakably Spanish with its long cruel points. And he halted, completely bewildered. No Spaniard ever reared this mound, with its undeniable marks of aboriginal workmanship. Yet how came that relic of Spanish caballeros hidden deep in the packed soil?

Brill shook his head and set to work again. He knew that in the center of the mound, if it were indeed an aboriginal tomb, he would find a narrow chamber built of heavy stones, containing the bones of the chief for which the mound had been reared and the victims sacrificed above it. And in the gathering darkness he felt his pick strike heavily against something granite-like and unyielding. Examination, by sense of feel as well as by sight, proved it to be a solid block of stone, roughly hewn. Doubtless it formed one of the ends of the death-chamber. Useless to try to shatter it. Brill chipped and pecked about it, scraping the dirt and pebbles away from the corners until he felt that wrenching it out would be but a matter of sinking the pick-point underneath and levering it out.

But now he was suddenly aware that darkness had come on. In the young moon objects were dim and shadowy. His mustang nickered in the corral whence came the comfortable crunch of tired beasts' jaws on corn. A whippoorwill called eerily from the dark shadows of the narrow winding creek. Brill straightened reluctantly. Better get a lantern and continue his explorations by its light.

He felt in his pocket with some idea of wrenching out the stone and exploring the cavity by the aid of matches. Then he stiffened. Was it imagination that he heard a faint sinister rustling, which seemed to come from behind the blocking stone? Snakes! Doubtless they had holes somewhere about the base of the mound and there might be a dozen big diamond-backed rattlers coiled up in that cave-like interior waiting for him to put his hand among them. He shivered slightly at the thought and backed away out of the excavation he had made.

It wouldn't do to go poking about blindly into holes. And for the past few minutes, he realized, he had been aware of a faint foul odor exuding from interstices about the blocking stone – though he admitted that the smell suggested reptiles no more than it did any other menacing scent. It had a charnel-house reek about it – gases formed in the chamber of death, no doubt, and dangerous to the living.

Steve laid down his pick and returned to the house, impatient of the necessary delay. Entering the dark building, he struck a match and located his kerosene lantern hanging on its nail on the wall. Shaking it, he satisfied himself that it was nearly full of coal oil, and lighted it. Then he fared forth again, for his eagerness would not allow him to pause long enough for a bite of food. The mere opening of the mound intrigued him, as it must always intrigue a man of imagination, and the discovery of the Spanish spur had whetted his curiosity.

He hurried from his shack, the swinging lantern casting long distorted shadows ahead of him and behind. He chuckled as he visualized Lopez's thoughts and actions when he learned, on the morrow, that the forbidden mound had been pried into. A good thing he opened it that evening, Brill reflected; Lopez might even have tried to prevent him meddling with it, had he known.

In the dreamy hush of the summer night, Brill reached the mound – lifted his lantern – swore bewilderedly. The lantern revealed his excavations, his tools lying carelessly where he had dropped them – and a black gaping aperture! The great blocking stone lay in the bottom of the excavation he had made, as if thrust carelessly aside. Warily he thrust the lantern forward and peered into the small cave-like chamber, expecting to see he knew not what. Nothing met his eyes except the bare rock sides of a long narrow cell, large enough to receive a man's body, which had apparently been built up of roughly hewn square-cut stones, cunningly and strongly joined together.

"Lopez!" exclaimed Steve furiously. "The dirty coyote! He's been watchin' me work – and when I went after the lantern, he snuck up and pried the rock out – and grabbed whatever was in there, I reckon. Blast his greasy hide, I'll fix him!"

Savagely he extinguished the lantern and glared across the shallow, brush-grown valley. And as he looked he stiffened. Over the corner of the hill, on the other side of which the shack of Lopez stood, a shadow moved. The slender moon was setting, the light dim and the play of the shadows baffling. But Steve's eyes were sharpened by the sun and winds of the wastelands, and he knew that it was some two-legged creature that was disappearing over the low shoulder of the mesquite-grown hill.

"Beatin' it to his shack," snarled Brill. "He's shore got somethin' or he wouldn't be travelin' at that speed."

Brill swallowed, wondering why a peculiar trembling had suddenly taken hold of him. What was there unusual about a thieving old Greaser running home with his loot? Brill tried to drown the feeling that there was something peculiar about the gait of the dim shadow, which had seemed to move at a sort of slinking lope. There must have been need for swiftness when stocky old Juan Lopez elected to travel at such a strange pace.

"Whatever he found is as much mine as his," swore Brill, trying to get his mind off the abnormal aspect of the figure's flight. "I got this land leased and I done all the work diggin'. A curse, heck! No wonder he told me that stuff. Wanted me to leave it alone so he could get it hisself. It's a wonder he ain't dug it up long before this. But you can't never tell about them Spigs."

Brill, as he meditated thus, was striding down the gentle slope of the pasture which led down to the creek-bed. He passed into the shadows of the trees and dense underbrush and walked across the dry creek-bed, noting absently that neither whippoorwill nor hoot-owl called in the darkness. There was a waiting, listening tenseness in the night that he did not like. The shadows in the creek bed seemed too thick, too breathless. He wished he had not blown out the lantern, which he still carried, and was glad he had brought the pick, gripped like a battle-ax in his right hand. He had an impulse to whistle, just to break the silence, then swore and dismissed the thought. Yet he was glad when he clambered up the low opposite bank and emerged into the starlight.

He walked up the slope and onto the hill, and looked down on the mesquite flat wherein stood Lopez's squalid hut. A light showed at the one window.

"Packin' his things for a getaway, I reckon," grunted Steve. "Ow, what the –"

He staggered as from a physical impact as a frightful scream knifed the stillness. He wanted to clap his hands over his ears to shut out the horror of that cry, which rose unbearably and then broke in an abhorrent gurgle.

"Good God!" Steve felt the cold sweat spring out upon him. "Lopez – or somebody –"

Even as he gasped the words he was running down the hill as fast as his long legs could carry him. Some unspeakable horror was taking place in that lonely hut, but he was going to investigate it if it meant facing the Devil himself. He tightened his grip on his pick-handle as he ran. Wandering prowlers, murdering old Lopez for the loot he had taken from the mound, Steve thought, and forgot his wrath. It would go hard for anyone he found molesting the old scoundrel, thief though he might be.

He hit the flat, running hard. And then the light in the hut went out and Steve staggered in full flight, bringing up against a mesquite tree with an impact that jolted a grunt out of him and tore his hands on the thorns. Rebounding with a sobbed curse, he rushed for the shack, nerving himself for what he might see – his hair still standing on end at what he had already seen.

Brill tried the one door of the hut and found it bolted. He shouted to Lopez and received no answer. Yet utter silence did not reign. From within came a curious muffled worrying sound, that ceased as Brill swung his pick crashing against the door. The flimsy portal splintered and Brill leaped into the dark hut, eyes blazing, pick swung high for a desperate onslaught. But no sound ruffled the grisly silence, and in the darkness nothing stirred, though Brill's chaotic imagination peopled the shadowed corners of the hut with the shapes of horror.

With a hand damp with perspiration he found a match and struck it. Besides himself only Lopez occupied the hut – old Lopez, stark dead on the dirt floor, arms spread wide like a crucifix, mouth sagging open in a semblance of idiocy, eyes wide and staring with a horror Brill found intolerable. The one window gaped open, showing the method of the slayer's exit – possibly his entrance as well. Brill went to that window and gazed out warily. He saw only the sloping hillside on one hand and the mesquite flat on the other. He started – was that a hint of movement among the stunted shadows of the mesquites and chaparral – or had he but imagined he glimpsed a dim loping figure among the trees?

He turned back, as the match burned down to his fingers. He lit the old coal oil lamp on the rude table, cursing as he burned his hand. The globe of the lamp was very hot, as if it had been burning for hours.

Reluctantly he turned to the corpse on the floor. Whatever sort of death had come to Lopez, it had been horrible, but Brill, gingerly examining the dead man, found no wound – no mark of knife or bludgeon on him. Wait! There was a thin smear of blood on Brill's questing hand. Searching, he found the source – three or four tiny punctures in Lopez's throat, from which blood had oozed sluggishly. At first he thought they had been inflicted with a stiletto – a thin round edgeless dagger – then he shook his head. He had seen stiletto wounds – he had the scar of one on his own body. These wounds more resembled the bite of some animal – they looked like the marks of pointed fangs.

Yet Brill did not believe they were deep enough to have caused death, nor had much blood flowed from them. A belief, abhorrent with grisly speculations, rose up in the dark corners of his mind – that Lopez had died of fright, and that the wounds had been inflicted either simultaneously with his death, or an instant afterward.

And Steve noticed something else; scattered about on the floor lay a number of dingy leaves of paper, scrawled in the old Mexican's crude hand – he would write of the curse on the mound, he had said. There were the sheets on which he had written, there was the stump of a pencil on the floor, there was the hot lamp globe, all mute witnesses that the old Mexican had been seated at the rough-hewn table writing for hours. Then it was not he who opened the mound-chamber and stole the contents – but who was it, in God's name? And who or what was it that Brill had glimpsed loping over the shoulder of the hill?

Well, there was but one thing to do – saddle his mustang and ride the ten miles to Coyote Wells, the nearest town, and inform the sheriff of the murder.

Brill gathered up the papers. The last was crumpled in the old man's clutching hand and Brill secured it with some difficulty. Then as he turned to extinguish the light, he hesitated, and cursed himself for the crawling fear that lurked at the back of his mind – fear of the shadowy thing he had seen cross the window just before the light was extinguished in the hut. The long arm of the murderer, he thought, reaching for the lamp to put it out, no doubt. What had there been abnormal or inhuman about the vision, distorted though it must have been in the dim lamplight and shadow? As a man strives to remember the details of a nightmare dream, Steve tried to define in his mind some clear reason that would explain why that flying glimpse had unnerved him to the extent of blundering headlong into a tree, and why the mere vague remembrance of it now caused cold sweat to break out on him.

Cursing himself to keep up his courage, he lighted his lantern, blew out the lamp on the rough table, and resolutely set forth, grasping his pick like a weapon. After all, why should certain seemingly abnormal aspects about a sordid murder upset him? Such crimes were abhorrent, but common enough, especially among Mexicans, who cherished unguessed feuds.

Then as he stepped into the silent star-flecked night he brought up short. From across the creek sounded the sudden soul-shaking scream of a horse in deadly terror – then a mad drumming of hoofs that receded in the distance. And Brill swore in rage and dismay. Was it a panther lurking in the hills – had a monster cat slain old Lopez? Then why was not the victim marked with the scars of fierce hooked talons? *And who extinguished the light in the hut?*

As he wondered, Brill was running swiftly toward the dark creek. Not lightly does a cowpuncher regard the stampeding of his stock. As he passed into the darkness of the brush along the dry creek, Brill found his tongue strangely dry. He kept swallowing, and he held the lantern high. It made but faint impression in the gloom, but seemed to accentuate the blackness of the crowding shadows. For some strange reason, the thought entered Brill's chaotic mind that though the land was new to the Anglo-Saxon, it was in reality very old. That broken and desecrated tomb was mute evidence that the land was ancient to man, and suddenly the night and the hills and the shadows bore on Brill with a sense of hideous antiquity. Here had long generations of men lived and died before Brill's ancestors ever heard of the land. In the night, in the shadows of this very creek, men had no doubt given up their ghosts in grisly ways. With these reflections Brill hurried through the shadows of the thick trees.

He breathed deeply in relief when he emerged from the trees on his own side. Hurrying up the gentle slope to the railed corral, he held up his lantern, investigating. The corral was empty; not even the placid cow was in sight. And the bars were down. That pointed to human agency, and the affair took on a newly sinister aspect. Someone did not intend that Brill should ride to Coyote Wells that night. It meant that the murderer intended making his getaway and wanted a good start on the law, or else – Brill grinned wryly. Far away across a mesquite flat he believed he could still catch the faint and faraway noise of running horses. What in God's name had given them such a fright? A cold finger of fear played shudderingly on Brill's spine.

Steve headed for the house. He did not enter boldly. He crept clear around the shack, peering shudderingly into the dark windows, listening with painful intensity for some sound to betray the presence of the lurking killer. At last he ventured to open the door and step in. He threw the door back against the wall to find if anyone were hiding behind it, lifted the lantern high and stepped in, heart pounding, pick gripped fiercely, his feelings a mixture of fear and red rage. But no hidden assassin leaped upon him, and a wary exploration of the shack revealed nothing.

With a sigh of relief Brill locked the doors, made fast the windows and lighted his old coal oil lamp. The thought of old Lopez lying, a glassy-eyed corpse alone in the hut across the creek, made him wince and shiver, but he did not intend to start for town on foot in the night.

He drew from its hiding-place his reliable old Colt .45, spun the blue-steel cylinder, and grinned mirthlessly. Maybe the killer did not intend to leave any witnesses to his crime alive. Well, let him come! He – or they – would find a young cowpuncher with a six-shooter less easy prey than an old unarmed Mexican. And that reminded Brill of the papers he had brought from the hut. Taking care that he was not in line with a window through which a sudden bullet might come, he settled himself to read, with one ear alert for stealthy sounds.

And as he read the crude laborious script, a slow cold horror grew in his soul. It was a tale of fear that the old Mexican had scrawled – a tale handed down from generation to generation – a tale of ancient times.

And Brill read of the wanderings of the caballero Hernando de Estrada and his armored pikemen, who dared the deserts of the Southwest when all was strange and unknown. There were some forty-odd soldiers, servants, and masters, at the beginning, the manuscript ran. There was the captain, de Estrada, and the priest, and young Juan Zavilla, and Don Santiago de Valdez – a mysterious nobleman who had been taken off a helplessly floating ship in the Caribbean Sea – all the others of the crew and passengers had died of plague, he had said, and he had cast their bodies overboard. So de Estrada had taken him aboard the ship that was bearing the expedition from Spain, and de Valdez joined them in their explorations.

Brill read something of their wanderings, told in the crude style of old Lopez, as the old Mexican's ancestors had handed down the tale for over three hundred years. The bare written words dimly reflected the terrific hardships the explorers had encountered – drought, thirst, floods, the desert sandstorms, the spears of hostile redskins. But it was of another peril that old Lopez told – a grisly lurking horror that fell upon the lonely caravan wandering through the immensity of the wild. Man by man they fell and no man knew the slayer. Fear and black suspicion ate at the heart of the expedition like a canker, and their leader knew not where to turn. This, they all knew: among them was a fiend in human form.

Men began to draw apart from each other, to scatter along the line of march, and this mutual suspicion, that sought security in solitude, made it easier for the fiend. The skeleton of the expedition staggered through the wilderness, lost, dazed and helpless, and still the unseen, horror hung on their flanks, dragging down the stragglers, preying on drowsing sentries and sleeping men. And on the throat of each was found the wounds of pointed fangs that bled the victim white; so that the living knew with what manner of evil they had to deal. Men reeled through the wild, calling on the saints, or blaspheming in their terror, fighting frenziedly against sleep, until they fell with exhaustion and sleep stole on them with horror and death.

Suspicion centered on a great black man, a cannibal slave from Calabar. And they put him in chains. But young Juan Zavilla went the way of the rest, and then the priest was taken. But the priest fought off his fiendish assailant and lived long enough to gasp the demon's name to de Estrada. And Brill, shuddering and wide-eyed, read:

". . . And now it was evident to de Estrada that the good priest had spoken the truth, and the slayer was Don Santiago de Valdez, who was a vampire, an undead fiend, subsisting on the blood of the living. And de Estrada called to mind a certain foul nobleman who had lurked in the mountains of Castile since the days of the Moors, feeding off the blood of helpless victims which lent him a ghastly immortality. This nobleman had been driven forth; none knew where he had fled but it was evident that he and Don Santiago were the same man. He had fled Spain by ship, and de Estrada knew that the people of that ship had died, not by plague as the fiend had represented, but by the fangs of the vampire.

"De Estrada and the black man and the few soldiers who still lived went searching for him and found him stretched in bestial sleep in a clump of chaparral; full-gorged he was with human blood from his last victim. Now it is well known that a vampire, like a great serpent, when well gorged, falls into a deep sleep and may be taken without peril. But de Estrada was at a loss as to how to dispose of the monster, for how may the dead be slain? For a vampire is a man who has died long ago, yet is quick with a certain foul unlife.

"The men urged that the Caballero drive a stake through the fiend's heart and cut off his head, uttering the holy words that would crumble the long-dead body into dust, but the priest was dead and de Estrada feared that in the act the monster might waken.

"So they took Don Santiago, lifting him softly, and bore him to an old Indian mound nearby. This they opened, taking forth the bones they found there, and they placed the vampire within and sealed up the mound – *Dios* grant until Judgment Day.

"It is a place accursed, and I wish I had starved elsewhere before I came into this part of the country seeking work – for I have known of the land and the creek and the mound with its terrible secret, ever since childhood; so you see, Señor Brill, why you must not open the mound and wake the fiend –"

There the manuscript ended with an erratic scratch of the pencil that tore the crumpled leaf.

Brill rose, his heart pounding wildly, his face bloodless, his tongue cleaving to his palate. He gagged and found words.

"That's why the spur was in the mound – one of them Spaniards dropped it while they was diggin' – and I mighta knowed it's been dug into before, the way the charcoal was scattered out – but, good God –"

Aghast he shrank from the black visions – an undead monster stirring in the gloom of his tomb, thrusting from within to push aside the stone loosened by the pick of ignorance – a shadowy shape loping over the hill toward a light that betokened a human prey – a frightful long arm that crossed a dim-lighted window. . . .

"It's madness!" he gasped. "Lopez was plumb loco! They ain't no such things as vampires! If they is, why didn't he get me first, instead of Lopez – unless he was scoutin' around, makin' sure of everything before he pounced? Aw, hell! It's all a pipe-dream –"

The words froze in his throat. At the window a face glared and gibbered soundlessly at him. Two icy eyes pierced his very soul. A shriek burst from his throat and that ghastly visage vanished. But the very air was permeated by the foul scent that had hung about the ancient mound. And now the door creaked – bent slowly inward. Brill backed up against the wall, his gun shaking in his hand. It did not occur to him to fire through the door; in his chaotic brain he had but one thought – that only that thin portal of wood separated him from some horror born out of the womb of night and gloom and the black past. His eyes were distended as he saw the door give, as he heard the staples of the bolt groan.

The door burst inward. Brill did not scream. His tongue was frozen to the roof of his mouth. His fear-glazed eyes took in the tall, vulture-like form – the icy eyes, the long black finger nails – the moldering garb, hideously ancient – the long spurred boot – the slouch hat with its crumbling feather – the flowing cloak that was falling to slow shreds. Framed in the black doorway crouched that abhorrent shape out of the past, and Brill's brain reeled. A savage cold radiated from the figure – the scent of moldering clay and charnel-house refuse. And then the undead came at the living like a swooping vulture.

Brill fired point-blank and saw a shred of rotten cloth fly from the Thing's breast. The vampire reeled beneath the impact of the heavy ball, then righted himself and came on with frightful speed. Brill reeled back against the wall with a choking cry, the gun falling from his nerveless hand. The black legends were true then – human weapons were powerless – for may a man kill one already dead for long centuries, as mortals die?

Then the claw-like hands at his throat roused the young cowpuncher to a frenzy of madness. As his pioneer ancestors fought hand to hand against brain-shattering odds, Steve Brill fought the cold dead crawling thing that sought his life and his soul.

Of that ghastly battle Brill never remembered much. It was a blind chaos in which he screamed beast-like, tore and slugged and hammered, where long black nails like the talons of a panther tore at him, and pointed teeth snapped again and again at his throat. Rolling and tumbling about the room, both half-enveloped by the musty folds of that ancient rotting cloak, they smote and tore at each other among the ruins of the shattered furniture, and the fury of the vampire was not more terrible than the fear-crazed desperation of his victim.

They crashed headlong into the table, knocking it down upon its side, and the coal oil lamp splintered on the floor, spraying the walls with sudden flames. Brill felt the bite of the burning oil that splattered him, but in the red frenzy of the fight he gave no heed. The black talons were tearing at him, the inhuman eyes burning icily into his soul; between his frantic fingers the withered flesh of the monster was hard as dry wood. And wave after wave of blind madness swept over Steve Brill. Like a man battling a nightmare he screamed and smote, while all about them the fire leaped up and caught at the walls and roof.

Through darting jets and licking tongues of flames they reeled and rolled like a demon and a mortal warring on the fire-lanced floors of Hell. And in the growing tumult of the flames, Brill gathered himself for one last volcanic burst of frenzied strength. Breaking away and staggering up, gasping and bloody, he lunged blindly at the foul shape and caught it in a grip not even the vampire could break. And whirling his fiendish assailant bodily on high, he dashed him down across the uptilted edge of the fallen table as a man might break a stick of wood across his knee. Something cracked like a snapping branch and the vampire fell from Brill's grasp to writhe in a strange broken posture on the burning floor. Yet it was not dead, for its flaming eyes still burned on Brill with a ghastly hunger, and it strove to crawl toward him with its broken spine, as a dying snake crawls.

Brill, reeling and gasping, shook the blood from his eyes, and staggered blindly through the broken door. And as a man runs from the portals of Hell, he ran stumblingly through the mesquite and chaparral until he fell from utter exhaustion. Looking back he saw the flames of the burning house and thanked God that it would burn until the very bones of Don Santiago de Valdez were utterly consumed and destroyed from the knowledge of men.

PEOPLE OF THE DARK

Strange Tales, June 1932

I came to Dagon's Cave to kill Richard Brent. I went down the dusky avenues made by the towering trees, and my mood well-matched the primitive grimness of the scene.

The approach to Dagon's Cave is always dark, for the mighty branches and thick leaves shut out the sun, and now the somberness of my own soul made the shadows seem more ominous and gloomy than was natural.

Not far away I heard the slow wash of the waves against the tall cliffs, but the sea itself was out of sight, masked by the dense oak forest. The darkness and the stark gloom of my surroundings gripped my shadowed soul as I passed beneath the ancient branches – as I came out into a narrow glade and saw the mouth of the ancient cavern before me. I paused, scanning the cavern's exterior and the dim reaches of the silent oaks.

The man I hated had not come before me! I was in time to carry out my grim intent. For a moment my resolution faltered, then like a wave there surged over me the fragrance of Eleanor Bland, a vision of wavy golden hair and deep gray eyes, changing and mystic as the sea. I clenched my hands until the knuckles showed white, and instinctively touched the wicked snub-nosed revolver whose weight sagged my coat pocket.

But for Richard Brent, I felt certain I had already won this woman, desire for whom made my waking hours a torment and my sleep a torture. Whom did she love? She would not say; I did not believe she knew. Let one of us go away, I thought, and she would turn to the other. And I was going to simplify matters for her – and for myself. By chance I had overheard my blond English rival remark that he intended coming to lonely Dagon's Cave on an idle exploring outing – alone.

I am not by nature criminal. I was born and raised in a hard country, and have lived most of my life on the raw edges of the world, where a man took what he wanted, if he could, and mercy was a virtue little known. But it was a torment that racked me day and night that sent me out to take the life of Richard Brent. I have lived hard, and violently, perhaps. When love overtook me, it also was fierce and violent. Perhaps I was not wholly sane, what with my love for Eleanor Bland and my hatred for Richard Brent. Under any other circumstances, I would have been glad to call him friend – a fine, rangy, upstanding young fellow, clear-eyed and strong. But he stood in the way of my desire and he must die.

I stepped into the dimness of the cavern and halted. I had never before visited Dagon's Cave, yet a vague sense of misplaced familiarity troubled me as I gazed on the high arching roof, the even stone walls and the dusty floor. I shrugged my shoulders, unable to place the elusive feeling; doubtless it was evoked by a similarity to caverns in the mountain country of the American Southwest where I was born and spent my childhood.

And yet I knew that I had never seen a cave like this one, whose regular aspect gave rise to myths that it was not a natural cavern, but had been hewn from the solid rock ages ago by the tiny hands of the mysterious Little People, the prehistoric beings of British legend. The whole countryside thereabouts was a haunt for ancient folk lore.

The country folk were predominantly Celtic; here the Saxon invaders had never prevailed, and the legends reached back, in that long-settled countryside, further than anywhere else in England – back beyond the coming of the Saxons, aye, and incredibly beyond that distant age, beyond the coming of the Romans, to those unbelievably ancient days when the native Britons warred with black-haired Irish pirates.

The Little People, of course, had their part in the lore. Legend said that this cavern was one of their last strongholds against the conquering Celts, and hinted at lost tunnels, long fallen in or blocked up, connecting the cave with a network of subterranean corridors which honeycombed the hills. With these chance meditations vying idly in my mind with grimmer speculations, I passed through the outer chamber of the cavern and entered a narrow tunnel, which, I knew by former descriptions, connected with a larger room.

It was dark in the tunnel, but not too dark for me to make out the vague, half-defaced outlines of mysterious etchings on the stone walls. I ventured to switch on my electric torch and examine them more closely. Even in their dimness I was repelled by their abnormal and revolting character. Surely no men cast in human mold as we know it, scratched those grotesque obscenities.

The Little People – I wondered if those anthropologists were correct in their theory of a squat Mongoloid aboriginal race, so low in the scale of evolution as to be scarcely human, yet possessing a distinct, though repulsive, culture of their own. They had vanished before the invading races, theory said, forming the base of all Aryan legends of trolls, elves, dwarfs and witches. Living in caves from the start, these aborigines had retreated farther and farther into the caverns of the hills, before the conquerors, vanishing at last entirely, though folklore fancy pictures their descendants still dwelling in the lost chasms far beneath the hills, loathsome survivors of an outworn age.

I snapped off the torch and passed through the tunnel, to come out into a sort of doorway which seemed entirely too symmetrical to have been the work of nature. I was looking into a vast dim cavern, at a somewhat lower level than the outer chamber, and again I shuddered with a strange alien sense of familiarity. A short flight of steps led down from the tunnel to the floor of the cavern – tiny steps, too small for normal human feet, carved into the solid stone. Their edges were greatly worn away, as if by ages of use. I started the descent – my foot slipped suddenly. I instinctively knew what was coming – it was all in part with that strange feeling of familiarity – but I could not catch myself. I fell headlong down the steps and struck the stone floor with a crash that blotted out my senses. . . .

* * *

Slowly consciousness returned to me, with a throbbing of my head and a sensation of bewilderment. I lifted a hand to my head and found it caked with blood. I had received a blow, or had taken a fall, but so completely had my wits been knocked out of me that my mind was an absolute blank. Where I was, who I was, I did not know. I looked about, blinking in the dim light, and saw that I was in a wide, dusty cavern. I stood at the foot of a short flight of steps which led upward into some kind of tunnel. I ran my hand dazedly through my square-cut black mane, and my eyes wandered over my massive naked limbs and powerful torso. I was clad, I noticed absently, in a sort of loincloth, from the girdle of which swung an empty scabbard, and leathern sandals were on my feet.

Then I saw an object lying at my feet, and stooped and took it up. It was a heavy iron sword, whose broad blade was darkly stained. My fingers fitted instinctively about its hilt with the familiarity of long usage. Then suddenly I remembered and laughed to think that a fall on his head should render me, Conan of the reavers, so completely daft. Aye, it all came back to me now. It had been a raid on the Britons, on whose coasts we continually swooped with torch and sword, from the island called Eireann. That day we of the black-haired Gael had swept suddenly down on a coastal village in our long, low ships and in the hurricane of battle which followed, the Britons had at last given up the stubborn contest and retreated, warriors, women and bairns, into the deep shadows of the oak forests, whither we seldom dared follow.

But I had followed, for there was a girl of my foes whom I desired with a burning passion, a lithe, slim young creature with wavy golden hair and deep gray eyes, changing and mystic as the sea. Her name was Tamera – well I knew it, for there was trade between the races as well as war, and I had been in the villages of the Britons as a peaceful visitor, in times of rare truce.

I saw her white half-clad body flickering among the trees as she ran with the swiftness of a doe, and I followed, panting with fierce eagerness. Under the dark shadows of the gnarled oaks she fled, with me in close pursuit, while far away behind us died out the shouts of slaughter and the clashing of swords. Then we ran in silence, save for her quick labored panting, and I was so close behind her as we emerged into a narrow glade before a somber-mouthed cavern, that I caught her flying golden tresses with one mighty hand. She sank down with a despairing wail, and even so, a shout echoed her cry and I wheeled quickly to face a rangy young Briton who sprang from among the trees, the light of desperation in his eyes.

"Vertorix!" the girl wailed, her voice breaking in a sob, and fiercer rage welled up in me, for I knew the lad was her lover.

"Run for the forest, Tamera!" he shouted, and leaped at me as a panther leaps, his bronze ax whirling like a flashing wheel about his head. And then sounded the clangor of strife and the hard-drawn panting of combat.

The Briton was as tall as I, but he was lithe where I was massive. The advantage of sheer muscular power was mine, and soon he was on the defensive, striving desperately to parry my heavy strokes with his ax. Hammering on his guard like a smith on an anvil, I pressed him relentlessly, driving him irresistibly before me. His chest heaved, his breath came in labored gasps, his blood dripped from scalp, chest and thigh where my whistling blade had cut the skin, and all but gone home. As I redoubled my strokes and he bent and swayed beneath them like a sapling in a storm, I heard the girl cry: "Vertorix! Vertorix! The cave! Into the cave!"

I saw his face pale with a fear greater than that induced by my hacking sword.

"Not there!" he gasped. "Better a clean death! In Il-marenin's name, girl, run into the forest and save yourself!"

"I will not leave you!" she cried. "The cave! It is our one chance!"

I saw her flash past us like a flying wisp of white and vanish in the cavern, and with a despairing cry, the youth launched a wild desperate stroke that nigh cleft my skull. As I staggered beneath the blow I had barely parried, he sprang away, leaped into the cavern after the girl and vanished in the gloom.

With a maddened yell that invoked all my grim Gaelic gods, I sprang recklessly after them, not reckoning if the Briton lurked beside the entrance to brain me as I rushed in. But a quick glance showed the chamber empty and a wisp of white disappearing through a dark doorway in the back wall.

I raced across the cavern and came to a sudden halt as an ax licked out of the gloom of the entrance and whistled perilously close to my black-maned head. I gave back suddenly. Now the advantage was with Vertorix, who stood in the narrow mouth of the corridor where I could hardly come at him without exposing myself to the devastating stroke of his ax.

I was near frothing with fury and the sight of a slim white form among the deep shadows behind the warrior drove me into a frenzy. I attacked savagely but warily, thrusting venomously at my foe, and drawing back from his strokes. I wished to draw him out into a wide lunge, avoid it and run him through before he could recover his balance. In the open I could have beat him down by sheer power and heavy blows, but here I could only use the point and that at a disadvantage; I always preferred the edge. But I was stubborn; if I could not come at him with a finishing stroke, neither could he or the girl escape me while I kept him hemmed in the tunnel.

It must have been the realization of this fact that prompted the girl's action, for she said something to Vertorix about looking for a way leading out, and though he cried out fiercely forbidding her to venture away into the darkness, she turned and ran swiftly down the tunnel to vanish in the dimness. My wrath rose appallingly and I nearly got my head split in my eagerness to bring down my foe before she found a means for their escape.

Then the cavern echoed with a terrible scream and Vertorix cried out like a man death-stricken, his face ashy in the gloom. He whirled, as if he had forgotten me and my sword, and raced down the tunnel like a madman, shrieking Tamera's name. From far away, as if from the bowels of the earth, I seemed to hear her answering cry, mingled with a strange sibilant clamor that electrified me with nameless but instinctive horror. Then silence fell, broken only by Vertorix's frenzied cries, receding farther and farther into the earth.

Recovering myself I sprang into the tunnel and raced after the Briton as recklessly as he had run after the girl. And to give me my due, red-handed reaver though I was, cutting down my rival from behind was less in my mind than discovering what dread thing had Tamera in its clutches.

As I ran along I noted absently that the sides of the tunnel were scrawled with monstrous pictures, and realized suddenly and creepily that this must be the dread Cavern of the Children of the Night, tales of which had crossed the narrow sea to resound horrifically in the ears of the Gaels. Terror of me must have ridden Tamera hard to have driven her into the cavern shunned by her people, where it was said, lurked the survivors of that grisly race which inhabited the land before the coming of the Picts and Britons, and which had fled before them into the unknown caverns of the hills.

Ahead of me the tunnel opened into a wide chamber, and I saw the white form of Vertorix glimmer momentarily in the semidarkness and vanish in what appeared to be the entrance of a corridor opposite the mouth of the tunnel I had just traversed. Instantly there sounded a short, fierce shout and the crash of a hard-driven blow, mixed with the hysterical screams of a girl and a medley of serpentlike hissing that made my hair bristle. And at that instant I shot out of the tunnel, running at full speed, and realized too late the floor of the cavern lay several feet below the level of the tunnel. My flying feet missed the tiny steps and I crashed terrifically on the solid stone floor.

Now as I stood in the semidarkness, rubbing my aching head, all this came back to me, and I stared fearsomely across the vast chamber at that black cryptic corridor into which Tamera and her lover had disappeared, and over which silence lay like a pall. Gripping my sword, I warily crossed the great still cavern and peered into the corridor. Only a denser darkness met my eyes. I entered, striving to pierce the gloom, and as my foot slipped on a wide wet smear on the stone floor, the raw acrid scent of fresh-spilled blood met my nostrils. Someone or something had died there, either the young Briton or his unknown attacker.

I stood there uncertainly, all the supernatural fears that are the heritage of the Gael rising in my primitive soul. I could turn and stride out of these accursed mazes, into the clear sunlight and down to the clean blue sea where my comrades, no doubt, impatiently awaited me after the routing of the Britons. Why should I risk my life among these grisly rat dens? I was eaten with curiosity to know what manner of beings haunted the cavern, and who were called the Children of the Night by the Britons, but in it was my love for the yellow-haired girl which drove me down that dark tunnel – and love her I did, in my way, and would have been kind to her, had I carried her away to my island haunt.

I walked softly along the corridor, blade ready. What sort of creatures the Children of the Night were, I had no idea, but the tales of the Britons had lent them a distinctly inhuman nature.

The darkness closed around me as I advanced, until I was moving in utter blackness. My groping left hand encountered a strangely carven doorway, and at that instant something hissed like a viper beside me and slashed fiercely at my thigh. I struck back savagely and felt my blind stroke crunch home, and something fell at my feet and died. What thing I had slain in the dark I could not know, but it must have been at least partly human because the shallow gash in my thigh had been made with a blade of some sort, and not by fangs or talons. And I sweated with horror, for the gods know, the hissing voice of the Thing had resembled no human tongue I had ever heard.

And now in the darkness ahead of me I heard the sound repeated, mingled with horrible slitherings, as if numbers of reptilian creatures were approaching. I stepped quickly into the entrance my groping hand had discovered and came near repeating my headlong fall, for instead of letting into another level corridor, the entrance gave onto a flight of dwarfish steps on which I floundered wildly.

Recovering my balance I went on cautiously, groping along the sides of the shaft for support. I seemed to be descending into the very bowels of the earth, but I dared not turn back. Suddenly, far below me, I glimpsed a faint eerie light. I went on, perforce, and came to a spot where the shaft opened into another great vaulted chamber; and I shrank back, aghast.

In the center of the chamber stood a grim, black altar; it had been rubbed all over with a sort of phosphorous, so that it glowed dully, lending a semi-illumination to the shadowy cavern. Towering behind it on a pedestal of human skulls, lay a cryptic black object, carven with mysterious hieroglyphics. The Black Stone! The ancient, ancient Stone before which, the Britons said, the Children of the Night bowed in gruesome worship, and whose origin was lost in the black mists of a hideously distant past. Once, legend said, it had stood in that grim circle of monoliths called Stonehenge, before its votaries had been driven like chaff before the bows of the Picts.

But I gave it but a passing, shuddering glance. Two figures lay, bound with rawhide thongs, on the glowing black altar. One was Tamera; the other was Vertorix, bloodstained and disheveled. His bronze ax, crusted with clotted blood, lay near the altar. And before the glowing stone squatted Horror.

Though I had never seen one of those ghoulish aborigines, I knew this thing for what it was, and shuddered. It was a man of a sort, but so low in the stage of life that its distorted humanness was more horrible than its bestiality.

Erect, it could not have been five feet in height. Its body was scrawny and deformed, its head disproportionately large. Lank snaky hair fell over a square inhuman face with flabby writhing lips that bared yellow fangs, flat spreading nostrils and great yellow slant eyes. I knew the creature must be able to see in the dark as well as a cat. Centuries of skulking in dim caverns had lent the race terrible and inhuman attributes. But the most repellent feature was its skin: scaly, yellow and mottled, like the hide of a serpent. A loincloth made of a real snake's skin girt its lean loins, and its taloned hands gripped a short stone-tipped spear and a sinister-looking mallet of polished flint.

So intently was it gloating over its captives, it evidently had not heard my stealthy descent. As I hesitated in the shadows of the shaft, far above me I heard a soft sinister rustling that chilled the blood in my veins. The Children were creeping down the shaft behind me, and I was trapped. I saw other entrances opening on the chamber, and I acted, realizing that an alliance with Vertorix was our only hope. Enemies though we were, we were men, cast in the same mold, trapped in the lair of these indescribable monstrosities.

As I stepped from the shaft, the horror beside the altar jerked up his head and glared full at me. And as he sprang up, I leaped and he crumpled, blood spurting, as my heavy sword split his reptilian heart. But even as he died, he gave tongue in an abhorrent shriek which was echoed far up the shaft. In desperate haste I cut Vertorix's bonds and dragged him to his feet. And I turned to Tamera, who in that dire extremity did not shrink from me, but looked up at me with pleading, terror-dilated eyes. Vertorix wasted no time in words, realizing chance had made allies of us. He snatched up his ax as I freed the girl.

"We can't go up the shaft," he explained swiftly; "we'll have the whole pack upon us quickly. They caught Tamera as she sought for an exit, and overpowered me by sheer numbers when I followed. They dragged us hither and all but that carrion scattered – bearing word of the sacrifice through all their burrows, I doubt not. Ilmarenin alone knows how many of my people, stolen in the night, have died on that altar. We must take our chance in one of these tunnels – all lead to Hell! Follow me!"

Seizing Tamera's hand he ran fleetly into the nearest tunnel and I followed. A glance back into the chamber before a turn in the corridor blotted it from view showed a revolting horde streaming out of the shaft. The tunnel slanted steeply upward, and suddenly ahead of us we saw a bar of gray light. But the next instant our cries of hope changed to curses of bitter disappointment. There was daylight, aye, drifting in through a cleft in the vaulted roof, but far, far above our reach. Behind us the pack gave tongue exultingly. And I halted.

"Save yourselves if you can," I growled. "Here I make my stand. They can see in the dark and I cannot. Here at least I can see them. Go!"

But Vertorix halted also. "Little use to be hunted like rats to our doom. There is no escape. Let us meet our fate like men."

Tamera cried out, wringing her hands, but she clung to her lover.

"Stand behind me with the girl," I grunted. "When I fall, dash out her brains with your ax lest they take her alive again. Then sell your own life as high as you may, for there is none to avenge us."

His keen eyes met mine squarely.

"We worship different gods, reaver," he said, "but all gods love brave men. Mayhap we shall meet again, beyond the Dark."

"Hail and farewell, Briton!" I growled, and our right hands

gripped like steel.

"Hail and farewell, Gael!"

And I wheeled as a hideous horde swept up the tunnel and burst into the dim light, a flying nightmare of streaming snaky hair, foam-flecked lips and glaring eyes. Thundering my war-cry I sprang to meet them and my heavy sword sang and a head spun grinning from its shoulder on an arching fountain of blood. They came upon me like a wave and the fighting madness of my race was upon me. I fought as a maddened beast fights and at every stroke I clove through flesh and bone, and blood spattered in a crimson rain.

Then as they surged in and I went down beneath the sheer weight of their numbers, a fierce yell cut the din and Vertorix's ax sang above me, splattering blood and brains like water. The press slackened and I staggered up, trampling the writhing bodies beneath my feet.

"A stair behind us!" the Briton was screaming. "Half-hidden in an angle of the wall! It must lead to daylight! Up it, in the name of Il-marenin!"

So we fell back, fighting our way inch by inch. The vermin fought like blood-hungry devils, clambering over the bodies of the slain to screech and hack. Both of us were streaming blood at every step when we reached the mouth of the shaft, into which Tamera had preceded us.

Screaming like very fiends the Children surged in to drag us down. The shaft was not as light as had been the corridor, and it grew darker as we climbed, but our foes could only come at us from in front. By the gods, we slaughtered them till the stair was littered with mangled corpses and the Children frothed like mad wolves! Then suddenly they abandoned the fray and raced back down the steps.

"What portends this?" gasped Vertorix, shaking the bloody sweat from his eyes.

"Up the shaft, quick!" I panted. "They mean to mount some other stair and come at us from above!"

So we raced up those accursed steps, slipping and stumbling, and as we fled past a black tunnel that opened into the shaft, far down it we heard a frightful howling. An instant later we emerged from the shaft into a winding corridor, dimly illumined by a vague gray light filtering in from above, and somewhere in the bowels of the earth I seemed to hear the thunder of rushing water. We started down the corridor and as we did so, a heavy weight smashed on my shoulders, knocking me headlong, and a mallet crashed again and again on my head, sending dull red flashes of agony across my brain. With a volcanic wrench I dragged my attacker off and under me, and tore out his throat with my naked fingers. And his fangs met in my arm in his death-bite.

Reeling up, I saw that Tamera and Vertorix had passed out of sight. I had been somewhat behind them, and they had run on, knowing nothing of the fiend which had leaped on my shoulders. Doubtless they thought I was still close on their heels. A dozen steps I took, then halted. The corridor branched and I knew not which way my companions had taken. At blind venture I turned into the left-hand branch, and staggered on in the semidarkness. I was weak from fatigue and loss of blood, dizzy and sick from the blows I had received. Only the thought of Tamera kept me doggedly on my feet. Now distinctly I heard the sound of an unseen torrent.

That I was not far underground was evident by the dim light which filtered in from somewhere above, and I momentarily expected to come upon another stair. But when I did, I halted in black despair; instead of up, it led down. Somewhere far behind me I heard faintly the howls of the pack, and I went down, plunging into utter darkness. At last I struck a level and went along blindly. I had given up all hope of escape, and only hoped to find Tamera – if she and her lover had not found a way of escape – and die with her. The thunder of rushing water was above my head now, and the tunnel was slimy and dank. Drops of moisture fell on my head and I knew I was passing under the river.

Then I blundered again upon steps cut in the stone, and these led upward. I scrambled up as fast as my stiffening wounds would allow – and I had taken punishment enough to have killed an ordinary man. Up I went and up, and suddenly daylight burst on me through a cleft in the solid rock. I stepped into the blaze of the sun. I was standing on a ledge high above the rushing waters of a river which raced at awesome speed between towering cliffs. The ledge on which I stood was close to the top of the cliff; safety was within arm's length. But I hesitated and such was my love for the golden-haired girl that I was ready to retrace my steps through those black tunnels on the mad hope of finding her. Then I started.

Across the river I saw another cleft in the cliff-wall which fronted me, with a ledge similar to that on which I stood, but longer. In olden times, I doubt not, some sort of primitive bridge connected the two ledges – possibly before the tunnel was dug beneath the riverbed. Now as I watched, two figures emerged upon that other ledge – one gashed, dust-stained, limping, gripping a bloodstained ax; the other slim, white and girlish.

Vertorix and Tamera! They had taken the other branch of the corridor at the fork and had evidently followed the windows of the tunnel to emerge as I had done, except that I had taken the left turn and passed clear under the river. And now I saw that they were in a trap. On that side the cliffs rose half a hundred feet higher than on my side of the river, and so sheer a spider could scarce have scaled them. There were only two ways of escape from the ledge: back through the fiend-haunted tunnels, or straight down to the river which raved far beneath.

I saw Vertorix look up the sheer cliffs and then down, and shake his head in despair. Tamara put her arms about his neck, and though I could not hear their voices for the rush of the river, I saw them smile, and then they went together to the edge of the ledge. And out of the cleft swarmed a loathsome mob, as foul reptiles writhe up out of the darkness, and they stood blinking in the sunlight like the night-things they were. I gripped my sword-hilt in the agony of my helplessness until the blood trickled from under my fingernails. Why had not the pack followed me instead of my companions?

The Children hesitated an instant as the two Britons faced them, then with a laugh Vertorix hurled his ax far out into the rushing river, and turning, caught Tamera in a last embrace. Together they sprang far out, and still locked in each other's arms, hurtled downward, struck the madly foaming water that seemed to leap up to meet them, and vanished. And the wild river swept on like a blind, insensate monster, thundering along the echoing cliffs.

A moment I stood frozen, then like a man in a dream I turned, caught the edge of the cliff above me and wearily drew myself up and over, and stood on my feet above the cliffs, hearing like a dim dream the roar of the river far beneath.

I reeled up, dazedly clutching my throbbing head, on which dried blood was clotted. I glared wildly about me. I had clambered the cliffs – no, by the thunder of Crom, I was still in the cavern! I reached for my sword –

The mists faded and I stared about dizzily, orienting myself with space and time. I stood at the foot of the steps down which I had fallen. I who had been Conan the reaver, was John O'Brien. Was all that grotesque interlude a dream? Could a mere dream appear so vivid? Even in dreams, we often know we are dreaming, but Conan the reaver had no cognizance of any other existence. More, he remembered his own past life as a living man remembers, though in the waking mind of John O'Brien, that memory faded into dust and mist. But the adventures of Conan in the Cavern of the Children stood clear-etched in the mind of John O'Brien.

I glanced across the dim chamber toward the entrance of the tunnel into which Vertorix had followed the girl. But I looked in vain, seeing only the bare blank wall of the cavern. I crossed the chamber, switched on my electric torch – miraculously unbroken in my fall – and felt along the wall.

Ha! I started, as from an electric shock! Exactly where the entrance should have been, my fingers detected a difference in material, a section which was rougher than the rest of the wall. I was convinced that it was of comparatively modern workmanship; the tunnel had been walled up.

I thrust against it, exerting all my strength, and it seemed to me that the section was about to give. I drew back, and taking a deep breath, launched my full weight against it, backed by all the power of my giant muscles. The brittle, decaying wall gave way with a shattering crash and I catapulted through in a shower of stones and falling masonry.

I scrambled up, a sharp cry escaping me. I stood in a tunnel, and I could not mistake the feeling of similarity this time. Here Vertorix had first fallen foul of the Children, as they dragged Tamera away, and here where I now stood the floor had been awash with blood.

I walked down the corridor like a man in a trance. Soon I should come to the doorway on the left – aye, there it was, the strangely carven portal, at the mouth of which I had slain the unseen being which reared up in the dark beside me. I shivered momentarily. Could it be possible that remnants of that foul race still lurked hideously in these remote caverns?

I turned into the doorway and my light shone down a long, slanting shaft, with tiny steps cut into the solid stone. Down these had Conan the reaver gone groping and down them went I, John O'Brien, with memories of that other life filling my brain with vague phantasms. No light glimmered ahead of me but I came into the great dim chamber I had known of yore, and I shuddered as I saw the grim black altar etched in the gleam of my torch. Now no bound figures writhed there, no crouching horror gloated before it. Nor did the pyramid of skulls support the Black Stone before which unknown races had bowed before Egypt was born out of time's dawn. Only a littered heap of dust lay strewn where the skulls had upheld the hellish thing. No, that had been no dream: I was John O'Brien, but I had been Conan of the reavers in that other life, and that grim interlude a brief episode of reality which I had relived.

I entered the tunnel down which we had fled, shining a beam of light ahead, and saw the bar of gray light drifting down from above – just as in that other, lost age. Here the Briton and I, Conan, had turned at bay. I turned my eyes from the ancient cleft high up in the vaulted roof, and looked for the stair. There it was, half-concealed by an angle in the wall.

I mounted, remembering how hurriedly Vertorix and I had gone up so many ages before, with the horde hissing and frothing at our heels. I found myself tense with dread as I approached the dark, gaping entrance through which the pack had sought to cut us off. I had snapped off the light when I came into the dim-lit corridor below, and now I glanced into the well of blackness which opened on the stair. And with a cry I started back, nearly losing my footing on the worn steps. Sweating in the semidarkness I switched on the light and directed its beam into the cryptic opening, revolver in hand.

I saw only the bare rounded sides of a small shaftlike tunnel and I laughed nervously. My imagination was running riot; I could have sworn that hideous yellow eyes glared terribly at me from the darkness, and that a crawling something had scuttered away down the tunnel. I was foolish to let these imaginings upset me. The Children had long vanished from these caverns; a nameless and abhorrent race closer to the serpent than the man, they had centuries ago faded back into the oblivion from which they had crawled in the black dawn ages of the Earth.

I came out of the shaft into the winding corridor, which, as I remembered of old, was lighter. Here from the shadows a lurking thing had leaped on my back while my companions ran on, unknowing. What a brute of a man Conan had been, to keep going after receiving such savage wounds! Aye, in that age all men were iron.

I came to the place where the tunnel forked and as before I took the left-hand branch and came to the shaft that led down. Down this I went, listening for the roar of the river, but not hearing it. Again the darkness shut in about the shaft, so I was forced to have recourse to my electric torch again, lest I lose my footing and plunge to my death. Oh, I, John O'Brien, am not nearly so sure-footed as was I, Conan the reaver; no, nor as tigerishly powerful and quick, either.

I soon struck the dank lower level and felt again the dampness that denoted my position under the riverbed, but still I could not hear the rush of the water. And indeed I knew that whatever mighty river had rushed roaring to the sea in those ancient times, there was no such body of water among the hills today. I halted, flashing my light about. I was in a vast tunnel, not very high of roof, but broad. Other smaller tunnels branched off from it and I wondered at the network which apparently honeycombed the hills.

I cannot describe the grim, gloomy effect of those dark, low-roofed corridors far below the earth. Over all hung an overpowering sense of unspeakable antiquity. Why had the little people carved out these mysterious crypts, and in which black age? Were these caverns their last refuge from the onrushing tides of humanity, or their castles since time immemorial? I shook my head in bewilderment; the bestiality of the Children I had seen, yet somehow they had been able to carve these tunnels and chambers that might balk modern engineers. Even supposing they had but completed a task begun by nature, still it was a stupendous work for a race of dwarfish aborigines.

Then I realized with a start that I was spending more time in these gloomy tunnels than I cared for, and began to hunt for the steps by which Conan had ascended. I found them and, following them up, breathed again deeply in relief as the sudden glow of daylight filled the shaft. I came out upon the ledge, now worn away until it was little more than a bump on the face of the cliff. And I saw the great river, which had roared like a prisoned monster between the sheer walls of its narrow canyon, had dwindled away with the passing eons until it was no more than a tiny stream, far beneath me, trickling soundlessly among the stones on its way to the sea.

Aye, the surface of the earth changes; the rivers swell or shrink, the mountains heave and topple, the lakes dry up, the continents alter; but under the earth the work of lost, mysterious hands slumbers untouched by the sweep of Time. Their work, aye, but what of the hands that reared that work? Did they, too, lurk beneath the bosoms of the hills?

How long I stood there, lost in dim speculations, I do not know, but suddenly, glancing across at the other ledge, crumbling and weathered, I shrank back into the entrance behind me. Two figures came out upon the ledge and I gasped to see that they were Richard Brent and Eleanor Bland. Now I remembered why I had come to the cavern and my hand instinctively sought the revolver in my pocket. They did not see me. But I could see them, and hear them plainly, too, since no roaring river now thundered between the ledges.

"By gad, Eleanor," Brent was saying, "I'm glad you decided to come with me. Who would have guessed there was anything to those old tales about hidden tunnels leading from the cavern? I wonder how that section of wall came to collapse? I thought I heard a crash just as we entered the outer cave. Do you suppose some beggar was in the cavern ahead of us, and broke it in?"

"I don't know," she answered. "I remember – oh, I don't know. It almost seems as if I'd been here before, or dreamed I had. I seem to faintly remember, like a far-off nightmare, running, running, running endlessly through these dark corridors with hideous creatures on my heels. . . ."

"Was I there?" jokingly asked Brent.

"Yes, and John, too," she answered. "But you were not Richard Brent, and John was not John O'Brien. No, and I was not Eleanor Bland, either. Oh, it's so dim and far-off I can't describe it at all. It's hazy and misty and terrible."

"I understand, a little," he said unexpectedly. "Ever since we came to the place where the wall had fallen and revealed the old tunnel, I've had a sense of familiarity with the place. There was horror and danger and battle – and love, too."

He stepped nearer the edge to look down in the gorge, and Eleanor cried out sharply and suddenly, seizing him in a convulsive grasp.

"Don't, Richard, don't! Hold me, oh, hold me tight!"

He caught her in his arms. "Why, Eleanor, dear, what's the matter?"

"Nothing," she faltered, but she clung closer to him and I saw she was trembling. "Just a strange feeling – rushing dizziness and fright, just as if I were falling from a great height. Don't go near the edge, Dick; it scares me."

"I won't, dear," he answered, drawing her closer to him, and continuing hesitantly: "Eleanor, there's something I've wanted to ask you for a long time – well, I haven't the knack of putting things in an elegant way. I love you, Eleanor; always have. You know that. But if you don't love me, I'll take myself off and won't annoy you any more. Only please tell me one way or another, for I can't stand it any longer. Is it I or the American?"

"You, Dick," she answered, hiding her face on his shoulder. "It's always been you, though I didn't know it. I think a great deal of John O'Brien. I didn't know which of you I really loved. But today as we came through those terrible tunnels and climbed those fearful stairs, and just now, when I thought for some strange reason we were falling from the ledge, I realized it was you I loved – that I always loved you, through more lives than this one. Always!"

Their lips met and I saw her golden head cradled on his shoulder. My lips were dry, my heart cold, yet my soul was at peace. They belonged to each other. Eons ago they lived and loved, and because of that love they suffered and died. And I, Conan, had driven them to that doom.

I saw them turn toward the cleft, their arms about each other, then I heard Tamera – I mean Eleanor – shriek. I saw them both recoil. And out of the cleft a horror came writhing, a loathsome, brain-shattering thing that blinked in the clean sunlight. Aye, I knew it of old – vestige of a forgotten age, it came writhing its horrid shape up out of the darkness of the Earth and the lost past to claim its own.

What three thousand years of retrogression can do to a race hideous in the beginning, I saw, and shuddered. And instinctively I knew that in all the world it was the only one of its kind, a monster that had lived on. God alone knows how many centuries, wallowing in the slime of its dank subterranean lairs. Before the Children had vanished, the race must have lost all human semblance, living as they did, the life of the reptile.

This thing was more like a giant serpent than anything else, but it had aborted legs and snaky arms with hooked talons. It crawled on its belly, writhing back mottled lips to bare needlelike fangs, which I felt must drip with venom. It hissed as it reared up its ghastly head on a horribly long neck, while its yellow slanted eyes glittered with all the horror that is spawned in the black lairs under the earth.

I knew those eyes had blazed at me from the dark tunnel opening on the stair. For some reason the creature had fled from me, possibly because it feared my light, and it stood to reason that it was the only one remaining in the caverns, else I had been set upon in the darkness. But for it, the tunnels could be traversed in safety.

Now the reptilian thing writhed toward the humans trapped on the ledge. Brent had thrust Eleanor behind him and stood, face ashy, to guard her as best he could. And I gave thanks silently that I, John O'Brien, could pay the debt I, Conan the reaver, owed these lovers since long ago.

The monster reared up and Brent, with cold courage, sprang to meet it with his naked hands. Taking quick aim, I fired once. The shot echoed like the crack of doom between the towering cliffs, and the Horror, with a hideously human scream, staggered wildly, swayed and pitched headlong, knotting and writhing like a wounded python, to tumble from the sloping ledge and fall plummetlike to the rocks far below.